# SOMEWHERE
# ALONG
# THE LINE

## MALLORY THOMAS

Formatting by Courtney Corlew

Cover design by Laolan Art

# Author's Note

THIS STORY CONTAINS ELEMENTS I love in a romance: fake dating, strong friendships, sweet family interactions, and mutual consent that occurs in the context of an emotional and physical adult relationship. It also includes elements that some readers may find difficult, including occasional cursing and coarse language, the death of a parent (off-page), depictions of anxiety and panic, interactions with law enforcement (non-violent), and sexually explicit scenes. If you're sensitive to any of these topics, *Somewhere Along the Line* may not be the right book for you.

This book is intended for an adult audience.

# Dedication

*For my daughter, who held a mirror up to my life and showed me where I was falling short of the person I want to be.*

*AKA for Sweet T, who came home from Kindergarten with a Mother's Day fill-in-the blank gift that said "My mom is good at <u>looking at her phone</u>" which convinced me to read again which led me to write again. (Yes, I was horrified and yes, I cried for hours.)*

# Where is Your *Somewhere*?

While this book isn't for young eyes, sharing the experience of writing and publishing this book with my daughter has been wonderful. She's my biggest fan! Now we're tracking where these words end up. Want to participate? **Scan the code below to add your location to our Where Is Your *Somewhere*? Project.** An elementary schooler in Tennessee thanks you :)

Where is your
*Somewhere?*

Scan to log your location for our traveling book project!

# 1
## *Piper*

CATCHING THIS TRAIN WOULD be easier if I wasn't missing a shoe. How am I supposed to convince my boss I'm worthy of a raise—that I can handle more responsibility—if I shuffle into the office on a naked foot?

Something is always amiss in my life but it's typically not this literal.

*One worry at a time, Piper.*

That's what Dr. Browne would say, and her words echo in my mind as I hoist myself up the station's stairs and steer my toes away from a sticky mess on the platform.

My anxiety about the promotion, and how it would fix my money issues, can have its turn later.

My lungs are desperate for air and my heart pounds reprimands in my chest as I dart into the third car through the disappearing space between the closing doors.

I'm right on time at 7:26 a.m.

The trek from my house takes twenty minutes, yet every morning I give myself fifteen. It's the story of my life, each day trying to stretch something into more, a little into enough, when that something isn't elastic to begin with.

Time. Money. Certain responsibilities.

No matter, I can take a marble block and chisel it into the David... well, maybe not *the* David, but perhaps something sort of resembling a man named David. Maybe one who dropped his cheap beer on the platform last night, chuckling with heavy eyes and this week's hook-up still tangled in his arms.

Close enough.

That's what I tell myself at my therapist's urging: I'm capable, I can figure things out, and it's okay if the details of my life are not perfect. Dr. Browne thinks positive self-talk is the answer to my anxiety. I think the jury's still out.

"You're on my shoe."

The sound echoes in my ears, the hair at the back of my neck standing up as I try to orient myself to where the voice is coming from. This is a collected voice, a makes-home-made-French-press-every-morning voice, a get-your-shit-to-gether-because-mine-certainly-is voice.

I recognize this voice. Not from a conversation, but from a tense work call this man conducted on the train last week, loudly enough for everyone in the third car to hear.

I couldn't drag my eyes away from him and not only because he was rude. He looked straight out of a Ralph Lauren catalog. It made my stomach somersault.

*What shoe?* I wonder, then suddenly remember—shoes! Ah yes, I'm missing a shoe. And upon surveying the situation—my eyes dragging down from the broad chest in front of me to the floor—I see my bare foot on top of this man's Cole Haan suede.

Worse, my toenail has edged a deep scratch across the top of the toe box.

An expensive toe box.

"Wow, holy shit. Sorry. Yikes, wow. Let me just—" I hobble on one leg, the weakest attempt at a smile settling on my lips as I grasp the cold metal pole between us for support. The suede tickles as I slide my foot off his and the man moves away, not making eye contact.

It's like he thinks spending a second more in my presence might cause my chaos to stick to him and impart something messy onto his otherwise immaculate (and immaculately fitting) navy suit.

"It's, uh... it's fine," he mutters, his hand raking into his mousy brown hair and then drawing down the side of his face. The motion projects *God, I'm tired* and *you aren't worth my time* in equal measure.

"I can pay to fix it," I reply, glancing down at his shoe and finally up to his face, my smile getting weaker by the second. I force the muscles in my cheeks to rise.

Do I have the money to fix his shoe? Absolutely not. But could I figure it out? Of course. I'm Michaelangelo... or something like that.

"Cole Haan, right?"

The man's blue eyes perk up and settle on mine, flashing a hint of curiosity before regaining their stoicism.

"They've got a program, Cole Haan does, a shoe repair program. You can send in damaged shoes, and they'll buff or fix or whatever else to make them look new again." The words tumble out of my mouth at a rapid clip. "My brother Kent does it—sends his shoes in. He's a banker. He knows things."

The man shifts uncomfortably, his gaze gliding down the length of my body before settling back on his defaced loafer.

*Good GOD, what am I doing right now?*

My brain is self-talking alright, but the talk isn't positive.

*Get it together. Can you act like a normal human for once? One with a brain and the ability to stop the words from spilling out of your mouth at sixty miles per hour, word vomiting on this specimen of a man who doesn't have the time or desire for this interaction?*

The answer is no, it turns out. I cannot. The spew continues.

"I said that 'cause I figured you're a banker like my brother. I mean, I can tell—I worked in corporate finance before things went totally to shit, which is another story for another time, but anyway, I said that so you know I know what I'm talking about. About the shoe repair, I mean."

If my body had a meter to measure the nervous energy flitting off it right now, the gauge would show max capacity.

"Really, it's fine." His mouth is attempting to approximate a smile, but it's not working. "It's just a shoe, the train is crowded, it's..." He gives half a shrug as the words trail off before turning his attention to his jacket and fiddling with a button between his long fingers.

Oooookay then. Had I known this morning would devolve into an awkward stand-off with Banker Man, I would've let myself miss the train.

The next few minutes pass in stony silence until a group of rowdy high schoolers gets off at the Robertson stop, opening seats near the back of the car.

The man darts to claim one by a window the second it's free, pulling out his phone with an intent look.

Not that I'm looking. At him. Or at his expression. Or at what he's doing with his perfectly groomed eyebrows, or how his thumb swipes at the screen in a way that feels obscene to someone imagining his thumb and this swiping motion elsewhere.

Which I am not... though the warmth building in my lap suggests otherwise.

I take a deep breath, air pushing at my ribs from the inside out, and find a seat of my own as far away from Banker Man as possible. With both feet planted on the floor, I push my hands down my thighs. It's a sensory thing, this action I've done for as long as I can remember—a means of providing necessary pressure to calm my racing mind.

My therapist says it's a strategy called "embodiment," and it works by bringing attention to your body from your head, into the present versus the past or the future. That's what I need. Because one thing is certain: my body must agree with my brain that this man—and this morning's pathetic exchange—are not something to fixate on.

It doesn't matter if he's exactly my type, over six feet tall with a starched collar and curated hair, plus the ability to make my heart flip at a glance. The fact he's my type is the reason I can't spend any energy on him.

I don't need another banker to come in and destroy my life. I don't need anyone at all, I remind myself.

It's not lost on me that this week marks two years since my corporate job (and my relationship with my corporate boyfriend) went up in flames. Every good thing in my life burned down in one afternoon, leaving me without a place or a person to witness the carnage, much less to bandage me up.

I will never let that happen again. The thought of it clenches at my chest, squeezing tight around my ribcage.

I never wanted the job at Fundament. I said as much to Kent, and, like the oppressive big brother he is, he'd already arranged it with HR.

"You won't make me a fool by quitting before you set foot in the door." Like the people-pleasing middle child I am... *was?*... I complied.

It made sense to put my business degree to use. While I would've loved to join a non-profit or an advocacy group, stepping onto the bottom rung of the corporate ladder felt like the smart move. One that could help me manage my student loans, afford an apartment on my own, and bankroll the trips I wanted to take. Gosh, I wanted to take those trips.

So, I set my heart aside, pulled on some (thrifted) Jimmy Choo pumps, and convinced myself that click-clacking away on a computer creating value was what I wanted. Because why wouldn't it be? That's what everyone else wanted for me, and everyone else seemed to know me better than I know myself.

It's no wonder I have anxiety.

And when a handsome, smart, clever, and charming man named Henry joined the firm and decided I was the sweetest thing he'd ever seen? I jumped in headfirst. I'd bring him coffee and he'd bring me salads and we'd sit around the conference table, him formatting pitch decks while I worked to make the numbers tie.

We laughed and climbed and built our American Dream on the backs of the nameless and faceless people we ignored because that's how capitalism works.

We were happy. It seemed like we were happy.

I thought *I* was happy.

Until the whole thing went to shit. Until Henry Sierra was screaming at me for fucking up his life and tanking the company, his face burning red and spit flying between his teeth.

That's enough to make you realize that whatever happiness you thought you'd found wasn't actually happiness. That existing in a world with people like Henry wasn't the way to get it.

*There will be no more bankers for Piper Paulson.*

The chill of the train car's metal frame radiates from behind me, sending a shiver down my back as I tuck my tote bag across my chest. The warmth from my breakfast seeps through the canvas, and it's a welcome distraction from the glances Banker Man occasionally throws in my direction. I hate that he's catching me looking at him, but it's only because he keeps looking here first.

His fault, I decide.

I fix my attention on how far I've come—on all I've accomplished since I walked out of the Fundament building and never looked back. The way I made it through that first year living at home given my sudden lack of income in this ridiculously expensive city. How I filled my days helping Mom prep projects for her first-grade classroom and dreaming about a future that felt like my own—not the product of everyone else's expectations.

It wasn't all bad, I tell myself now, choosing to ignore the itch that starts on my skin when I think about the twin bed that sheltered me at age eight and again, unwittingly, at twenty-six.

Then there's Sami, the absolute best college roommate-turned friend-turned adult roommate-turned-wannabe life coach. Sami, who has never once made me feel like I'm anything other than perfection wrapped in sunkissed skin and a graphic tee. It's hard to believe she can fit so much support and encouragement into her tiny, five-foot-nothing frame.

Sometimes I think her magic is hidden beneath her mass of shiny black curls.

When I got the job offer from Hope First six months ago (after interviewing at no fewer than eighteen non-profits), we spent the night at our new place watching *Titanic* and drinking champagne, stopping only to discuss how Leonardo DiCaprio went from being the hottest man on Earth to a serial age-gap dater with a surprisingly round face.

It was the start of a new chapter, one I was eager to fill with all sorts of goodness I had been missing, desperately, for far too long.

And now things are looking up. I've spent the past two years building a mosaic out of my life, placing one broken shard into the picture at a time, and it's finally starting to make sense... if you stand far away and squint a little. I tally the pieces I've added lately:

A great new job, even if it does pay fifty percent less than I used to comfortably make at Fundament.

The ability to help people, moms and their kids, who need support as they navigate life without a partner.

The cutest coach house apartment with Sami that is slowly coming together, filled with flea market finds in every color imaginable and our very own stackable washer and dryer.

Enough money to buy the groceries I want to buy most weeks.

Painting, even though it's just with the kids at work on Thursday afternoons. Our weekly painting class lights up a part of myself previously buried under mounds of numbers and paperwork. It's helping me breathe again.

"Your stop?"

That voice, the never-forgets-a-birthday, always-returns-his-voicemails, custom-tailors-his-clothes voice pops my brain bubble for the second time this morning. I blink up at him towering over me, his blue eyes reflecting bits of silver from the pole he's grasping as he stands.

"You always step off here. Didn't want you to miss it."

He shifts his bag up his shoulder and clears his throat as he steps past me to join the mass of people waiting for the doors.

I'm frozen for a second, maybe ten, as my brain orients itself away from its replay of the last two years and to the reality that I *am* about to miss my stop.

I jump up with a start, my canvas bag full of notebooks and a sausage ball breakfast, nearly whacking the sweet old lady sitting beside me. "So sorry!" The words are an exhale as I catch my balance, the train slowing with a jolt.

Missing this stop would mean being late for work. With a possible promotion hanging on my performance at the upcoming gala, I'm in no position to slack off. My bank account nods in agreement.

The realization hits me as I move toward the train's doors. It takes out my senses for a second, the feeling that happens when you stand up too fast and everything blurs. I regain my focus on the back of the man's perfectly styled head, the head that floats tall above several people standing between us.

Banker Man knows my stop.

Of course, I've been studying him these past few weeks, wondering if he'll continue to ride in the third car of the 7:26 a.m. B Line train. This car filled with comers and goers I don't recognize, the man's presence a point of comforting consistency in my otherwise unpredictable days.

So far, he has. Every day he's here.

*Maybe he's been watching me too?*

I let the question swirl in my mind. The thought sends a tingle straight down my spine, sprouting goosebumps on my arms.

The doors open, and I want to say something to him, to tell him thanks for prompting me about the stop. But by the time

I'm off the train, he's halfway down the platform steps, walking toward whatever Important Banker Building he'll spend his next eight (Twelve? Sixteen?) hours within.

A small ache stirs in my chest as I turn the opposite way toward my building, and I try to smother it. The goal is to feel nothing for this man. Yet, in these past two minutes alone I've felt gratitude, then hope, and now disappointment.

*Smother, smother, smother.*

Tomorrow, I'll keep my thoughts in line. Odds are we'll both be on this train again tomorrow.

2

*James*

THE WOODEN PLATFORM GROANS under my feet as I speed walk away from the station and into the city, a place that offers blissful anonymity if you bob and weave with the mass of humanity lining the streets.

Being anonymous sounds a hell of a lot better than being James Newhouse right now, especially after that embarrassing show of disinterest—or maybe annoyance or awkwardness, I'm not sure which one—in front of the woman on the train.

It's not often I find myself intrigued by someone, much less wanting to make a decent impression. But since I first saw her several weeks back, I can't keep my eyes to myself.

Each morning, she boards the train like she's one banana peel away from slipping legs over head, her stuff threatening to float through the car like millennial confetti. I find myself wondering, every ride, how she can own so many vintage t-shirts, each one grazing the curve of her collarbone and hanging loosely at her waist.

More practically, what kind of downtown job allows a woman with faded Bob Marley t-shirts and an ever-changing hairstyle to do meaningful work?

If there was any hope of learning more about this woman, of coming to understand how she seems to exist so concerned and unconcerned at the same time, it's gone now. It disappeared the second I stared her down for scuffing my shoe like I'm some sort of meathead.

Damn it.

My focus snaps to the buzz in my pocket, a merciful distraction that stops me from dwelling on my behavior with the woman this morning. A surge of cortisol travels my nerves as I spot a text from Hunter, my boss and Trion's CFO. I'm sure of the text's contents before I read it; each one is some version of the same:

*"Get your ass in here. This sell-side process has turned into a fire drill and our investors are going to shit themselves if we don't sort this out today."*

Is it really a fire drill if *everything* is a fire drill? I don't think so, but my thoughts on the matter aren't welcome. Hunter's made that clear.

My bag digs into my shoulder as I increase the speed of my steps. I steel myself for whatever lies ahead of the revolving door that spits me into the lobby. The turnstile clicks as I pass my keycard over the sensor, letting me through to the elevators.

I try to soak in these last moments of silence before the workday erupts in front of me, knowing that lava will nip at my toes the second I reach my desk.

"Jamessssss," my co-worker Kyle shouts as he does a half spin on his chair and shoots me a nod of greeting. "How'd it go with your dad this weekend? Everything good?"

I don't have the time nor the energy to go into detail about the mess that was my weekend. Helping my dad begin pack up my childhood home was hell, but I'm not going to cry about it in the office.

"Yeah man, it was good to be with him but better to be gone, you know?"

Kyle nods, spinning a pen on top of his thumb before tucking it between his ear and his shaggy blond mop. He turns back to his spreadsheet.

I'm positive Kyle *doesn't know*, not the half of it, but other than reminiscing about our first jobs and sharing hot sauce in the company's kitchen, Kyle and I aren't friends. Not tell-you-my-family's-baggage kind of friends.

The smooth leather of my chair—an ergonomic model I requested in a detailed proposal to HR—greets my ass as I boot up my computer. Spreadsheets appear across two monitors with my calendar on the third. Evaluating the day's needs, I'm not sure how to fit Hunter's fire drill into the ten free minutes I have between meetings.

We both know that's not his problem. The work will get done because it always gets done. It has to, so I'll be the one to do it.

There are no feelings or boundaries at Trion, the premier investment bank in the city. No "me" that exists as an embodied human within these walls. Instead, I'm a cog in a wheel, a James-sized piece that cranks and cranks to keep the rest of the bits moving.

It suits me, this sort of detachment. Ever since Mom died it's easier this way, existing with an emotional range that's purposefully narrow. I've truncated the ends of the spectrum, shielded myself from feelings other than "fine." Keeping myself from caring about anything or anyone avoids a slide into "bad" territory.

Unfortunately, this practice means I never inch up to "good" either, but that's a price I'm willing to pay. I stay neutral and focused, letting everything roll off my back while I keep my feelings at arm's length. It's kept me upright so far.

This self-preservation strategy, which typically works well, is why my penchant for admiring the woman on the train is so unnerving. I see the internal warning signs (Slow down! Curve ahead! Stop!), but I can't seem to heed them.

Every morning, I'm tangled up with one feeling or another as she boards, stands or sits, reads or looks out the window and thinks. I never know what mystery feeling will spring up into my belly or throat to catch me by surprise. Sometimes it's anticipation, sometimes it's attraction, sometimes it's curiosity, and often, to my dismay, it feels a little like hope.

Like there could be a *what if* between us if only I permit myself the risk of discovering it.

Instead, I spend my time on the train staring at my phone, or at my shoes, pretending to be busy with something important. I'd rather assess what she's wearing, how her strawberry blonde hair is fixed, or what she's eating for breakfast which looks, if I'm not mistaken, like Bisquick sausage balls.

That's her breakfast every day on repeat.

*God, I need to get a life*, I think with resignation. My work requires every inch of my brain, and reserving space to contemplate sausage balls is not prudent.

I try to set the thought aside and focus on my monitors. It works for three seconds before a tab stuck to the folder next to my mouse brings up a memory of the first time I saw her three weeks ago.

She boarded the train with her hair held back by a Rosie the Riveter-style bandana. Equal parts put together and messy, she was wearing the type of outfit that happens when you're working on something and lose track of time. When the minutes spent untangling a problem and finding a solution matter more than picking out cohesive clothing. She was that image personified, the carefree nature of it in contrast to the stress she also wore that day.

Her eyes—a deep brown—seemed worried, the corners of her eyebrows pulled in and her mouth spread tight in a line. She bounced her knee with a speed that betrayed anxiety as she flipped between her phone and a notebook every other minute of the ride.

I didn't know what was bothering her that morning, only that I wanted to help. To comfort her. I wanted to wrap her up, my arms around her shoulders, and pull her body against mine. The thought, flitting across my mind so quickly I couldn't catch it if I tried, scared the crap out of me.

I've been stealing glances ever since.

A *ding* from my email jolts me back to reality. If I'm not

careful, I will be the one wearing the stress today. I stuff my feelings into a small room somewhere inside and do my best to board up the door. Successful James is detached James, and that's who Hunter will get today. Detached James keeps the cogs turning.

I type without thinking, my fingers knowing the answer to the question that popped into my inbox without consulting my brain. It's nice to work on autopilot.

Kyle is at my office door before I can finish the email, his arms draped over his chest. The stance would threaten to wrinkle his striped button-down shirt had it not been a non-iron—the unofficial official working uniform shirt of bankers nationwide (with a vest, of course, if it's below sixty degrees).

"Did you get the latest turn from GPC?" Kyle says this as if his definition of "fire drill" doesn't include urgency.

My chest heaves a sigh, my fingers finding my forehead and stretching the skin to release tension. I do a mental scan of what I've seen come through my inbox and what I haven't.

"Yeah, their analyst sent it over last night, came in about three in the morning." Without trying, I set myself up for a conversation closer so good my face relaxes into a grin. "I'll take a look at it. If it's anything like the last one, I'll spend all day correcting errors. They don't make analysts like they used to."

With that, Kyle gives me a smirk that sneaks out from behind his beard. We were in the same investment banking analyst cohort after college and barely survived those two years of torture.

While he's only been working at Trion with me for a year, the fraternity born out of months of communal suffering runs deep. It's nice to know I can trust someone here, even if I'm not willing to share my family history with him.

"I'll pass it over to you when I'm done reviewing it, hopefully by end of day."

Kyle offers a sort of salute, signaling his agreement before turning back to the bullpen and making his way to the office on the left.

I release a big exhale, a bit overwhelmed and still distracted, as I stretch my fingers across the keyboard and narrow in on my growing to-do list.

The shriek of the alarm clock rattles my bones, its bright wail in stark contrast to the dark sky. It's as black now as it was at 2 a.m. when I rolled into bed; morning comes quickly when sleep rarely exceeds five hours.

I check my phone and groan, unsure which is worse: the fluorescent numbers showing 6:30 a.m. or the string of notifications piling up from Hunter. Neither is great.

I stumble to the kitchen to start the kettle before pouring myself into today's iteration of the work fit: tailored pants, a button-down shirt with a button collar, a leather belt, and a vest or blazer that complements. I keep a few ties at the office in case of emergency—there's no sense in restricting my ability to breathe any further. The mystery woman on the train does a fine job of that already.

Each day's outfit selection process—choosing from an equal number of coordinating separates and mixing and matching at will—is a fitting analogy for everything else in my life of late. Plug A and then B into the equation and it'll spit out C. No thoughts and no feelings are required. Simply feed the algorithm and things run smoothly. The system hasn't let me down yet.

The kettle whistles on the white granite counter as I head to the hallway to grab a pair of shoes. I run my finger across the scratch that sits atop my favorite loafer, and a twinge of regret shoots through me, as fleeting as it is sharp.

Is it because of the imperfection? Or because of how badly I bungled the conversation that followed its discovery?

Maybe I *should* look into the Cole Haan repair program. It would certainly be easier to fix the shoe than replace my broken social skills, the ones that left me unable to talk to the woman on the train yesterday.

Today requires a different pair of shoes. I don't need a visible reminder of my failure every time I take a step; it'll taunt me enough without prompting.

My hands and feet take over out of habit as I finish up my morning routine: I pour hot water into my insulated tumbler, grab a sachet of black tea and slip the string through the cup's notch, and check my teeth for evidence of my ham and spinach omelet. Then I slip my laptop into my messenger bag, turn off the lights, grab my keys, and lock the door.

My phone shows 7:08 a.m. as I begin the walk to Carmack station. I'll board the train at 7:15 like I do every day then endure eleven slow minutes of watching familiar landmarks flash by the window. My eyes will stay busy on the interstate split, the jewelry store with a metal door, the bustling elementary school carpool line.

After too long, the train will scream into Roosevelt station and she'll board.

Those eleven minutes of waiting and the fourteen minutes after, when I share her air, are the best parts of my day. I don't think about work, about my inbox that becomes more overstuffed minute by minute. I don't think about Dad, or the house, or the questions he's asking about the fate of Mom's things. About whether I want any of it before it gets donated or goes to auction as if they're items a stranger can appraise for value and not the vestiges of her life.

I try not to think about Mom at all, for that matter, about the hole she left in our family. Most of all, I avoid wondering if she'd be proud of me, and what she'd think about the way my life is turning out.

Instead, for twenty-five minutes, a measly 1.736% of each day, I let myself exist beyond the demands of my life—to wonder about a different existence. I ponder the opportunity cost to give up everything I've built, perhaps to become the dad helping his five-year-old son out of the carpool line before waving him off to kindergarten.

To wonder, in this other imaginary life, whether the woman on the train might have packed the lunch he'll take out at a tiny round table circled by even tinier chairs.

It's a pleasant thought, and I let it waft through my brain as I stride up to the platform. It's pleasant the way dreaming about becoming a surf instructor while living off backyard fruit trees is pleasant. It's simple escapism, not a plan.

And that's fine, of course, because I already have a plan. Follow the steps, keep the cogs turning, increase the market value, make the calls (literally and figuratively) that Dad can't or won't make, and keep everything else at a distance.

Yesterday and tomorrow, last year and next month, the plan chugs along just like this train. Today will be no different.

Except, it turns out, it is.

I make my way into the train car, or more accurately, into a sea of white flared pants and bedazzled jackets, the scent of hairspray overtaking the train's usual aroma of body odor, last night's party, and too much cologne.

The words exit my mouth before I realize I'm saying them aloud.

"Why the hell is this train filled with Elvis impersonators?"

## 3
## *Piper*

BREAKFAST IN HAND—AND BOTH shoes *very* much on my feet—I skip down the steps of our coach house, shuffling past the main house that sits in front of ours, where my sweet eight-year-old neighbor is arguing with her mom about her hair.

Nostalgia pinches my heart as I think about my own mother and what I put her through in my adolescent years, demanding a different hairstyle every morning and then whining when she dared to touch the brush to my head.

The slight chill of this late September morning is a welcome change as I wave to them through their kitchen window and hurry past. It's going to be one of those sweater roulette days that will have me tugging on and yanking off my faded, jersey quarter-zip every time I change locations.

We'll call that my workout for today.

I make the left turn at the light on the corner of my street, jaywalking as I close in on the final two-minute sprint before the B Line train pulls into my station and promptly leaves. I pick up the pace, emulating those Olympic power walkers with their swinging arms and stern faces, the ones willing their legs to go a smidge faster without breaking into a jog.

Who am I kidding? *This* is my workout for the day.

I spot the elevated platform, swipe my fare card, and take the stairs two at a time until my feet screech to a halt. They echo the sound of the incoming train.

While I may be a mess, all wild hair and frayed jeans and overstuffed tote, I'm not late for the train today. That's a win.

Minding the gap, I step into the third car and freeze.

*Holy shit.*

A burst of laughter escapes my lips. The city's annual Elvis convention is today. KingCon, as it's called, is a day-long bar crawl that stops at nearly every music establishment in the city, offering nostalgia, strong drinks, and the chance for grown-ups to play hooky.

Does 7:26 a.m. feel like an appropriate start time for the public pre-game that's happening currently? Not in my mind, but these folks have other ideas.

The car is packed full of impersonators—tall ones, short ones, old ones, little baby college student ones—and these multiplied Elvises (Elvi?) occupy nearly every square inch of space. They croon and snarl and dart hooded eyes at each other as one leads a rendition of "Jailhouse Rock" and the others happily join.

I scan the crowd, playing a surreal game of Where's Waldo as I look for a single open seat amid the sea of collars and sparkles. Spotting one, I weave my way toward the back of the car, thankful I won't have to shoulder my bag between two greasy aficionados for the next fourteen minutes.

I plop down with a heaving groan and settle myself into the plastic curve of the chair, bumping my knee against the guy staring out our shared window. His pants communicate a not-here-for-Elvis vibe.

"So sorry, gosh, what a morning, yeah?" I say as I search through my bag for my sausage balls, planning to eat and scroll and wonder what compels a person to attend KingCon. "If you had told me when I woke up this morning I'd step into Graceland-made-over, I wouldn't have believed you."

The man clears his throat and shifts his knee to the right, breaking our point of bodily contact. He turns his head, and we meet eyes. My stomach plummets to my feet.

"Wow, *wow*, okay..." I sputter as my gaze traces the hard lines of Banker Man's face, the way his nose curves down just a bit at the end, his perfect white teeth giving a slight bite to the corner of his bottom lip. The rise and fall of his chest silently occupy the seconds as I figure out what the hell is happening and what to say next.

"Wow. So sorry. I need to stop saying wow. I don't know why I'm saying it. I don't mean wow. I guess I mean... hi?" I say it like a question, offering up my words in both apology and invitation.

A pink flush creeps up my neck, made worse by the heat this man's body throws in my direction.

"Sorry, I didn't mean to bump into you," I say. "Again. Literally. I guess also figuratively but mostly literally... for the second day in a row." I bring my focus to my faded jeans, smoothing my hands down my thighs as I steady my breath.

"Wow, indeed," he replies, and in that small moment I think I catch the hint of a smile. It's nothing more than a wisp. He settles back into his seat, his long legs careful not to nudge mine. "I mean... *hi.*"

"Are you mocking me?" I blurt, unsure if I can handle any more embarrassment in front of this man who's only ever seen me at... not my best.

Who I am on the train each morning, even outside of the last twenty-four hours, is not what I'd put on Instagram.

He senses my defensiveness and softens, catching my eyes with an expression that might betray fondness if I believed this man knew what fondness is.

"I'm not sure what I'm doing, to be honest," he says. He looks around and gives an amused sigh, scrubbing his right hand through his hair. "This Elvis thing has me feeling like I'm in a simulation. Let me try this again." He takes a deep breath. "Hey."

"Just hey?" I squeak, desperate for him to say something, anything, to make up for the avalanche of words I unloaded a few moments ago.

"Okay, how about..." he bites is bottom lip in thought again, nestling it between his teeth. I try not to stare as he releases it and takes another breath. "Hey, I'm James, and I accept your apology for bumping my leg. And you were right yesterday, I am a banker. I didn't know I was so easy to read."

He looks relieved to have gotten the words out.

"How was that? Better?" he asks.

What would be better is if it wasn't one hundred degrees on this train, but I refuse to peel off my top layer. Not in front of this man, this *James*, who looks like he's never sweat a day in his life.

"I will accept that," I reply, forcing an expression that I hope projects confidence and doesn't betray the chaos erupting in my chest. "And yes, you *are* easy to read. I know your type from a mile away."

"Do you?" His eyes quirk, prodding me with a look that asks me to prove it.

"Yep. You own the same pair of pants in approximately eight different shades of black, gray, and navy. You answer your phone without thinking, and you agree to whatever is asked of you without reservation. You listen to classic rock, you take your coffee black, you pride yourself on your typing speed and your ability to navigate Excel, and you wonder if your life expectancy is inversely correlated to the number of deals you get across the line."

I feel a strange sense of pride in nailing him so thoroughly.

I immediately make myself promise to never think the phrase "nailing him so thoroughly" *ever* again as the blush creeps further up the side of my neck. "Tell me I'm wrong."

James pauses, searching my face like he's looking for something he didn't know he lost.

"You're wrong," he deadpans, jostling his tumbler. "It's black tea, not coffee, and I have ten pairs of identical neutral pants, not eight. Better luck next time." His lips curl into a cheeky grin before he settles them down in their usual straight line.

He looks like he's trying to convince himself not to say what he's about to. "So, what's your deal, then?" he asks, "other than mowing down strangers on the train and paying concerningly close attention to their pants?"

Heat rushes through me at the accusation that I may have stolen a glance, or several, at the man's lower half.

"Well, for one, I do not look at everyone's pants." Only yours, I think, and only because the way those tailored pants hug your quads should be a crime. "And I don't usually run into people either."

"Does miss *eyes-up-here* have a name?"

"Piper." The name comes out in a half-whisper. I don't know if I can keep up this banter for a second longer with what it's doing to my insides.

"Ah, Piper. Like the Pied Piper. That explains your charisma."

"Are you mocking me again?" I reply sharply, the difference in volume between this exchange and the last causing the twin Elvises behind us to jump.

"No, I'm really not trying to. Sorry. Piper is a great name. Lovely, even."

I nod, eyes narrowing, and he nods, a hint apologetic. My phone's lock screen shows it's only been six minutes since I boarded this train. We have another eight minutes to go.

James and I settle into an awkward silence, him scrolling his emails and me admiring the get-up of a man in his early seventies who is brandishing a guitar with "Burning Love" embroidered in script on the strap.

"You're right, you know." James breaks the tension with a tentative glance my way. "If someone had told me this morning I'd be packed in this sardine can with sixty clones of Elvis, I wouldn't have believed it either."

"I'm always right." Will he call me out given the error I made guessing his beverage a few minutes before? He seems to consider this option but stays silent. I accept the olive branch of his statement and offer him one of my own.

"My question is how these people afford to take a day off work, buy these costumes, and spend all their fare money going between neighborhoods to drink their way around the city. My wallet could *never*."

The words slip out with a chuckle, my brain forgetting for a moment that this man can't commiserate with my pay-check-to-paycheck lifestyle. I let my eyes linger on what must be a father-son pair; they're identical in features in addition to outfits.

"Maybe they're all related," I wonder aloud, pointing to the dynamic duo. "Surely, those two are. Then at least they're saving money with a Family Fares commuter pass. If I could convince my sister to move to the city, I could pocket some extra cash each month that way."

James looks at me curiously, and I wonder if he's decided that a person for whom a bit of petty cash would make a difference isn't worth his conversation. I can't blame him. If I had disposable income, I'd look at me funny too.

He takes a beat, chewing on the words and seeing how they

taste before spitting them out. "We could create a Family Fares account."

He says it like it's the score of last night's game or the weather forecast for this upcoming weekend. Like it's nothing out of the ordinary, like he isn't an incredibly hot stranger—well, I guess he's just barely *not* a stranger now—and like he didn't just offer to tie himself to me for the sake of my grocery budget.

"We..." I gesture wildly between us, circling my hand in front of his chest and mine. "You and me...could split... a family pass."

Hearing the words come out of my mouth makes me dissociate from my body. I'm watching this conversation from another dimension, equally stunned in both worlds.

"Yes, *we*..." he says leisurely, mirroring my hand motion and drawing out the words for emphasis, as though speaking slowly will help my brain comprehend, "could split a family pass. I can't imagine the MTA employs people whose job it is to check the relationship status between pass holders. They can't even staff enough people to keep the platforms salted in the winter. I'll go into my commuter account, add you, and I'll bring you the new card next week."

Again, James says this as though he's rattling off a list of items he needs from Home Depot and not like he's proposing we commit transit fraud (is that a thing?) by falsifying our relationship to the state government. He looks as unfazed as I look incredulous.

"You'll add me as what, exactly?" Skepticism drips from my

voice. I hope it hides my ascending glee at what I know he'll say next.

"As my fake wife, I guess, though I'd obviously leave the *fake* part off the application. I'll need your last name to add to the portal unless you want me to list you as Mrs. James Newhouse."

He means this as a joke, of course, meant to lighten the mood. Instead, the tension between us grows taut as we consider, briefly, the weight of what he's just said. He scrambles to redirect the line of thought.

"Listen, I know we're strangers and this is an insane proposition, but look around, Piper. This idea isn't even close to being the wildest thing happening on the train today. It doesn't have to be a big deal. You agree, I update my account, and you save money on the fare. A plus B equals C. Honestly, you don't have to pay for your portion. It won't cost me much more each month—won't make a dent."

He shrugs like it's nothing, shifting in his seat as he stretches his fingers and rolls out his neck as if trying to release the tension that's built during this conversation.

"You must be joking." I'm pretty sure this is when I roll my eyes. "Yesterday I ruined your shoes and today you repay me by literally offering to cover my commute? What's in it for you?"

"The warm fuzzy feeling that comes from being kind?" He smirks and I can't help but nudge his shoulder with my own, a tactile plea for him to be honest with me. I regret the second I shift back to my own space, feeling the place where he was acutely and becoming instantly aware of all the places I'd like him to be.

"Okay, how about this? You join my commuter account and in exchange, I get some of...whatever it is you bring for breakfast every day. You make some for yourself and bring some for me."

James gestures to the bag of sausage balls in my lap, which, I admit, look less like a set of individual balls and more like a brownish-beige glob of cholesterol in a Ziploc. I immediately regret thinking the phrase "set of balls" and yet here we are.

"So, to confirm," I eye him with intention, one eyebrow raised as I lean tentatively into his half of the two-seater bench, "I moonlight as your wife, you cover my daily train fare, and I bring you the Midwest's favorite potluck staple in return?"

James nods, accepting the terms as if this is a totally reasonable thing we've decided on. He sticks out his hand to make it official. "Well, Miss..."

"Paulson."

"Miss Piper Paulson." He cocks his head to the left like he's working out how my name fits with my features. "You've got yourself a deal."

I cautiously extend my right hand, unsure how we went from "sorry I messed up your shoe with my toenail" to "yes, I'll pretend to be your wife and bring you breakfast sausage rolled in a biscuit" within twenty-four hours.

James grips my hand firmly but with a conscious effort to match my strength—to not squeeze too hard. I notice the valleys between his knuckles, the uncalloused skin of a man who makes a living in an office and not out in the sun. The warmth and weight of his fingers settle around my hand as he gives a gentle shake, lingering for just a moment longer than seems necessary.

Though, is a handshake necessary at all for an arrangement like this?

He throws a small smile my way as we pull back our hands, choosing to sit the remaining three minutes in silence. Energy thrums through me as I turn over the conversation in my head, my mind racing as fast as my heart.

*This doesn't mean anything*, I whisper to the spinning wheels in my brain. Goodness knows I don't have the time or headspace for it to mean anything even if it could.

Still, the knowledge that I'm sharing something with this stranger-turned-not-stranger lights up like a spark I want to shelter and nurture. We're not only sharing a commute, we're sharing a commute *and* a secret. I forgot that secrets could be this fun.

The train slides into the downtown station and I gather my things, careful not to bump James as I sling my tote over my shoulder and ball up the napkin that accompanied my (apparently intriguing) breakfast.

He stands and smooths out the top of his pants, catching my eye briefly before I take a sudden interest in the peeling plastic on the seat in front of me. James straightens with an exhale, shakes out his limbs, and proceeds to tuck away his levity along with his phone.

In an instant, James transforms back into the stoic, no-non-sense Banker Man I had previously assumed him to be. I wonder if it feels as stiff on the inside, this commitment to discipline and pragmatism, as it looks from the outside.

We shuffle toward the doors without talking, focused on making our way through and past the throng of Elvi to cross onto the platform. He goes right as I go left, both of us stepping into the spaces we belong, him to his spreadsheets and me to my advocacy work.

I don't feel any wistfulness at this moment, no pang of desire for us to venture in the same direction. Splitting off here feels right; the two of us can exist as a "we" on the train, and in name only. Nowhere else.

Halfway down his set of stairs, James turns with a shout.

"Piper!" he yells, with a measure of authority I'd expect from a man in such a nicely tailored suit. I swivel on my heels to face the direction of his voice. "You better keep taking this train so I can bring you your fare card."

I smirk, rolling my lips between my teeth as I see his wager and decide to raise him one. "Of course! Wouldn't miss it... *hubby*."

If James reacts to this uncharacteristic burst of boldness, I don't see it. I'm flying down the stairs, two at a time, before I have the chance to regret this morning and the delight that came with it.

# 4
## James

THERE AREN'T ENOUGH TASKS in the world to distract me from the image of Piper standing across the platform and calling me "hubby."

*Hubby.*

Lord knows I'm trying, sitting here at my desk as I plead with some assignment to steal my attention. It's been three and a half hours since we parted ways at the station, and I can't scrub that final picture from my mind.

Her one raised eyebrow over a mischievous brown eye. The singular twitch of her mouth as she spoke. The lightness in her voice before she skittered across the platform. The way her jeans, comfortably worn, hugged her hips and pulled tight across her ass as she walked away.

My stomach twists into a painful knot as I realize how screwed I am. What compelled me to make the Family Fares offer? Hell if I know. I'm not sure what made me able to talk to Piper in the first place. Maybe I had a contact high from all the Elvis-inspired hairspray floating through the car.

That's the only plausible explanation because while I am

many things—loyal, motivated, decent—I am not impulsive. Or rather, I'm usually not impulsive. Today, I guess I am.

I repeat to myself the words I managed to tell her so confidently, willing myself to believe them:

*It doesn't have to be a big deal.*

I can count myself a Good Samaritan and we can exchange occasional pleasantries on the ride in. It'll be just like any other business arrangement... except that the sight of her waist dipping in from her hips makes me sweat, and I want to wrap her hair around my palm and pull.

Except for that.

Kyle drums his fingers on the doorframe as he ducks his head to enter my office, breaking me out of the daydream. "Hey man, I'm thinking Sombreros for lunch, want to join?"

Every day he asks me, and every day I decline. One, Sombreros is disgusting, and two, taking forty-five minutes out of the middle of the day means adding forty-five minutes to the end. After weighing the very short list of pros and the very long list of cons, saying "yes" is never an option.

I've got to hand it to Kyle, though. The man is persistent.

He continues, "Listen, I know how you feel about lackluster Tex-Mex, and dude, you're not going to offend me if you decide to bail *again*, but you look like you could use a break." Kyle says this with concern, his brown eyes narrowing as his fingers continue to drum on the metal frame. "Something is up with your face today and frankly, it's not a good look."

I rub my hand over the side of my cheek, pulling and pushing the skin as I weigh whether to scoff. I know he's right, though I'd never admit it to him. If Kyle could sense something off about me after sixty seconds of standing in my doorway, it won't take long for others to follow suit.

Maybe I should go out to lunch—I'm not getting anything done in the office anyway.

"Alright, alright, I'm in," I reply, and I'll be damned if Kyle doesn't perform a touchdown dance as I gather my things. "But I'm not splitting the queso with you. Cheese shouldn't congeal like that."

We make our way to Kyle's go-to hole-in-the-wall and slide into a booth that's not meant for people over six feet. I scan the menu and settle on fajitas, trying to ignore the stickiness of the laminated page under my fingers. This lunch special offers me one crucial benefit—the ability to pick and choose what goes into the tortilla based on look and smell.

It's not much, but I'll take it.

"So, what's your deal?" Kyle asks around a mouthful of chips from the bowl in front of us. I fiddle with my straw, trying to decide if it's worth opening this particular can of worms when I'm not sure I'll be able to get the squiggly suckers back in.

"Are you asking me to talk about my feelings, Kyle?" I deflect his question with my usual detachment. "Because if you brought me here so we can *share our hearts,* you should know I require a significantly nicer restaurant, not to mention a bottle of cab, before putting out."

"Are you for real right now?" He flicks a chip into my chest with a glare. "Maybe this is foreign to you because you stay shut up in your office for fifteen hours a day, but there's this thing some people have called *friends.*"

An exaggerated eye roll accompanies the taunt. "James, we've known each other for what, ten years off and on? I've always known you have a cold, dead heart, but I didn't realize it was this bad. If you want to unload, feel free. If not, we can talk about statistical analysis and financial forecasting and pretend you're not drinking a midday margarita to cope with whatever situation you have going. Your call, man."

The realization that his perception is entirely, painfully true makes me wince. I tally another point in the *easy-to-read* column.

How have I gone two-and-oh in the span of five hours?

With nowhere else to hide, and no steaming platter of fajita veggies yet in front of me, I decide to risk sharing.

"Something happened on the train today."

The words come out slowly, like molasses that clings to the sides of the bottle until it can't hang on any longer. I'm not sure how much of this story I'm willing to divulge, so I buy time with a long swallow. The curved top of the booth angles sharply into my back; the pain distracts only slightly from the tension in my chest.

"There's this woman, her name is Piper, and we share the same commute. I've been seeing her every morning on the train for weeks, and today we had an exchange."

To call the situation an "exchange" feels disingenuous, but I'm not sure there's a more appropriate way to say, "*We were flanked on all sides by costumed men while we agreed to defraud the government."*

"We talked for a few. I'm pretty sure I offended her twice. She called me out on my banker bullshit, I insulted her breakfast, and she griped about how much she's spending on train fare."

I study Kyle's face, looking for a hint about how this story is landing. He gives me nothing.

"It was probably a meaningless exchange," I continue, "but it has me messed up. Because as you so kindly pointed out earlier, I stay locked in my office for fifteen hours a day, I have no friends, and I keep a cold, dead heart. Flirting on the train wasn't on today's agenda, and neither was spending the hours since overanalyzing it."

I leave the story there for now, not venturing to the part where I offered to create a family commuter account. That's not a crucial detail for Kyle to know at the moment.

"So, you're telling me," Kyle lights up with a smirk now that I've (mostly) laid everything out, "that Mr. Stoic-and-Staid, one Mr. James Newhouse, is flustered? Some girl on the train has you all riled up? I've gotta be honest, man, I don't know what I was expecting but this... this is better than I could've hoped."

He leans back in the booth, fingers interlaced behind his neck.

A firm kick to the shin tempers his gloat. He shoots me a glare to show his annoyance, though the kick did seem to bring his energy down a notch.

"Okay, but seriously, this is good. It's good to see a crack in your armor for once. Sounds like she can keep you on your toes. I hope in six months you're leaving at seven o'clock every night to take her out, if only so I can stop fighting you for the binding machine for these damn pitch decks in the evenings."

"Sorry to disappoint," I reply with a shrug, "but this...whatever this is with her... it's a no-go, a non-starter. You know I don't have time with all the shit happening at work and everything going on with my dad. Also, I'm pretty sure she hates guys like us. I'd ruin her for all of mankind, given my stone-cold heart, and while I don't know much about her, I know she deserves better than that."

He looks at me with incredulity, digging his fork into his enchilada which recently arrived. My fajitas are nowhere to be seen.

"You have got to be kidding. You finally meet someone who breaks through *this*," Kyle motions in my general direction, "and you're just going to what, ignore her every morning for the sake of your ego?"

"What do you want me to say, Kyle?" I huff, my frustration building. "I haven't dated in years, not seriously at least, since everything went down with Sydney. You might not remember this, given how busy you were dicking around when we were twenty-six, but I'd planned to propose. I would've had she not left me for someone more available—someone not beholden to their job and the needs of their family.

"The demands of my job haven't changed in the years since, and my family situation is worse than ever. It wouldn't be fair to wrap Piper up in that mess. It's a bad idea."

Our server shows up with a steaming cast-iron skillet to save me before I say anything else.

"Just...don't write this off just yet. Will you promise me that?" Conviction oozes from every line of Kyle's face.

I can promise exactly nothing but I nod anyway. I've spent more relational energy today than I have in years; I have nothing left to give. The emotional hangover might even be worse than this sorry excuse for a fajita plate.

I should've stayed at the office.

The next week comes and goes without incident, and this includes my morning commute. Whatever tension existed between Piper and me on the day of Elvis-gate has thankfully dissipated. While my heart rate still ticks steadily up when I see her on the platform, I've been able to control myself enough that our new B Line routine feels borderline business-like.

Piper gives me a nod or an eyebrow raise when she boards and I reciprocate. We find each other as the huddle forms to exit the train and trade a single remark before heading in opposite directions on the platform.

Our growing collection of quips and jests swarms my mind during today's ride home from work, just like it has every night since the game started.

*"Wow, I can't believe you own khakis, Banker Man. Will add it to my list of notes about you."*

*"I didn't take you for a Led Zeppelin girl, but your shirt suggests otherwise."*

*"How's your tea today? Still going with black or are you hiding mango passionfruit in that travel mug?"*

*"If you're not careful, you're going to take someone's eye out swinging your tote bag around. I just hope it's not mine."*

*"Ahh, there he is. I was worried the financial district was going to be down a money man today. How would they have coped?"*

*"Don't you ever get tired of eating the same thing every morning? You know, I'm still waiting for my share of that breakfast."*

I hate to admit that these little barbs are easily the highlight of my day. The promise of seeing Piper, of making her smile or glare or roll her eyes... it's enough to get my butt in gear every morning, to make sure I make it on the train.

Not that I have ever missed it, but I certainly won't now.

This harmless tit-for-tat is exactly what I can handle at the moment. It's enough to remind me that my heart isn't *entirely* made of stone and that I'm capable of something approximating fun, but it's not so much that it costs me anything. Other than the extra fare money each month, which hardly counts.

It's good this way.

I haul myself into the house after another late night, releasing a groan as I take in the growing pile of letters scattered all over the floor on account of the door's mail slot. This is what happens when you're never around—the responsibilities accumulate until you can't ignore them anymore.

I grab the stack of mail and head toward the kitchen, kicking off my shoes and carefully dropping my bag on the bench that makes a nook of the foyer.

The microwave clock reads 11:32 p.m., and I note, with appreciation, that it's not quite as late as usual. After grabbing a beer from the fridge, I settle at the counter, the cold metal of the barstool seeping through to my skin as I rifle through the mail, sorting it into piles.

"Trash, trash, shred, trash, keep..." I dictate aloud, assigning each letter to its respective stack.

There are four items of consequence, the rest a mass of flyers, advertisements, and junk mail. I feed those to the recycling bin with a thud as I thumb through what remains.

First up, a credit card bill even though I am positive I've signed up for paperless e-statements at least twice. I set it aside to bring to the office tomorrow. That's tomorrow's problem for tomorrow's James.

Next, my eyes linger on a donation request postcard from a local non-profit. It's the sort of thing I'd typically toss... if I didn't have a house full of furniture in the suburbs that I need to help clear out. Based on the stock images plastered across the front, it looks like the organization provides resources for low-income families.

I slide the postcard across the counter where it lands next to the empty fruit bowl. Mom loved helping other people; she was compassion personified. Donating her things to help other families get on their feet feels like the right move.

I vow to give the advert to Dad the next time I see him and tell him to set up a pick-up appointment when he's ready.

Maybe this will motivate both of us to start packing up the house in earnest.

With the postcard out of the way, a notice from our estate lawyer glares at me from the counter. My heart stops for a second at the startling reminder that Mom is not only *not here*, she's *dead*. A shiver sends prickles of cold down my back.

It shouldn't be shocking, after so many months, but the finality of her death still catches me off guard. I place the letter on top of the credit card bill to look at tomorrow. Maybe then I'll have the energy to deal with it.

Last but not least, I pick up an envelope from MTA with "Card Enclosed" stamped on the left side under the return address. Adrenaline runs through me as I toy with the envelope, bending it carefully with both hands to feel the edges of the new fare cards tacked to the letter inside.

I tear open the back and peel the cards from the paper, sticky adhesive pulling at my skin as I flip one between my fingers. I take out my wallet and tuck both cards into a slot.

While I knew this letter was coming—I did order the cards in the commuter portal after all—seeing Piper's fare card in the flesh makes my stomach tumble to my knees. It has been easy enough to pretend the silly agreement we made, an extension of the insanity that surrounded us that morning on the train, only existed in theory. With this physical evidence in my pocket, that's no longer possible.

*This doesn't have to be a big deal.*

The mantra flashes behind my eyes without conscious thought. I swivel off the bar stool and adjust my pants, my hand briefly palming the wallet in my back pocket.

The last swig of my beer tingles on its way down before I toss the bottle in the bin atop the discarded mail, a shrine to the evening's activities. I suppose I'll give Piper the card tomorrow morning during our exit meet-up on the train. I could say something like,

"I'm not trying to make a pass at you, but here's your pass." ABSOLUTELY. FUCKING. NOT. My face burns in embarrassment from having even had the thought.

Instead, I'll try something like, "Look what arrived. It's a great day for free commuting." Somehow that's even worse. Why am I so bad at this? It's likely the whole haven't-dated-for-years thing.

I'll just stick to something simple like, "Hey, I got your pass. Don't lose it. I don't want to get charged for a replacement." I could say that if I wanted to look like an asshole... which I don't.

"Hey, this is for you." Simple, short, direct. Nothing is implied, there's no risk of insult, it's not cheesy, and it doesn't betray the nerves that spring up whenever I interact with her. It'll have to do.

# 5
## *Piper*

IT'S 6:45 A.M. WHEN I swing open the metal door to the office, and I'm thrilled to find I'm the only one here. There's something about a quiet space at the start of a workday that feels hopeful.

While I dread morning meetings, like the one at 7:15 with today's prospective donor, it's nice to start before the day's chaos ensues. Plus, I can't blame folks for wanting to meet before they head to work, even if it means *my* work starts when the sun's barely up.

The 6:30 a.m. train was empty and felt especially so without a Banker Man exchange to look forward to. It's become a source of amusement, wondering what sort of line he'll give me as we split up at the doors.

I wonder whether he'll ever be James, in my mind, or whether Banker Man is the best he'll get from me. I should stick with Banker Man. It's less personal. Less likely to mean something it shouldn't mean. More likely to dampen the nervous energy that flits under my skin when I wonder whether he'll miss me today too.

Slinging my tote over the back of my chair, I unload its contents to their respective homes on my desk. The laptop gets plugged in, my lunch gets tucked in the bottom left drawer, I place my notebook to my right and my water bottle to the left. I pick out a file from the bottom right drawer and scan the profile of this morning's donor to familiarize myself before he arrives.

Like most of our donors, Mr. Nowak is older and trying to find purpose in retirement after a lifetime of, *checks notes*, corporate law. He's interested in seeing the proposal for the Hope First scholarship program. He wants to learn how any funds he provides would be allocated.

I could talk about the program all day, and I might if I'm not careful. My fingers find a pen to jot down a few thoughts to structure the conversation, and more importantly, my anxious mind:

Mentorship

College application support

FAFSA help

Grant opportunities

Matching funds

One-to-one reporting from recipients to donors

Lasting generational impact

Those points sum it up. My phone buzzes with a text, vibration breaking the silence and causing a startled yelp to leave my mouth.

Sami

> GIRL. I don't know about you, but this morning has been a doozy. 😵

It's only 7:08 a.m.

Piper

> How can it be that bad when it's barely past seven? 🐷

Sami

> Well, the fact that I'm awake at seven is a big part of the problem. I wanted to catch you for breakfast but didn't realize you'd be gone so early. Can we meet for happy hour tonight and I'll fill you in? The Velvet Stool has half-price apps if we make it before six.

Sami follows the text with a gif of a pleading penguin, its smooth fins held together in prayer in front of its sweet little face. I can't fight the grin that's spreading across my cheeks.

Piper

> Yes pleaseeeee!

My fingers fly across the screen as I try to wrap this conversation in a bow before Mr. Nowak arrives.

See you there, 5:45 pm? I'm always down for whatever greasy, cheesy thing they're selling for half-off. And to commiserate. Obviously. 🍷🍕🍴

Sami

Today is going to be good. I'm not sure why, but I can feel it.

Each fallen leaf crunches and splinters under the balls of my feet as I walk to meet Sami for our half-apps date. Hearing every crisp, dry edge pop under the pressure of my steps is supremely satisfying. I'm shimmering from the inside out as I stroll through the neighborhood, my brain bathing in the glow of a truly great day; everything turned out exactly right.

I run through each hour in my mind, trying to wring my memory of every last drop, wishing I could bottle up today's wins for a future tomorrow.

The donor meeting went flawlessly. I secured a ten-thousand-dollar initial pledge for the scholarship program. The jelly didn't seep through the bread of my PB&J sandwich for lunch. Alberts & Sons agreed to provide an in-kind donation for the fundraising gala I'm in charge of next month. My art class students were eager to work and, thankfully, not eager to fight.

But the best part of today? Having a salary that covers the occasional half-priced app with my roommate. A roommate who is proof I don't live with my parents anymore. It's not much, this string of good news, but it's mine, and that's enough.

After things blew up with Henry, I couldn't imagine having days like this again. I couldn't imagine anything, actually. The picture I painted of the rest of my life was wiped clean in one explosive afternoon, and for almost two years I stared at the blank space left over, unsure how to draft a new plan.

While I may never receive an apology for how things ended with him or the company, it's an act of defiance to enjoy myself on the new path I'm cobbling together.

The thought prompts a little twirl, the wind picking up my skirt as I spot the bar in the distance. What do they say, *living well is the best revenge*?

Today, I believe it.

The Velvet Stool has a heavy wooden door that I haul open before elbowing my way past a throng of suits to find Sami perched at a high top. The light catches her dark hair and bounces off the martini glass in front of her.

"Your girl has arrived!" I squeal as she jumps down to wrap me in a hug. If you weren't aware we are roommates who see each other every day, you'd think this was a reunion after five years apart. It's just how we operate. I love every bit of it.

"Tell me," I say as I slide into my seat, "what happened before 8 a.m. that made you in dire need of a drink?"

Sami launches into her story, bemoaning our (now) broken dishwasher and how she walked downstairs into a cascade of bubbles I managed to miss by thirty minutes.

I decide *not* to volunteer that I started the dishwasher before I left.

"And then, when the maintenance man finally arrived, a full two hours after the service window," Sami says before taking a gulp from her martini to build suspense, "he looks at me, this scruffy old man who could desperately use a belt, and goes, 'You need to clean the filter.' As if that's a thing we're supposed to know. Why the hell do I need to clean a filter if the entire purpose of a dishwasher is to be a cleaning machine?! That's literally its *only job*."

She presses the tips of her fingers to her scalp, pushing her hair back from her forehead in frustration. "Plus, he charged me seventy-five bucks for the visit even though he didn't even touch the thing."

"Ugh, I'm so sorry. That's absolutely absurd." I try my best to muster up some anger on her behalf, if only to dampen the glow I waltzed in here with. "I'll clean the filter. I'm sure there's a tutorial on YouTube. It can't be that bad."

The door chimes as it opens, Sami's head turning toward the sound as I spot the bar's newest suit.

"Well, that's a man if I've ever seen one," Sami chuckles, her head swinging back my way as she continues. "What I wouldn't give to have had him show up at our place today instead of Mr. Butt Crack."

Her smile falls as her hazel eyes settle on my face, recognizing in my expression that I recognize *him*.

"Piper... you good?" She grabs my hand as my gaze follows James. I hope she doesn't notice that the sight of him makes my palms clammy.

He scans the room, trying to decide where to land. I'm trying to decide whether to slide under this table.

"Yeah, I'm fine. Sorry."

"Sure seems like you are the one with something to tell here, Piper. And to think I wasted fifteen minutes talking about our damn dishwasher when we could have been talking about how you know that fine man. And I do mean *fine* man."

Sami shoots me a smirk, egging me on to spill every detail.

"It's nothing, really, we ride the same train every morning."

The words come out choked as I watch James turn our way and spot me in my seat. Thank God for the wine Sami ordered before I arrived. I take a big sip as he starts to approach, his long legs making their way here with too much speed.

My roommate couldn't hide her glee if she tried.

James comes to stand to my left as he pulls out his wallet and fumbles through it, looking for something.

"Hey, this is for you." He places a fare card on the table, silently sliding it in my direction. I wrap my fingers around it. "I planned to give this to you this morning on the B Line, but you were notably absent." He clears his throat.

Sami nudges my leg under the table and I give her the eye.

It's the universal sign between women that takes the place of a conversation that would go something like,

"What is happening??"

"I don't know!!"

"Okay, act cool."

"I *am* acting cool, you act cool!"

"This is bananas!"

"I'll explain it later, just stop being weird!!"

James clears his throat again, his eyes drifting between the two of us and the card under my palm. He must be wondering where we disappeared to just now between our glances.

"Wow, thanks!" I offer brightly, perhaps too brightly. "And sorry, again, with the 'wow.' I don't know why I always say that with you. I mean, not *with* you. To you." My free hand finds my thigh, smoothing my skirt with the hope it will soothe my nerves. "What are you doing here?"

He shrugs, glancing around as he takes in the place. "I come here occasionally if I have a long night ahead of me and need a quick break. They make the best Old Fashioned in town and I'm picky."

"Of course you are," I reply with a laugh, excited to have this new piece of information to tuck into my expanding repository of Banker Man facts. "That tracks."

Sami kicks me again and I shoot her another look. She nods her head ever so slightly in James's direction, and I realize she's waiting for an introduction.

"Ah yes, sorry. James, this is Sami. We've been roommates for the better part of ten years. I guess you could say she puts up with me."

Extending a hand, James glances my way with a slight smile before he turns to greet her. "Nice to meet you, Sami."

"Nice to meet you, too. And for what it's worth, I don't just put up with her." Sami takes his hand, giving it a firm shake before letting it drop and leaning in my direction. "Piper keeps me sane and fed. It's a good situation."

Her face beams as her eyes dart between James and me, trying to piece together the story. She'll never get there on her own. We hang in silence for what feels like hours but must be seconds.

"Well, I guess I'll leave you to it," James says awkwardly. He looks a bit forlorn, though maybe it's exhaustion. "I've only got twenty-five minutes before I have to be back at the office. Anyway, I'll see you on the train?"

He tosses the question my way, and I'm not sure if it's rhetorical. When no one speaks, I answer.

"Yes! See you on the train. Thanks again for the card." For some unknown reason, I take this opportunity to wave at him... which is embarrassing because he's standing a foot away from me and hasn't yet turned to leave. I want to shrivel myself into a ball and bounce away.

James rocks back on his heels like he cannot figure out how to end this interaction while preserving our dignity and then decides to mirror my wave. I'm pretty sure Sami is having a medical event across the table, but I can't confirm because my eyes are still locked with James's. He gives a final soft smile and turns toward the bar, walking so stiffly he looks like he needs every bit of that Old Fashioned.

Sami comes alive with a gasp the second he's out of earshot. "PIPER ELISE PAULSON, YOU BETTER START TALK-ING," she shout-whispers. Her eyes are nearly as wide as her grin, downright giddy as she waits for my answer.

I swirl the wine glass in my hand and take a deep breath and then a deep sip, wondering where a person begins with a story like this. Might as well start at the start, I decide.

"Well, as I told you, we take the same train every morning. A few days ago, I managed to literally run into him as I boarded, during which time I ruined his shoe with my toenail."

My cheeks pull into a grimace at the memory; I fully expect Sami to call out the shitshow that is my life.

Instead, she just grins, a quiet chuckle coming out with her words. "That sounds right. And then?"

"And then the next day was KingCon. You know how it is; the train was totally packed. The only open seat in the whole car was next to his, so I took it. At the time, though, I didn't realize it was him—he was obscured by the mass of Elvis fans. We recognized each other after I sat down. I apologized again for the shoe, we traded names, the usual stuff."

Sami's pursed lips tell me she's not buying what I'm selling, this attempt to make the interaction sound casual.

"Uh huh," she squints, trying to read my thoughts. "So, tell me. Why exactly did that man, that six-foot-tall, blue-eyed, suit-wearing man," she shoots a glance toward the bar where James is sitting alone, nursing his drink, "saunter right up to you and give you a train pass? If you ride the same line every morning, he must realize you have a fare card."

My heart pumps a steady thrum as I shift in my chair. Without the absurdity of KingCon as a backdrop, the agreement I made with James feels silly, reckless even. Whatever delusion led me to say yes that morning has since disappeared.

"Well, we were talking about all the Elvis costumes, and I mentioned how expensive the whole thing must be, doing the KingCon bar crawl. I guessed the attendees probably didn't care about paying the fares to wander around the city, that maybe some of them were related and traveling on a Family Fares card. Saving money that way."

"Piper. No. *No...*" Sami grips the edges of the table with her petite hands, and I can see the story starting to knit together in her mind. If there was no judgment before, it's likely to come now.

"And then he offered to set up a family pass and add me to his account," I continue. "I think he got the sense I'm broke, which I am, and he wanted to do something nice. It's not a big deal."

No way is my nonchalance coming across as anything but forced. I'll keep trying.

"Let me get this straight to make sure I understand," Sami leans forward, not breaking eye contact, "You meet this guy, James, on the train. You mess up his shoe. You sit by him the next day, tell him your name and that you're poor, and he offers to pay for your commute?"

"Yes. That's the gist." When Sami puts it like that it sounds ridiculous. I suppose it is ridiculous.

"Girl, he is *in. to. you!*" She whistles and I hush her before anyone, before *someone*, can take notice. "You think guys are out here being chivalrous for fun? In this economy?"

She leans back in her seat, pleased as punch to be a witness to this romantic development of mine. "So, what are you going to do about it?"

"Sami, there is nothing to do about it. I'll take the train like I always do, and we'll say hi and goodbye. That's it."

"Hmmm. I can see that going super well for you."

I cover my face with my hands, scrunching up my features behind my palms as though it may help me disappear from this conversation altogether.

"You know as much as I do that I can't pursue this. He's a banker, just like Henry. It's taken the last twenty-four months to put myself back together after he tore my life to pieces, and I am finally back on track. I know the kind of guy James is, and I'm not interested."

"You sure? Cause you looked *very* interested when you watched his ass walk away from this table." Sami is impossible. Mostly because she's always right.

"There is a difference between being attracted and being interested. Even if I were, I'm too much of a mess for him. I'll never be put together enough or articulate enough to exist in his world. I tried that, remember? I'm not looking to get involved with another guy who will only want me until he really knows me. There's no need to lengthen the roster of men I've scared away."

Sami considers this with a nod. She shepherded me through

the breakup with Henry and knows the toll it took on me, on us. She wants to protect me almost as much as I want to protect myself.

"I get that, I do," she replies.

Her empathy softens the space between us as she continues. "If you don't want me to push you on this, I won't. But I'm telling you, Piper, I saw the way he smiled at you, the glint in his eye when you laughed at his drink order. He feels something toward you, whether you want him to or not."

I drain my drink, letting the wine tingle my throat before setting the empty glass on the table. I'm not sure where we go from here.

Then it hits me.

"Oh shit!" I jump up with a start. "Sami, we've gotta go home. I need to make more sausage balls."

# 6

## *James*

AFTER LAST NIGHT'S EXCHANGE, I'd be thrilled if Piper skips this morning's commute like she did yesterday's. I seem fairly incapable of having a normal conversation with her, and I don't have the energy to stick my foot in my mouth, not ahead of today's pitch at work.

I go through my usual morning routine, black tea in hand, my jacket scratching at the back of my neck as I head out the door. It's 7:08 on the dot, right on track for what should be a busy, if uncomplicated day.

One can certainly hope.

The B Line arrives at Carmack at 7:15 and I step on, finding a seat near the doors so I can make a quick exit if necessary. It's a beautiful day, sunny, and the ride is peaceful... as peaceful as it can be on public transit.

My pulse increases as we pull into Roosevelt. My eyes start scanning the crowd for Piper before we even stop.

She boards in a rush, as though she made a ten-minute walk in five minutes flat, her tote bag trailing a second behind her as she pulls it through the doors. She spots me immediately and breaks into a grin before shuffling through the car and plopping down in the seat beside me.

So much for an uncomplicated day.

Piper's buzzing, and I'm not sure if it's from excitement or nerves. Maybe she had too much coffee this morning? She turns in her seat, her knee bumping mine like it did the last time we found ourselves here. I'm not sure she's noticed.

"This," she rustles through her tote like she's digging for gold, "is for you!"

The bag of sausage balls swings from her fingers like a pendulum in an old cuckoo clock, ticking-tocking back and forth as she awaits my reaction. Her brown eyes are so earnest I can't pull away. Her gaze sends blood rushing south and my heartbeat thumping in my ears.

"Wow!" I say, realizing she may be rubbing off on me already. "To be honest, I didn't know if you were going to hold up your end of the deal. Thank you."

I take the bag and open it carefully, savoring the familiar smell. It's home and childhood and easy mornings and everything good. My eyes close without my consent.

"Why would I slack on this if we made a deal?" A jolt of cortisol races through my veins, pulling me out of my nostalgia. "We shook hands, remember? I resent you thinking I might take you for your money without delivering on my end."

She's joking, I think, but this is clearly a sore spot. I don't like the fact that it's there. I like even less that I touched it.

"Sorry, you're right. Thank you for these. If you don't mind, I'm going to save them for lunch." I press together the zipper seal and tuck the package into my shoulder bag to save for later. It would be a shame for them to get squished before we leave the train.

"James, I don't need your pity. If you don't want the sausage balls, you can say so."

She deflates, sinking into her chair and picking at a string near the hem of her skirt. Piper has no idea how much I want these damn sausage balls, much less why.

Foot, meet mouth.

I reach for her leg, my hand extending toward her before my brain knows it's happening. I grip her thigh gently, the warmth beneath my fingers spreading heat up my arm. "Hey, look at me."

She lifts her cautious and questioning eyes to mine.

"I'm not doing you a favor here. I meant what I said last week—this breakfast," I pat the bag in my lap, "is what's in this arrangement for me. I appreciate you bringing it for me." I lift my hand slowly, moving it from her thigh to my own, watching her straighten and soften as we both take a breath.

***BANG!***

The sound ricochets off the metal siding and surrounds us, loud and disorienting. Piper and I operate from muscle memory, years of lockdown drills at school propelling us to dive into the well in front of our seats and raise our arms to shield our faces.

The area between our row and the row in front of us is tight—not meant for two adults to crouch comfortably.

I step over Piper and sit, positioning my back as a barrier to the aisle of the car before pulling her to me, tucking her into the pocket between my arms and chest.

I'm sure I do this to help optimize the tiny space and not because I feel protective over this woman I barely know. She collapses, her head heavy under my collarbone and her body twisted up between my legs.

Smoke fills the car. I don't know what the hell is going on here, but I've got her. My autopilot kicks in, no thinking or feeling, and I act accordingly.

"You okay?" I shout, my mouth grazing the soft, warm shell of her ear. Her legs curl up as she scoots into me, trying to make herself smaller. She's definitely not okay.

"I want you to breathe with me." I tuck my chin to the top of her head, my arms wrapping around her curved back as she inhales again and again, too shallowly. "I'm here with you. Try to slow your breathing down."

I tighten my grip on her sides, tracing small circles with my fingers, hoping it projects confidence and not my deep-seated fear that something might happen to her on my watch.

My senses are at DEFCON 1 as we wait, my breath stretching my lungs and lingering there, held, for whatever comes next.

Nothing comes.

No new noises after the first crack; no repeated pops to indicate gunfire. Is it over?

I peel my focus from Piper and risk glancing around. A heavy haze blankets the space, making it almost impossible to see anything. It's quiet now, the sound of the bomb (*was it a bomb?*) having mercifully dissipated. Whispers and coughs replace it.

My eyes spot movement near the front of the car, and I whip my head to see a lone figure darting between rows. I strain toward the image, willing myself to focus, to cut through the smog so I can make out what's happening.

The person looks to be grabbing items out of bags people left abandoned on their seats. Within a second, he's gone, hidden somewhere among the rest of us crouched down for cover.

*Holy shit.*

The sound and smoke were just a diversion for theft.

The train pulls into the downtown station in near silence outside of the familiar screech of friction on the track. No one moves, no one talks. Piper is still whisper-close, our tiny piece of square footage existing for me and her and no one else.

I assess where I am in space, focusing on details, to bring myself back to our current reality. My feet are on the floor, hip-width apart and knees bent, my soles pressing against the linoleum. Piper's shoes are between mine but twisted sideways, notably small in comparison to my wingtips. Her hips are settled right below my knee, and her curled-up legs rest on my left thigh.

My arms envelop her top half, my sweaty hands stretched across her back to grip her sides, with less force now that the threat is over. *Is it over?*

The weight of her rests against my sternum (and also my groin, which I'm ignoring) with her head tucked just below the hollow of my throat. Her wavy hair catches against my stubble as her breath pushes her slightly up my torso with each inhale. I count each one.

My blood pulses wildly in my neck, in my limbs, down to the tips of my fingers. I want to blame the adrenaline still coursing through me from the sound and smoke, but I know it's not that.

It's not only that.

It's been years since I've held a woman like this. The thought flashes faster than I can catch it:

*Piper fits here.*

The train doors open, and a rush of fresh air fills the car: cool, clear, and clean. If anyone exits the train, I don't see it.

"I called 911!" A man shouts from several rows back. "We're supposed to stay here. The police are on the way."

Piper takes a deep breath, her chest pushing into mine as it expands fully for the first time since we've been in this position. I regret the way it draws my attention, the feel of her breasts against me as she inhales. She's still shaking, still curled into a ball within the confines of my body, and she makes no effort to move. It's more than fine by me.

"Hey, we're safe," I whisper in her ear, feeling her relax just a bit in my arms. "It's over, we're good. Are you alright?"

She glances up and nods, holding my eyes and searching for something. Perhaps she needs more convincing that we're going to be fine or assurance she can stay here until she's ready to move.

Maybe it's both.

"You can stay like this, you know... with me." I tuck her hair behind her ear then lightly hold the back of her head to my chest, my palm stretching from the nape of her neck to her crown. "We'll stay here until the police come, and then we'll talk to them together. We're going to be fine. You're going to be fine."

We sit in silence for a long while, our bodies intertwined on the floor as people around us stretch and take stock of what's missing—mostly cell phones and credit cards. I feel Piper's heart slow as the minutes pass. She unfurls bit by bit as the train fills with chatter plus a few tense laughs as we wait for the police.

"Thank you. I...ugh... I... I had a panic attack." She's sitting across from me now, her knees pulled up to her chin as she wraps them with her arms.

Given that we're still tucked between the seats, she's close enough that I can feel her breath as she utters the words. Even so, I notice her absence acutely, the place that she occupied between my limbs now cold and hollow.

"Thank you," she says again, and I know she means so much more than that.

"Of course," I whisper, and I mean more than that too, though I shouldn't.

A throng of passengers huddles along the side of the station, shaken and sweaty. Piper and I join their ranks. At some point, my gratitude will turn to anger, but right now I'm just thankful we're off the train in one piece.

Two pieces, if you count both me and Piper. Two pieces, because we're not a unit. What we experienced this morning doesn't change our relationship; we're still near-strangers who happen to find themselves witnessing wild events on the B Line.

I will myself to believe it, even while I can't convince my hand to leave the curve of her lower back.

I guide Piper in front of me, my fingers pressed to the base of her spine as we take our place near the other commuters. Turns out the police want to talk to you when you've witnessed a crime, so now we wait.

The excuse to spend extra time with her this morning has my heart palpitating. It doesn't help that Piper's trying to dissolve into me as we stand here, her head pressing against my shoulder and her body leaning into me as though she can't bear the weight of her own bones. The panic attack this morning drained her.

An officer with a clipboard inches his way toward us, jotting notes as his boots thunk with each step closer. He's taking fare cards and transcribing names on a list. He pauses in front of us, eyes narrowing as they dart between Piper and me, and points.

"You two, you're together?"

My stomach tumbles as I glance at Piper, unsure how to proceed. She smiles weakly, leaving the ball in my court. I can't blame the guy for asking given that my arm is currently draped around her waist, keeping her anchored to my side.

"You got your card with you?" he asks. "We're going to cross-reference this written list against the database of all the cards swiped on this line before this stop. Will help us know who was still on the train during the incident."

I pull out my wallet and hand over my card. The officer gives it a quick once over.

"Ah, gotcha—a family pass. That must make you..." He glances down at the name on the rectangular piece of plastic and then over at Piper, "...Mrs. Newhouse."

My whole body stiffens, every nerve rising to attention. He turns back to me as he continues.

"I've got you and the Mrs. recorded here." His pen taps against the list, and I can't help but wonder if there's a more advanced technology that could be used instead of a clipboard.

"We'll pull your full names and contact info from the profile associated with your MTA account. You'll get a call from a deputy within a few days as we'd like you two to come down to the station and give witness statements."

I nod, not daring to look at Piper as I digest what he's saying.

"And between you and me," the man catches my eye, "my gut says this incident will lead to a damages case. Don't be surprised if you get called to testify. Lawyers love having a family man on the stand."

His unexpected slap on the shoulder before moving to the next person in line makes me jump. It's enough to startle Piper away from my side and spring her back to life. The softness of her body draped against mine is replaced with static.

We stand frozen for two minutes or ten—I can't be sure. Neither Piper nor I are willing to make the first move to address what just unfolded.

And to think, I assumed the smoke bomb would be the beginning and the end of the day's surprises.

"Well, alright," Piper offers, breaking the silence as she shuffles her feet. "Seems we're going to have to... figure this out."

"Yeah. I guess so." We're still facing outward, side-by-side, as though the traffic passing in front of the platform has suddenly become binge-worthy.

"The officer said they'd reference your commuter profile—I'm assuming that's the one you added me to? What exactly does it look like?"

"It shows that we hold a joint account under the Family Fares program. My name is the primary contact, your name is listed with 'spouse' as the designation, and it has my address, phone number, and billing information."

Piper nods, a slow bobbing of her head that I catch in my peripheral vision. A motion that says, *I'm processing this.*

"I had to agree to the terms and conditions before purchase—acknowledge that the information provided was true." It hurts coming out of my mouth, these words that barely squeeze past the giant lump in my throat.

"There was a warning about falsification with a threat of fines, loss of transit privileges, that sort of thing. I checked the box anyway, confident we'd never be in a situation where the validity of our relationship would come into question."

I still haven't made eye contact, feeling the breeze tickle the back of my neck as we stand there, still frozen.

"You had no way of knowing this would happen." Piper sounds like she's trying to comfort me, but I can tell she's spiraling. The shakiness of her voice gives it away. "Neither of us did. I agreed to this too, remember?"

It's silent for another moment as we peer at the cars, each turning over ideas and solutions for how to proceed and coming up empty.

"If you want I could..." she starts to say, directly on top of the "We could decide to..." that spills out of my mouth.

We finally dare to glance at each other, and before I can make sense of what's happening, a high-pitched giggle cuts through the tension and breaks it up like confetti. The floodgates are open, and all the stress, fear, and uncertainty of the day comes tumbling out of Piper in squealing, heaving waves. Her laugh makes me laugh and soon we're clutching our stomachs, trying to catch our breath as tears slip down our cheeks.

It's a sweet relief, this sort of laughter after the heaviness of the morning. The harder we try to rein it in, the worse the fit gets. We gasp like hyenas until we're wrung dry, until our abs are sore.

"As I was saying," I compose myself enough that the words are (mostly) intelligible, "we could decide to see this through. I mean, if you're up for it."

There's a lot I don't say right now about ethics and lying and loyalty. I'm not even sure what I mean by "see it through," if I'm being honest.

I can't read the look on Piper's face as spins the suggestion around in her mind, swaying side to side as she thinks.

"We *could*..." she murmurs, rubbing her hands down her arms, her fingers pressing against the soft wool of her jacket as she considers her options. "We could. I'm not sure that we *should* keep up this charade considering what happened this morning and what may be asked of us, but we could."

She pulls her lips between her teeth, and I have to restrain my eyes from lingering on her mouth.

"How about this," I say, nudging her gently with my elbow which she rewards with a small smile. "Take some time to think about what you want to do. We can make a plan to come clean before we give our statements, or we can let the folks at the station think what they want to think. I'll defer to you entirely. Just let me know what you decide."

I pull a business card from my wallet, a chuckle escaping with my exhale as I consider how comically formal this feels. This woman spent the better part of the morning tucked between my legs, after all.

"Here's my cell. Shoot me a text when you're feeling settled, and we can make a plan. No rush—the officer said it would be a few days before we hear from anyone with next steps."

Piper takes the card and nods, toying with it for a second before slipping it in the back pocket of her tote.

"I will." She smiles, a bit of hesitation pulling at the right side of her lips. She turns to head out, presumably in the direction of wherever she works, before spinning around to face me. "And seriously, thank you, James. For all of it."

"Of course," I parrot my words from earlier. Like before, I mean it.

# 7
## Piper

THE EVENTS OF THE morning replay in my head as I walk to work, the scenes flipping through my brain like cards in a toy View-Master:

The mixture of surprise and eagerness on James's face when I sat down in the seat beside him on the train.

The way he grabbed the bag of sausage balls from my grasp, immediately opening them and stealing a smell.

His hand resting timidly on top of my leg as he asked for my eyes, and the electricity sparking under his fingers.

The ear-splitting *POP!* and my immediate belief that I wouldn't live long enough to leave the train.

My dive to the floor, James catching me in his arms and tucking me into his chest as I buried my face in his shirt.

His whispers in my ear, his hands smoothing my hair and then tracing circles on my back as I sat frozen.

The heat of him as I lay surrounded, James's heart beating a steady thrum I worked to emulate.

*How safe I felt during such a scary moment simply because James was with me.*

I let my mind dwell there for a while, lingering in the warmth of the memory as I cut across the street. It's outrageous to feel any positive emotion about the day's events, I know that, but I can't help it. I'm so used to taking care of myself (and frankly, everyone else) that being so intentionally, tenderly cared for by James has me floating.

The pitchy blare of a car horn brings me down to Earth.

Is something wrong with me? Maybe I hit my head when I ducked down. Although this new endearment toward James might be a normal reaction—the logical result of having a near-death experience together.

That's why they make the people on *The Bachelor* do those bungee jumping dates, right? Getting through something scary with another person makes you feel bonded.

*Stupid dopamine response.*

Once this high wears off, I am sure I'll float back down to the realization that nothing has changed between us. No cocktail of brain chemicals could convince my *right* mind that any real relationship with James Newhouse is a good idea.

I glance at my phone, slowing my steps briefly on the sidewalk to note the time: 10:25 a.m. Nearly two and a half hours after I typically start work.

No one knows where I am or what happened, and by the look of my notifications, people are concerned. If this morning's incident has hit social media, much less the news, it would explain why I have seventeen missed calls.

I pick up my pace, willing my feet to move faster so I can get to my desk and start letting folks know I'm safe. Our building's lobby is empty as I slip inside and up the stairs unnoticed. Praise the Lord I don't have to give the whole team a play-by-play yet. I need to call Mom first.

"PIPER?!" The yell almost ruptures my eardrum as Mom's voice bounces off the walls of my office. She's not even on speakerphone.

"Where have you been? I've been worried sick all morning. I heard what happened. You know I know you take the train every day. I understand that you're busy, but how hard would it be to send your mom a quick text to say you weren't in that train car?"

She's talking a mile a minute, and while I feel her exasperation, I smile at my own frantic cadence echoed in my ear.

"Actually, Mom," I take my bag from my shoulder and drop it near my feet, "I *was* in that train car. I just got to my office. It was a crazy morning, but I'm okay. Really, I'm fine. It was just some smoke, that's all."

"This is absolutely not fine! Do you need me to come up there? I can load up the car now and be at your house by dinner. I can't believe this. I knew you moving back to the city was a bad idea. I talked to your sister the other day and she said you never even called her back last week..."

I stretch the phone several inches from my ear, filling my lungs with a deep breath before I re-engage.

"I hear you Mom, I do. Everything is okay; you don't need to drive up here. Promise. Hey, I've gotta go. I need to let everyone else know I'm okay. Love you!" I end the call before Mom has a chance to argue.

I plop down in my rolling desk chair to scroll through my notifications and send the required texts—to Sami, my sister Gemma, a friend from high school who also works in the city, my brother Kent, my grandpa Bud, and the lady who does my hair who knows I ride the B Line.

They all want the full story, but I don't have it in me to tell it just yet. They'll have to settle for knowing I'm safe.

There's one more message I need to write, my eyes lingering on the screen as I consider it. James said this was my call—that I could choose how we address the issue of our relationship (or rather, our "relationship")—but that doesn't feel right.

We both agreed to this fake-marriage-for-benefits thing; we should also agree on how to deal with it in the aftermath of today's events. Besides, I can't risk he rats me out Prisoner's Dilemma-style when we go to the station to give our statements.

We need to get our stories straight.

I type James's number directly in the text message's "to" field, ignoring the option to create a contact card. A contact card implies repeated contact... which is not going to happen.

James and I will talk, we'll figure out a plan, and then we'll go back to exchanging soft smiles on the train each morning. The endearment I felt toward James on the walk to the office is my signal to back away. I can't risk drifting from the path I've painstakingly rebuilt solely because this man comforted me this morning.

Piper

Hey. It's Piper. I know you told me to take some time but waiting makes me anxious. We need to decide whether to come clean about our faked family account and I don't want to make the choice alone. I can't choose something that will impact your life without hearing your thoughts on the matter.

I add no emojis or exclamation points and hit send. This text is all business, a farce now that I know the smell of his aftershave and can feel the ghost of his fingers on my back.

He replies almost immediately.

James

Hey. It's James.

*Obviously...*

James

I'm sorry I jumped to conclusions earlier about keeping this charade going. I want to understand your perspective and come up with a plan that makes us both comfortable. We should talk through it together.

Is it just me, or is there a shocking level of emotional intelligence and self-awareness in these few texted lines? Hats off, Banker Man.

> Piper
>
> Not a problem! I'm sorry I shut you down earlier. I just need to process our options before we decide. What's easiest for you, a phone call?

> James
>
> To be honest, I'd rather live through another homemade smoke bomb than talk on the phone. Can we meet up later? We can go somewhere near the Roosevelt stop, presuming you live around there.

I pause for a second, weighing which direction to take this conversation. Meeting in person is a bad idea. It'll feel like a date whether I want it to or not, and the fact that I *do* want it to is a red flag.

That said, James and I might be able to wrap this up in an hour over drinks while a series of emails or texts could last for days. I'd rather make the decision tonight. The butterflies in my stomach at the thought of having a drink with James have nothing to do with it.

> Piper
>
> Sure, I can do that. 7 p.m.? There's this place, Tempest Tapas, which could work. It's casual and tends to be quiet on weeknights. Decent food, too, if you'll be hungry.

James

Sounds great, I'll see you at seven. Thanks for reaching out.

I exit the thread and turn my phone face down on the desk as I mull over his words. "Thanks for reaching out." Didn't have much of a choice given we may need to show up *as spouses* at the police station soon, but I appreciate his graciousness.

"Piper! I heard what happened!" Jenny, Hope First's development coordinator, spots me through the window next to my desk and makes a beeline for my office. "You have to get out here, this thing on the train is all anyone has been talking about. Are you okay? What was it like? Did you think you were going to die? I would've been losing my shit!"

My stomach cartwheels at being put on the spot like this. I'm not ready to answer these questions, but a crowd gathers at my door regardless.

Wiping my damp hands on my skirt, I stand up from my workspace and follow everyone to the lobby—a large landing at the bottom of the stairs with two armchairs. My coworkers gather around like first graders ready for story time, sitting crisscross applesauce on the floor as I lord above them from my seat, their eyes attentive and eager.

"Is it true that everyone huddled together in the back of the car? I heard you were packed like sardines in there!" Sadye, twenty years old and our newest intern, may be the most eager of all.

"Well, I mean, it was crowded because it's the train. When

the incident happened, everyone kind of stuffed themselves between the rows, the seat backs promising a bit of protection. I wouldn't say people were huddled though, everyone stayed spread out."

This is a version of the truth I'm comfortable sharing. She didn't ask if *I, specifically,* was huddled together with someone. We can stick to the broader facts here.

The friendly interrogation goes on too long before I shoo everyone back to their respective desks. I've got eight hours of work to fit into four with a hard stop at 6:35 p.m. All other burning questions will have to wait.

The train drops me at my stop, and I'm jittery with nerves as I head across the outdoor platform and down to the sidewalk. I'm not sure why I'm anxious; I basically spooned with James Newhouse for an hour this morning and whatever happens tonight will certainly be less awkward.

Except, of course, that the spooning didn't feel awkward at all. Which is concerning.

I lengthen my stride as I approach Tempest Tapas, a coffee-house-turned-bookstore-turned small plates joint I frequent with my sister when she comes to town. It's a small comfort knowing this meeting will take place on my turf. I may not be at ease in James's presence, but at least I'll be in a familiar swivel chair that presses in on all sides.

I turn the corner and there he is: Banker Man in all his glory. It's easy to forget how tall he is since I usually see him sitting on the train. He has his knee-length pea coat atop his outfit, but it's unbuttoned so his blue oxford shirt peeks out when he moves. His hands are tucked in his pockets until he sees me and pulls one out for a wave.

James looks exactly like the kind of guy I could fall for, the kind of guy I *have* fallen for, all lean muscle and careful hair with a business school vocabulary and a penchant for stealing the check.

If the first step in fixing a problem is to admit you have one, pass me on to step two. I know this guy, I know his type, and I know the damage a smile like his can inflict.

I won't be fooled twice.

"Hey, thanks for meeting me." Again, he leads with gratitude, and it catches me off-guard.

"Oh. Yeah! Thanks for the suggestion." Should I go in for a hug or a handshake? A high-five? If a standard protocol exists for greeting your week-old fake husband, I haven't learned it yet. My shoulders settle for a small shrug.

"This place is one of my favorites," I say. "I typically come here with my sister, but I suppose you will have to do. There are some chairs near the front in a reading nook-type area. Could be a nice place for us to talk."

He nods, opening the door and then gesturing for me to walk in ahead of him. His familiar scent—the one I learned this morning—greets me as I pass.

"Piper's got a sister. Noted."

I swivel around to ask what the hell *that* means and while I've stopped moving for a second, James hasn't. In an instant my face meets his chest, his hands catching my hips to steady me. He presses in softly, anchoring me to the floor as I regain my balance.

There can't be more than an inch between us. It's shameful how much my lower half wants to close the gap.

"Wow," I blurt, as usual, because apparently I can only conjure up one single word when it comes to this man. "I mean, thanks. Sorry. What were you saying about my sister?"

I step back and turn forward as we walk in tandem to my favorite chairs. We keep two feet of distance until we're safely seated.

"I was just saying," he adjusts himself in his pants, "that I didn't know you have a sister. Felt like something important to note."

"How so?"

"Well, if we have to pretend to be married, we should at least know the basics of each other's lives. If we decide to go forward with this thing, I mean."

My cheeks flush, and I hope the light is dim enough that he doesn't notice. "Gotcha," I choke out, concerned he mentioned marriage and I'm already losing my resolve to stay casual. Has it even been five minutes? "Let's talk about it then."

"Let's." James swivels his chair my way and leans forward, dropping his hands between his knees. If he could be more of an ogre, this conversation would be easier.

"Here's what I'm thinking," I say. "We have two choices,

really, and they both come with risks. Choice number one is to come clean at the station when we give our statements. We try to get ahead of our lie—to go on the offensive, if you will."

I don't know if James cares about sports. I also don't know if I'm using this sports-sounding word correctly, but it doesn't stop me from continuing.

"We tell them we shouldn't be on the same Family Fares account and that we don't want to go further in this process without being honest about the nature of our association."

He nods and presses his fingers together, stretching them toward the back of his hands. His knuckles crack with the pressure.

"With this option, we wouldn't have to lie—even by omission—to a bunch of officers *and/or* the State if we are called to testify. But we'd have to walk into the police station and literally confess to a crime, which is horrifying."

My anxiety is rising rapidly, and with it, the propensity for words to pour out of my mouth. "Do you know the potential consequences of fare evasion? I researched it today and *wow*, it's way worse than I expected. We're talking fines, community service hours, restitution, suspended riding privileges, even arrest or jail time.

"Why didn't we look into this before signing up together? We really should have because I don't have the money to pay a fine, I won't be able to keep my job if I'm barred from public transit, and we both know I'd be a hot commodity in prison."

James breaks into a laugh, and I get the sense he's picturing me in an orange jumpsuit, bartering with a seasoned inmate for a pen to turn into a shiv.

"*I'm serious,* James! I'd be hard-pressed to become a social worker someday if I have a criminal record!" He seems to note the social work info, tucking it alongside the fact about my sister. I throw myself back in the chair and it rocks under the force of my stress.

"And option two," James picks up where I've left off, "is we go down to the station, we give our statements, and we let them think what they already think. A 'don't ask, don't tell' sort of deal."

"And the risk," I reply with a huff, "is we get busted, and I end up in jail anyway, probably with some additional hard time for misleading a police officer and lying under oath."

It's a funny thing, James's expression just now. He's amused, but it's not at my expense. He's appraising *down-the-rabbit-hole-Piper* and appears to think it's delightful and not terrifying. Huh.

"Listen," James continues, "I feel strongly that neither of us will end up in prison. There is also no guarantee that this theft case will go to trial. Even if it does, they won't ask us to state the nature of our relationship on the stand. Lawyers only care about details that can help them win. Our marriage, or lack thereof, wouldn't be one of them."

His tone projects confidence like he's given this some thought and is comfortable with his answer.

"My suggestion is we not make waves," he says. "We do what the officers ask us to do, and we let them believe what they want to believe. Their job isn't to suss out if we're secretly hiding something. Their focus will be on finding today's thief and recovering the stolen property. We can help them with that." He taps his fingers on the top of his thighs as he waits for my thoughts.

James makes a good point. I may be overthinking this. My ability to catastrophize knows no bounds.

"Okay, I hear that, and you may be right. But I see two more risks you failed to mention and they're worth discussing."

His face lights up at the suggestion and he resumes his listening posture, his hands between his knees as he leans in with curious eyes.

"You've seen me when I'm nervous or under pressure. I panic, I talk too fast, I can't control my limbs. The words spill out before I can put together complete sentences. Either that, or I freeze and hyperventilate. Is it really a smart idea to trust me to *not make waves* if this scenario escalates to a trial?"

It pains me to bare my faults like this, especially when he might agree I am an unpredictable mess.

"First, I do think you're trustworthy. You made good on your promise to bring me sausage balls, remember? Second, we can consider today a dry run of Piper-under-pressure. So what if you showed me what you consider to be your worst attributes? I showed that I can handle you."

My soul exits my body as the words come out of his mouth. I sit, slack-jawed, as James speaks, wishing I could scoot closer.

Wishing I could release some of this tension that's been building in my center since he bumped into me in the foyer.

"So that was your first concern, yeah?"

I nod. He has no idea I want to crawl out of my skin, or rather, to crawl straight into his lap.

"What is your second concern?"

"You're right that we should get to know each other, at least a bit, in case this thing goes beyond a station visit."

A smile turns up at the corners of his mouth that lifts his cheeks slightly.

"But what if we agree to this and you realize, in a week or two, that I'm much, much more than you signed up for? What if you regret being stuck with me? By then, it'll be too late."

James tilts back in his seat, letting out a gruff laugh until he catches my expression and notes my concern. It's like he can't possibly conceptualize the scenario I just described.

"Not a fucking chance, Piper. I can promise you that." He doesn't break eye contact as he says it.

*Well, okay then.*

"So, we're really doing this?" I ask, craving one more nudge of encouragement before this decision is finalized.

"Yes, we're doing it, and it's going to be fine." He calls the waiter over and orders an Old Fashioned. I'm protective over this haunt of mine, and I wonder how he'll rate his drink against The Velvet Stool. He motions for me to order, and I pause for a moment.

Is drinking a good idea when I'm feeling the way I am? James is so self-assured, like he knows exactly what he wants at all times, while I'm winging my whole life based on vibes and my available cash.

"I'll have a glass of the house white," I say, ignoring my

conviction I'd make better decisions sober.

He gives a soft nod like he's adding my drink order to his list. "Sister, social work, chardonnay." He swivels his chair again to face mine. "Fear of public speaking. Convinced I'll run. What else, Pipes?"

"*Pipes?!*" I screech. "You can't be serious. I take it back; I want a fake divorce from this fake marriage. Where do I fake sign? Certainly, someone has a pen around here..." I lean to my left and right, making a show of looking for an escape route.

"Seems I hit a nerve?" James smiles, ducking his head so we're at eye level and looking at me like he wants nothing more than to watch me explain myself.

"I *hate* nicknames! Hate them with a passion. If I wanted someone to call me something other than Piper, I'd introduce myself that way."

"Gotcha, so Pipes it is then." He smirks and throws me a wink. I cannot stand this man, and I also cannot stand that I want to climb him like a tree.

"I *just* told you I hate nicknames. What, in that very clear sentence, made you think doubling down on 'Pipes' was the right call?"

"Piper, we're supposed to be married. What is marriage if not an excuse to do the things that annoy another person without consequence?" I hate to admit he's got me there. "Be thankful I didn't choose Pipsqueak."

I grab the pillow from behind my lower back and toss it at him roughly, the move admittedly losing effect when he catches it with one hand.

"Okay then, Banker Man, enough about me. What should I know about you?" I'm as eager to peel back his layers (figuratively... mostly figuratively) as I am to remove myself from the hot seat.

"I'm not complicated," he replies, his arms stretched comfortably across the back of the chair, legs splayed wide. "I work a lot. Occasionally sleep. I like whiskey. No siblings; I'm an only child. I'm close to my dad. I enter into morally-gray arrangements with strangers on the train. Nothing crazy."

There's a difference between sharing facts and letting someone in, and James is sticking with the former. I appreciate the wisdom and vow to do the same. While we've made things official tonight, in one sense of the word. This is a relationship based on a lie, and it's a relationship that will end when the need to lie does.

I can't forget that.

Our drinks arrive and we shoot the shit for a while, talking about the weather and the "joy" of public transit, our theories about what the thief did with the stuff he stole this morning and whether he'll end up in jail.

James swirls his Old Fashioned as he talks, alternately attentive to me and to the glass in his hand which he acknowledges is pretty good "for a spot like this." I don't press him on what he means and choose not to be defensive.

Watching him as he talks, I try to piece together all the versions of James I've met into a cohesive whole. Aloof James, Protective James, Tender James, Funny James, Keeps-Me-At-Arm's-Length James... I hate that there are more to uncover, and I hate that I want to be the one who finds them.

"It's getting late," I say when I finish my drink and the awareness sinks in that I've enjoyed the evening too much. "Where do we go from here?"

"How about this." James sets his empty glass on the table beside him and motions to the waiter for the check. "I'll text you tomorrow and we can set a time to get into the nitty gritty before our visit to the station. We should do it in the next day or two since we don't know when they'll call us down."

I nod, interested to know what he means by "nitty gritty" but willing to let the question keep me company in the meantime.

"That would be great," I reply. "Can I Venmo you for my wine?" I slide my eyes to his and he raises his eyebrows in return, reminding me silently that he's aware I'm broke. My poor financial state is why we're in this mess, after all.

"Let me get it, Pipes." The name makes me cringe, but I like the look of it leaving his lips. "And let me walk you home. You don't need to begin *and* end your day as the victim of a crime."

"No need, I'm perfectly fine." What I am is both giddy and offended by the suggestion. "I walk from the train to my house every night, and it's further than the walk from here."

James rises from his seat and walks toward my chair, spinning it toward the entrance as he hands two twenties to our server.

"I'm not saying you need me to walk you home, Piper." He waits for me to stand and then leads me toward the door, his hand resting on the small of my back. It prompts a line of goosebumps to erupt along my spine.

"I'm saying that I want to."

# 8

## James

"I PROMISE, DAD, I'M working on it."

I drag my ass to my desk chair, dropping my shoulder bag at my feet and the morning's sausage balls on my desk. They were a pleasant surprise from Piper who tossed them my way as we split directions on the platform.

"God, that's good," I mutter to myself as the warm, buttery ball of biscuit starts to dissolve on my tongue.

"What are you saying?" My dad's voice enters my ear and reminds me he's still on the line.

What *was* I saying before I spaced out, high on whatever drug Piper puts in these things?

"Sorry, I, uh... I said I'm working on the house stuff. I know you want to be closer to town and you need my help getting the house ready to list. I found an organization that could use a lot of the furniture; once we have things pared down, we'll reach out to an agent. It's going to take time."

The phone is tucked between my ear and shoulder since my fingers are dusted with crumbs and slick with grease. Dad rattles on about the landscaping and having one opportunity to make a strong first impression.

My phone buzzes with a text, and the vibration causes it to slip down my arm before landing with a thud on the floor.

"Damn it," I whisper, picking up the phone to more of my dad's questions while noting a new message from Piper.

"You there, Jamie?"

"I'm here, Dad," I reply, though I'm not really. I'm tied up reading Piper's message and noting the nervous anticipation that grips me against my will.

Piper

Thanks for last night. Best first date with a fake husband I've ever had. Let me know about this nitty-gritty meet-up. I'm intrigued 😊

She uses the winking face emoji in place of punctuation. I wait for the rest of the sentence before I realize it's not coming.

"James, are you listening to me?"

No, but that's not his fault. "Sorry, I'm here. I got a text and got distracted. What were you saying?"

"I was saying we need to schedule the guys to come stretch the carpets before we meet with a realtor."

"Yes, you're right, I'll add it to my list. But that isn't the priority right now, the priority is..."

*Buzz.*

Another message. Again from Piper. This time it's a gif: a cat dressed like Sherlock Holmes, its head shifting back and forth as it peers through a magnifying glass held between its paws. A chuckle escapes my lips. She couldn't be cuter if she tried.

"James, if now's not the right time…" Dad starts, and while his voice is measured, I can tell he's annoyed. "If there's something more important than this, just call me back later. It's fine."

It's not fine because if I end the call now he'll sit in the house, swimming in memories of Mom as he tries to decide on his own which things of hers to let go.

I can't have him doing that for either of our sakes.

"Now is a fine time, Dad. Let me mute my notifications; I'll text her back later. It's nothing urgent." I rock back in my chair, raking my hand through my hair as I settle in for the rest of this conversation. It's eating into my workday.

"You'll text who back? Her?"

The pitch of Dad's voice ticks up and hot discomfort seeps through my chest. I've made an error of disastrous proportions just now.

Dad's been goading me for years to prioritize my personal life—it kills him that Mom won't see me get married. He feels responsible for helping me get there, as though shepherding me into a happy ending would mean he's done right by her.

"It's nothing, Dad. Sorry, I just mean that I *can* talk now. You want to talk about carpets?" I hope he'll take the bait. I know he won't.

"Well, I don't anymore!" Dad chortles and my jaw sets as I steel myself for the interrogation to follow. "C'mon Jamie, throw your old man a bone. Who is this young lady who's making you laugh on a Friday morning when you're supposed to be paying attention to your dad?"

I roll my eyes, glad he's not here to see it. "Listen," I reply, "I'm only telling you this because you won't let it go if I don't." I try to sound firm as though it could stop him from pressing. "Her name is Piper, and we've been talking. It's nothing serious, and it's not going anywhere, so don't get your hopes up. We're just getting to know each other."

"Piper? That's a lovely name. You've been seeing her for a while?"

I exhale and pick up a pen from my desk, spinning the cold metal tube between my fingers.

"We're not *seeing each other*, Dad. We met on the train and we get off at the same stop. It's been a fun distraction but that's really all it is. Things are nuts right now with work and the house; I have no room in my life for anything else."

I need to wrap up this call before I say more, and because my inbox is accumulating at a rapid clip.

"James, I've been telling you this for years..."

Here it comes. The same story I've heard since I turned twenty—the age my parents were when they got married.

"There's nothing worth more than sharing your life with somebody. You think you have all the time in the world, that marriage is something you can put off until you're settled, or more successful, or have whatever it is you've decided you need. But the best part of building a family is getting settled *together*, being successful *together*, and you're willfully missing it.

"You're thirty-two, and the good ones are mostly taken. Try not to let this one go. I don't know about her but I do know about you, and it's been years since you've let a woman catch your attention after Sydney broke your heart. That's not nothing."

He's right, but I won't tell him that.

"Geez, Dad, I don't even know this woman's address (*that's a lie—I walked her home last night*), and you're practically volunteering to officiate our wedding. I don't need this pressure or your guilt trip about 'wasting my best years.'

"Look, you know as well as I do these past eighteen months have been brutal. I've watched grief eat you alive as you try to move forward without Mom. Forgive me if I'm not eager to sign up for more hurt. I know how this will end if I get caught up with Piper, and I can't do that right now. Not to me, not to her, and not to you."

My forehead finds its way to my desk, my arms slack at my sides as though my will to live has drained from my body entirely. The only pieces of me left are sinew and bones.

"My life is fine, Dad. I mean it. Sorry I let this conversation go sideways. I'll drive up this weekend, and we can make a plan for the carpets and the landscaping and whatever else we need to address. Love you. I'll see you soon."

I press the red END button and linger with my cheek pressed to the cool wood, taking a deep breath as I hear my office door open.

"JAMESSSS, my man, I'd ask how it's going but I can see it's not great." Kyle walks over and gives me a rough slap on the back.

I lift my head slightly before deciding I'd rather melt into the desk.

"Just stopping by to chat about the term sheet but if you want to keep talking about Piper, I'm game for that too," he says.

"You're an asshole, you know that?" I sit up and stretch, shaking out my arms and rolling my neck. "It's still nothing, by the way—this situation between Piper and I. 'Cause I'm dead inside and all that."

"You're looking dead, alright."

I push some life back into my legs and stand from my chair, gesturing my head toward the door. Kyle leads the way back to his office where we'll go through the document together.

I swipe my phone from the desk and type a quick note on my way out, Kyle's back toward me keeping him oblivious.

James

Brandt Park, 6pm? I'll meet you by the fountain and we can walk and talk.

Piper gives the message a thumbs up and I slip my phone into my pocket. The rest of the day better be nothing but spreadsheets and emails. I need to pull my head out of my ass before I see her later.

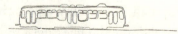

It's 5:45 p.m. and I can't remember the last time I left the office this early. I got enough done to head out, though I'll need to log on this weekend to finish up a few tasks. It's a beautiful night for a walk, not too cold and not totally dark, the sort of fall evening that makes you nostalgic for high school football games and the way you thought you had the world at your feet.

I haven't been down to Brandt Park in years, having routinely ignored what the city has to offer in favor of my computer screen. I make a mental note to tell Dad I stopped by, and even if I leave the fake wife out of it, he'll be glad I touched some grass.

Piper is standing at the back side of the fountain, and the sight of her checking her phone and looking around occasionally to take in her surroundings lifts a smile to my cheeks.

Is she texting Sami, the roommate who seemed *very* interested in our situation when I ran into the two of them the other night at the bar? I add Sami to the running list of questions I've been collecting for tonight. I wonder if she's been collecting questions too.

"*Pipes!*" I bellow and watch her jump at the sound before she catches my figure heading toward her. I'm surprised she's here early. Frankly, I'm surprised I'm here early.

She starts walking my way and I take in the sight of her, appreciating that the distance means I can let my eyes hang on her frame a bit longer than usual.

She's wearing a skirt—this one hits her mid-shin—and she has boots underneath with fuzzy socks curled over the top. Her printed T-shirt looks vintage and comfortably worn, resting under a thick sweater that hangs loosely over her shoulders; she pulls it across her chest as she walks. Her hair is different than I've seen it, gathered to one side of her neck, maybe in a braid.

A figment of desire flashes behind my eyes and I watch myself grab it gently, tugging her hair to pull her close to me, to tilt her chin up to mine for a kiss.

*Stop.* I shake my head, attempting to cage in the image and replace it with the email that's still open on my laptop, also begging for my attention.

"How's it going?" I ask. I want to seem friendly but not overeager. Not like I just pictured her mouth on my mine, the thought briefly setting my skin on fire.

"It's going!" Piper responds, and we stand there for a beat, looking at each other and waiting for someone to take the lead. It should probably be me, so I start walking.

"I figured we could walk around and get to know each other," I say. "Share some facts about ourselves and then make a plan for our visit to the station. Officer Knowles called me today and said we can stop by whenever so I told him we'd try for Monday; we can compare schedules and decide on a time. Does that work for you?"

"Sounds great," she agrees before stepping in front of me and turning so we're facing each other. She keeps the pace purposely slow now that she's walking backward. "You want to go first? Tell me, what makes Mr. James Newhouse tick?"

Piper smiles, a sneaky bend to her lips like she's spotted something shiny after weeks of looking for gold.

"Well, I told you I'm an only child. That's a big one. I'm pretty sure that's why I have such stunted social skills."

She gives me a look that says my self-deprecation isn't landing. I won't do it again.

"I grew up in the suburbs, about forty minutes from here if you're driving and using the express lane, and my dad still lives there. He's retired now." I'm not sure if this is useful information, but Piper listens attentively as she strolls, glancing over her shoulder sometimes to make sure the path is still clear.

"That's a good start," she says, her brown eyes filled with curiosity and her expression encouraging. She wants me to keep talking. I'll do whatever she wants.

"Um, I've been working at Trion, the investment bank, for about seven years now. Mostly mergers and acquisitions. I'm very fast with a spreadsheet."

My stunted social skills are fully on display, and I have no idea what I'm saying, much less why. I push through my sudden queasiness to share more.

"I live near Carmack and Lafayette, so one stop ahead of you on the B Line. No roommates, which seems relevant, since I already know you have one." I give her a grin and watch as she replays the memory of our chance meeting a few days back.

God, that feels like forever ago; so much has happened since then.

Piper's face softens as she picks up the baton, mercifully taking the onus of being vulnerable away from me.

"I do, just Sami. We've been in the coach house for about a year, and it's been an awesome spot for us." She turns so we're walking side-by-side, and I narrow my stride to accommodate for our height difference.

"She's my best friend, as I told you the other night, and my partner-in-crime. We're not the best influences for one another but we certainly have fun." She lets out a small breath as she smiles. I wish I could catch it somehow.

"And what does fun look like for Miss Piper Paulson?"

"Ahh, yes. Well, I'm broke, so that puts a damper on things." She laughs without a hint of embarrassment. "Lots of free stuff. I like to wander around flea markets and look at everyone's treasures. I visit museums when admission is waived with proof of residency. Sami and I play board games and watch rom-coms and talk about the meaning of life. And I make sausage balls."

"For that, I am grateful." I give a small bow of my head to show my appreciation. She accepts the gesture with a nod before continuing.

"This isn't necessarily *fun*, but I also started a new job recently at a non-profit downtown. We help single-parent families get back on their feet. We connect them to community resources and offer classes for both moms and kids. I teach a weekly painting class, which is the absolute best. We're also planning to launch a scholarship program soon. I secured our first donor a few days ago actually."

She projects nonchalance as though this isn't an accomplishment; I can't let that slide.

"That's really incredible, P." I decide to try out "P" as a nickname to see how it lands. The usual nickname-induced eye roll is absent from her face, and instead she gives me a warm, if uncertain, glance. She doesn't acknowledge it further. "They must feel so lucky to have you."

"I feel lucky to be there. I'd been in a rough spot for a while and it's nice to do meaningful work again, especially for a good cause. I worked at a bank in town a few years back, though I won't mention the name since you'll know people there. Things went south both personally and professionally, and it's taken a long time to put the pieces back together. I'm happy to be on a better path now."

Piper gazes down as she's talking, only making eye contact with the tops of her shoes. I'm desperate to learn more but decide not to push.

"Did you grow up around here?"

She looks at me fondly and her whole body relaxes, seemingly glad for the change of subject.

"No, I grew up about six hours south of here. I've been in the city for about five years though, off and on, so it feels like home. My mom would love to have me back in my hometown again, but she's grateful I'm here with Kent at least. That's my brother."

"The banker?"

"That's him. He lives on the northside. It makes my mom feel better that he's local in case I need him, though we basically never see each other. I would've bet my life on her driving up and dragging me back home when I talked to her after the smoke bomb. She was livid I hadn't called her to tell her I wasn't on the train, then horrified when I told her I was."

*That's my opening.* "Speaking of the smoke bomb, let's talk about Monday."

I'm confident nothing we've discussed tonight is relevant for a trip to the station to give witness statements. If anything, this plan to meet up and talk—a hopeful scheme to create some convincing level of comfort between us—has only made me aware of how unnatural I feel when Piper's around. My measured, predictable, analytical self goes out the window. I'm alternately tongue-tied and awkward or brazenly flirty.

We may have to further our lie and pretend to be newlyweds, if only to explain why I can't keep my eyes off her.

I guide Piper to a nearby bench and we sit, her body twisting toward me. Her cheeks are flushed from the chill breeze or, if I'm lucky, from being here with me.

"Alright, *hubby*, what'cha thinking?" She waits expectantly for my answer, her brown eyes on mine and her lips barely parted.

Good God, that word coming out of her mouth again sends a thrill up my spine and blood rushing downward. I shift, trying to get comfortable on the damp, wooden bench, but it's futile. Everything about this situation—about having Piper's attention and her body within arm's reach—is out of my comfort zone.

I can't name the feelings bubbling up in my chest. I don't recognize the thoughts swirling in my head about what I would do if this was a date, about how I'd tuck my arm around her waist and pull her into my side where I already know she fits.

About how if she was truly my wife, I'd lift her legs onto my lap and tilt her chin, guiding her lips to mine to search her mouth slowly, my fingers threading through the back of her hair, tugging.

*Stop.*

*Fucking hell.*

*I need to stop.*

Instead of indulging another second of fantasy, I offer logistics. "It makes sense to go down to the station early and get things wrapped up. We should go together, being married and all that."

She bites her top lip and I can tell she's thinking.

"If you want," I continue, "I can meet you at your place at seven and we can take the F Line to the main terminal. It should be a short walk from there."

Piper nods and the jostling of her knee draws my attention. The discussion of giving these statements is enough to make her nervous, to set her heart pounding.

Without thinking, I let my hand find hers, and while I don't know what I'm doing, being held eased her anxiety on the train. She wraps her fingers around mine, small and soft and cold, and scooches a bit closer on the bench. My brain tries to put up caution tape, but my heart bulldozes through it, flopping wildly in my chest as I graze my thumb over hers.

"You're gonna do great, Pipes." She smiles softly, joining the grin with the eye roll I was missing earlier. "We'll go in, describe what happened, and we'll leave. I'll be there the whole time and I can cover for you if you get tripped up. Easy peasy."

I can tell she does not think this will be *easy peasy,* but she seems to relax a bit at the idea that it could be. She makes to

stand and I wait for her to withdraw her hand from my grip...
but she doesn't.

We continue our loop along the path, a heavy silence settling
between us though it's not awkward. If silence could feel warm
it would feel something like this.

Neither of us mentions that our hands are still intertwined
and that it appears from the outside like this was the purposeful choice of two people who *like* each other. Our hands swing
as we walk, keeping us in step, and while I try to concentrate
on the path, my mind is stuck on her fingers looped between
mine.

It feels so casual, walking like this, but casual meaning ease,
not lack of care. Strolling around the park tonight, being with
Piper—I'm lighter, more agile than I've been in months. Is it
from being with her? Or is this lightness what happens when
I veer from my usual work-sleep-rinse-repeat?

It must be the latter.

That's what I tell myself as we stroll hand-in-hand, the sky
losing the sun. What feels so pleasant about this evening is
the break from my normal, stressful routine, not the woman
who's keeping herself warm tucked to my side.

This is part of the process—we're getting comfortable with
each other before Monday's song and dance—and it's a good
thing.

*It doesn't have to be a big deal.*

Piper's phone chimes in her pocket and she pulls her hand
away to reach for it. "It's Sami," she mutters, as though she
wishes it were someone else or no one at all. "She's waiting for

me at the restaurant over there." She points across the street to a rooftop bar lit with string lights.

"We agreed to have dinner at seven and also that she would keep an eye out in case you brought me here to murder me." Piper looks at me sheepishly, her face an apology at the need to be cautious. I hate that she needs to be.

"Then let's get you to Sami." My shrug tries to hide my disappointment at having to pass her off to someone who already gets so much of her time. We make our way to the bar with a purpose we previously lacked. We stop by the door, and I wave up to Sami who is hanging conspicuously over the railing, peering down to spy on us.

"I should probably keep my hands to myself," I say, gesturing up to the balcony before sliding my palms into my jacket pockets.

"Probably should." Piper smirks. "See you Monday, Mr. Newhouse!" She gives me a wave, the same one she always does, tight to her side.

"See you Monday, Ms. Paulson," I grin, warmth blooming dangerously in my chest as I think about spending the morning with her.

She turns and the door closes behind her. Sami retreats, running to greet her friend before Piper makes it up the stairs.

Meandering back to the office, I duck in to take care of the tasks I abandoned earlier for this evening's stroll. Plus, if I don't, I'll do nothing but think about Piper.

I need to at least try to keep my brain intact. This whole charade will end on Monday, most likely, when we leave the station. After that, we'll go back to our usual exchanges on the train.

I can enjoy Monday for what it will be—a few hours pretending I exist in a different life—without letting my thoughts or feelings move beyond that. It'll be a one-time indulgence, like a cheat day on a diet, before returning to business as usual.

That's all it will be.

## 9
## *Piper*

MONDAY ARRIVES AND WITH it my nerves. Ever since our evening in the park, the thought of seeing James makes my pulse climb. It's not that I'm anxious about him, really—he's clearly in control of himself—I'm worried about me, about how I felt holding his hand on Friday.

Something stirred in my chest when he wove his fingers through mine, and I've been trying to name it since. The bad news? It wasn't the safe indifference I'm trying to maintain.

The front steps of the main house are cold under my legs while I wait for him to show up. I slide my hands over my skirt and tap my knees as I think, forcing myself into positive self-talk that would make Dr. Browne proud:

*It'll just be a few hours.*

*We can pretend to be married.*

*I can give the police my statement.*

Hopefully we can make this field trip quick—go in, say the things, and get out. There is so much to do before the fundraising gala next week; I wouldn't be able to extend the morning with James even if I wanted to. Which I don't.

I watch him turn the corner and unfortunately, he looks as handsome as ever. Tailored pants, fitted button-down shirt, open pea coat, bag hung effortlessly on his shoulder and styled hair. James is a beacon of put-together perfection. I wonder if he gets tired of it, looking this pretty.

I wouldn't.

"Hey, Banker Man!"

James breaks into a grin at my shout. If he's sticking with a nickname, so will I.

"You ready for this?" I brush dirt off my butt as I stand and walk down to the sidewalk.

"Absolutely!" He picks me up in a hug and twirls me around, my feet floating through the air before I can protest. It makes me laugh, this gesture, and I'm surprised by how much I like it—both his hug and my laughing.

"Are *you* ready for this?" James tilts his head to catch my eyes, and he looks different than I've seen him before. Lighter, less stressed.

Thank God because my nerves will go further through the roof today and one of us needs to stay calm.

"I can be ready," I reply, nudging his side with my shoulder. I feel around in my tote and grab his bag of sausage balls. I already stress-ate my own on the stoop. Tossing them his way, I watch as he grabs the bag and holds it to his heart before tucking it in the pocket of his coat.

Strangely, I've never seen him actually eat one. I want to believe him when he tells me he saves them for lunch. Given we're together this morning because of a mutual lie, though, maybe I shouldn't presume honesty.

We walk toward the station in lockstep, not to my usual Roosevelt stop but further west to Monroe where we'll catch the F Line. It feels easy between us as we make our way over, nothing substantial by way of conversation but enough to keep my mind busy as we stroll. We take the stairs up to the platform and swipe our fare cards—evidence of our ruse that we tuck in our pockets—and we wait.

After riding the train together for weeks, this moment feels different. James and I aren't riding together as two individuals in a shared space, we're taking the train together as two people in a unit. It feels strange, different, but good.

James finds us seats as we enter the third car (because we're creatures of habit), and we settle in for the ride. "You okay?" he asks after noticing that my leg is bouncing faster than a metronome.

"Yep, I'm fine," I choke out, the least convincing affirmative that has ever been uttered.

He takes his left hand and steadies my right knee, splaying his fingers across my thigh with just enough pressure.

"Breathe, Piper," James instructs, and I take a deep inhale and release a long exhale as his thumb slides back and forth, his pinky finger slipping occasionally to graze between my thighs.

I'm not sure if distraction was James's plan all along, but I'm distracted all right. My heart rate ticks up instead of down, which may defeat the purpose of this meditative exercise, but I'd rather be wound up with want than anxiety.

We sit just like this, his hand steadying my leg as we stare out the window and comment on landmarks, favorite restaurants, and the old metro post office James visited on a field trip as a kid. The thought of a tiny James Newhouse in a turn-of-the-century government building fills me with delight. I'm sure he was the cutest first-grader alive, likely attentive and curious too. I like hearing his version of the world we're seeing outside.

The train screeches to a stop, much sooner than I'd like, as we pull into the main terminal. We join the huddle near the doors and the overwhelming urge to offer a one-liner in our usual style appears in my throat. Unfortunately, I can't think of anything—how rude of my brain to abandon me this way.

"After you, my dear."

James says this with a cheeky grin as he guides me onto the platform. For the first time, we both turn right after leaving the train, making our way to the stairwell and down the steps to the street together.

He circles around to position himself nearest the traffic, grabbing my hand as we weave through the morning's commuters. It's a six-minute walk from here to the station, and James decides it's time for a pep talk.

"Alright, P, the hardest part is over."

*Is it though??* I give him the side-eye as he continues.

"That's what they say, right? The first step is the hardest, and we've already made it through steps one and two, the walk and the ride."

He's so endearing with this encouragement that I'm almost tempted to believe him. Almost.

"I'm pretty sure the hardest part will be living a lie in front of a few police officers but please, go on." It's a snarky comment, I know, but James doesn't care.

"It'll be simple. We'll go in, I'll introduce both of us, and I'll state that we're here to give witness statements. We'll sit in a waiting room and they'll call us back, probably separately, to give our account of the day. Your only job is to tell the officer what happened on the train that morning. You don't have to volunteer details that aren't relevant, like why you have a different last name, for example."

"Lots of married women keep their last names!" I interject, willfully missing his point. He levels me with a look. "Okay, fine. I'll try to stick to the facts." I smile, but it's not convincing.

We arrive at the door and he pulls it open, letting me duck under his arm to enter the station. Our first stop is a set of metal detectors where an officer searches my bag. Nothing in there but a few notebooks, empty snack wrappers, and a card I meant to mail two months ago.

The officer decides I'm not a threat and I wait for James to walk through so we can approach the desk together. I'm standing, fidgeting, as he comes up behind me, wrapping his arms across my chest and lowering his mouth to my ear.

*"Time to be married, P."*

The whisper leaves goosebumps on my neck, tiny artifacts that he kisses away with light brushes of his lips near the start of my jaw. I tally another point for this man's distraction game because whatever I was worried about three seconds ago? It escapes me completely. The only thing on my mind is the tickle of his breath and the softness of his mouth against my skin.

"We're here to give statements for the smoke bomb incident?" He moves himself to my right and drops an arm to my waist, pulling me tightly against him as he signs us in. "Piper and James Newhouse."

I don't miss his purposeful arrangement of our names—how he interjects his first name to separate mine from his last.

The officer gestures for us to sit down and we claim two seats under a window on the far wall. I realize I have no idea how else a person might end up in a police station waiting room or what sort of people may join us this morning. My body scooches closer to James.

"You're doing great," he murmurs, the heat behind his words warming the side of my face. He nudges his nose into the hollow of my cheek. "Keep it up."

Do I have a thing for praise? Apparently I do because my stomach tumbles to my feet. James moves his arm to my shoulder and gives it a squeeze before rubbing his hand up and down tenderly, stopping to knead the muscle at points before resuming his path.

"Why is this so easy for you?" I whisper, in awe of the way he exists in this space, his confidence and deftness in contrast with our environment.

"Because, Piper, pretending to be into you is the easiest thing I've ever done." The chuckle that accompanies this statement surprises me. Is it because he just made a joke or because the answer is so obvious he can't believe he had to say it?

"James Newhouse?" An officer appears at a door in the corner of the room with a clipboard in hand. James stands, pulling his hand from my arm and leaving me strikingly aware of its absence.

"Please come with me." The officer glances down at his notes before turning my way. "Ma'am, my partner, Officer Wyndham, will be with you shortly. Giving your statements should take thirty minutes tops and then you can be on your way."

James bends down and presses a kiss to my cheek, his hand sliding behind my ear as he grips my jaw gently. "See you soon, P. You're going to be fine."

And with that, he disappears and takes every bit of distraction with him.

Was it always this cold in the waiting room? That must be the reason for my shaking hands—not my nerves.

Officer Wyndham approaches the door two minutes later and leads me back to a small room, barren except for a table in the center. She pulls out a chair and I take a seat, grateful I'm not here to defend myself. I'd fold in a second.

My mind pulls up the image of James in the other room, undoubtedly sitting back and talking calmly like he's a guest on a late-night show. I try to channel his energy, and it helps slightly.

"Alright, can you confirm your name?"

*Shit.* "Piper Paulson."

The officer writes it on the form and doesn't glance up,

unconcerned or unknowledgeable about my supposed union. "Can you tell me about the events of Thursday, September twenty-eighth in your own words?"

Her eyes search mine as I talk. She nods and writes between glances at my face.

The whole story spills out in one breath, about boarding the train, taking a seat, talking with James, how normal it all felt, how nothing seemed weird until the ear-splitting noise and the smoke. I don't know how helpful this account will be given I spent the rest of the ride curled up in a ball with my eyes closed.

I affirm that I didn't notice any movement in the car after the smoke deployed and that nothing of mine was missing when I took stock of my bag.

Officer Wyndham asks a few questions about other people on the train that morning, and I couldn't remotely have less information for her. My focus was on James the entire ride, both before and after the incident.

When we're done (*!!!!*), I sign to attest that the information provided is true and the officer thanks me for my time. The waiting area is empty when I return, understandably so given James (who was not pseudo-paralyzed during the incident) likely has more to say than I did.

He emerges ten minutes later and greets me with a soft smile before mouthing the words, "You did it," and grabbing my hand to pull me up from my seat. Our fingers stay linked as we sign out and leave the station.

A rush of endorphins buzzes beneath my skin—the kind, I imagine, a runner experiences when they finish a marathon.

Frankly, I also feel like I could collapse on the sidewalk right now, so the analogy tracks.

While the weather is threatening, dark clouds cluttering the sky, it doesn't dampen my mood. James knew I could handle giving a statement this morning and I did. Pride expands to all corners of my limbs.

"And that, Mrs. Newhouse, is how it's done." He smirks as he unhooks our hands and wraps his arm around my waist. My stomach flutters beneath his fingertips.

While I'll never believe omitting the truth about our ruse was an ethical choice, I'm glad we decided to go for it.

What else could I do if I had the guts to try versus letting my anxiety talk me out of it before I begin? I'm not saying the ends justify the means (we did commit fare evasion, after all), but I'm thankful to have stretched myself this way regardless.

"I know we should get to work but... what if we stopped for coffee?" James points to a coffee shop ahead on the left, and it looks as warm and nice as I currently feel. "Like when you get ice cream as a kid after a flu shot, but this time it's coffee as a reward because we're adults?"

I should say no. Tell him I'm too busy. That a possible promotion hinges on my performance at a fundraising event next week and I need to get to work to focus on it.

"But what if," I ponder aloud instead, "I put ice cream *in* my coffee? Would I still be an adult?"

"Yes, and you'd also be Italian. It's called an affogato." He says this like it's common knowledge.

"When did you become a coffee connoisseur? Was it the

same time as the whiskey?"

He nods without a hint of irony, missing my sarcasm. "Yep. I took a year after high school and studied in Florence. Had the time of my life. Drank lots of coffee and whiskey that year."

This man is full of surprises today, and I relish that he's letting me in a little deeper than he did at the park.

"I need to know way, way more about this gap year but... Italy isn't known for whiskey. Unless you're referring to Rome, Kentucky?" I laugh.

"Italians care *immensely* about their spirits, in fact. I did a whole lot of drinking that year; the coffee in the morning was a necessity to pull me out of the stupor from the whiskey the night before."

The door chimes as we enter the shop, the scent of coffee and cinnamon wrapping me up like a hug. We mosey over to the counter and I study the menu posted on the wall as though I'm not already certain about what I want. James gestures at me to order first.

"Hi, I'll take a hot coffee with oat milk and two pumps of hazelnut. Thanks so much!" Does this drink make me basic? I don't care if it does.

James raises his eyebrows in my direction before turning to place his order. "Hmm, I'll have a medium coffee, dark roast, no cream or sugar." He turns to walk toward the register, but I stop him with both hands pressed firmly on his pecs, eyes wild.

"JAMES NEWHOUSE, *how dare you*?" My expression contorts, angry and offended, and James is buying it. A look of confusion settles over his features before morphing to concern.

"I'm sorry?" he says earnestly, and I know he has no idea what he's sorry about. Still, I can appreciate the impulse to apologize first and sort out the details later.

"I told you, the first day I sat next to you on the train, that you drink black coffee. You told me I was wrong, and if I'm not mistaken based on your order just now, I was right about you."

I crack a smile and watch relief flood his face as he grips his hands over mine, keeping them planted on his chest.

"See, there's where you're wrong, P. I had black tea *that day*. I never said I don't like black coffee."

He can't contain his grin as he walks me backward to the register before peeling my fingers off his torso as he turns to pay. We keep one set of hands connected as he signs the receipt; I don't offer to pay and he doesn't ask.

A table near the window calls us to sit, the warmth from my mug spreading from my hands to my arms, offsetting the cold wafting from the glass pane.

"Thanks for the drink," I say as I raise my mug for a "cheers" and James taps his gently on the rim. He takes a long sip of his coffee, pleasure apparent on his face as he swallows.

It makes me wonder what he looks like doing other pleasurable things, this man who is usually so measured. I wonder what it would take to put the expression there myself.

I'm lost in the thought, my cup millimeters from the table when James slides his hand under it, gripping the base.

"Shit, Pipes!"

The outburst snaps me to attention as I try to make sense of what's happening.

"You need to take a drink. You can't toast and then put your cup on the table." James is emphatic like this near miss is *echelons worse* than being a victim of a crime, which we have been. He keeps his hand under my drink until I lift it dramatically and take a sip.

"Better?" I smirk. "I didn't take you for the superstitious type." I lick a bit of foam from my top lip, his eyes lingering on my mouth as I do it.

"Better. And I'm generally not superstitious—I don't care about black cats or broken mirrors or bad luck. What I do care about is not sentencing you to seven years of bad sex. That's what'll happen if you toast and don't drink after."

He chuckles before raising his mug for another sip, and I'm almost certain there's a flush creeping up his neck.

"Gotcha. And now that you've stopped the curse, good sex is guaranteed?" Tomorrow's Piper—heck, even Later-Today's Piper—will regret playing this game, but I can't help myself. I want to stay in this bubble a bit longer, the one where we pretend we're the kind of couple who gets coffee together on a dreary morning and teases each other across the table.

James sets his mug down and rotates it under his fingers. He's got something to say—I can tell because he's pulling his bottom lip through his teeth at the corner of his mouth—and he's trying to decide whether to say it.

I shoot him a narrow-eyed glance and he nods, leaving his cup on the table to stretch an arm across the back of his chair.

"It is if I have anything to do with it."

My entire body turns feverish as James sits across from me, comfortable and unfazed, bringing an ankle to rest on his opposite knee. I remove my hand from my mug to diffuse some of the heat prickling across my skin. My cheeks turn pink as James holds my gaze.

"Good to know," is all I can muster.

A rumble of thunder breaks the tension, and I startle in my seat, my arms almost knocking over my coffee in the process. The rain starts, just a drizzle, but James and I both know it'll pick up soon. It's time to get moving.

"We should've taken my car," James says, studying the raindrops slipping down the window with regret.

"You have a car?!" I reply. This is shocking news. No way would I take the train every morning if I had the option to drive.

"I do, though I don't use it much. It's not worth the cost to park at the office." He shrugs and then stands, this new piece of information hanging in the air. A thought crosses my mind.

"So, I know this whole thing was supposed to wrap up today..." I'm careful not to define "thing" because I couldn't tell you for the life of me what is happening between us, "but is there any chance that you and your car could do me a small favor?"

I give James my sweetest smile and throw in some batted eyelashes for good measure.

"I need to pick up a few items for our fundraising gala next weekend and I could do it in half the time, maybe a third, if I wasn't canvassing the city by train."

"Are you asking me to run errands with you?" James eyes me curiously, amusement fluttering across his face as he considers the request.

"Just one errand! But if it makes the task more compelling, I can bring sausage balls and promise not to criticize whatever classic rock you play while you're driving."

He takes both of our mugs and reaches to place them in the dish container on the counter behind him. I'm frozen as I wait for his answer.

"I could go with you on Friday. I'll pick you up at nine."

I hadn't considered asking him to take time off work for this escapade, but if he wants to keep his weekend free, that's fine by me.

"You are the BEST, James. Thank you, thank you. I promise you won't regret it." He likely will regret it but there's no sense in telling him now.

His arm wraps around my shoulder and we step from the coffee shop onto the sidewalk, turning toward the B Line stop about half a mile ahead. The financial district isn't far—he could head to his office from here—but I like that he wants to walk with me anyway. Especially since it's really starting to spit.

I drop off at the station entrance and head up the stairs before pivoting to give him a wave and a smile. "See you Friday!" I shout, though he interjects before I can finish the sentence.

"See you tomorrow, P, since you're not planning to walk to work." James laughs with enough force that I can hear it clearly from my perch. "I'll see you tomorrow, and Wednesday, and

Thursday on the B Line."

He throws up a hand before turning down the street, crossing diagonally at the intersection and heading toward his building, quickening his pace to get out of the rain.

It's always a treat to catch a glimpse of James from behind, but the view doesn't obscure the sting of something sharp twisting in my chest as I board the train alone.

Today was meant to be the end of... whatever this is between us... and I was confident being done was the right call for both of us. But is it really so bad if he helps me with gala prep? Spending another morning together won't hurt, will it?

I don't let myself linger on the question. I don't want to consider the answer.

# 10

## James

I WAKE UP BEFORE my alarm for the first time in years. Rubbing my eyes with a stretch, it hits me it's Friday. That explains why I slept past 8 a.m.; I have the day off. This is only the second day I've missed at Trion in seven years. The other day was Mom's funeral.

Tension crowds my shoulders as I roll out of bed, my muscles twisted up and angry this morning. I'm not anxious I'll miss a fire drill at work—my bigger concern is how to function today without the usual pings to distract me from thinking.

When I'm at the office, I operate from muscle memory, knowing what to do and how to do it to get results. It's comfortable and controllable. It's why I never take time off. Freedom for my brain to wander doesn't turn out well.

Facing the closet, I skip over my work clothes to swipe through the small section that houses everything else. When's the last time I wore something casual? The thought sets my stomach in a knot to match my shoulders.

I pull on a blue knit sweater and some chinos, tucking in the shirt before threading my favorite belt through the loops. My hair is a mess from the rare good night's sleep, and I weave some pomade through it to loosen it up further. It's controlled but less uptight than my typical style. I grab my glasses, choosing to ditch my daily contacts.

Whether I think Piper will like the outfit has informed all my choices this morning, and it's messing with me. I shouldn't care what she thinks about my clothes. My logical brain knows I need to be careful with her, for both of our sakes, but my lizard brain doesn't want to be.

My unrestrained self craves more of what we had on Monday—more time, more touching, more teasing.

I shake the thought from my head. *Focus on keeping things friendly, James.* Piper and I have fallen back into a pattern of daily waves and quips on the train since our date to the station, and it's good. That's what this whole charade was supposed to be.

Nothing more.

My car pulls up to Piper's house two minutes before nine and she's sitting on the stoop just like she was on Monday. She's wearing jeans instead of a skirt along with a crew neck sweatshirt printed with Binghampton Class of '84 and (presumably) the college seal. It might be original based on how comfortably worn and well-loved it looks. Her hair is strung up loosely in a ponytail, a few waves hanging down near her ears.

Piper looks relaxed, an easy smile and soft eyes gracing her pretty face. I'm glad to see it.

She jumps as I lean on my horn, easily startled by the sound.

The finger she raises playfully before grabbing the passenger side door is unexpected; the uncharacteristic boldness of it has my heart flying against my ribs. A loud gasp leaves her mouth before her legs hit the seat.

"Excuse me, who are you and what have you done with Banker Man?" Her eyes are wide as she takes me in, stopping at every difference from my usual appearance. She clocks my hair, my glasses, my sweater, and my pants, her gaze drifting from top to bottom and back again with a small exhale.

"Ahh yes, well, I'm not Banker Man today. I'm Errand Boy, and that requires a different uniform." My chuckle makes her laugh as we pull out onto the street. The feeling in my chest is a lot like pride when I hear her giggle like this, stretching and warming me from the inside out.

I want more of it... if only to distract me from the fact that we are alone together in my car.

For all the vulnerable moments I've had with Piper, this may be the most dangerous. She angles her body toward me and I'm captive. It will be like this all morning—there is nowhere to escape whatever thought or emotion might materialize for either of us. It's terrifying and thrilling.

Taking a Ziploc out of her tote like she does every morning, Piper tosses a bag of sausage balls my way. I catch it without looking, my eyes focused on the road and place it in the center console.

"Alright, I have to ask, though I may not like the answer..." She tucks one knee to her chest, a cautious curiosity rising in her face. A flash of nerves shoots through me.

"What's your deal with the sausage balls?" she says. "I've never seen you eat one and yet every morning you're eager to take them. You act like they're God's gift to breakfast, but you never indulge."

I let out a laugh, turning toward her to take in an expression that's intrigued, not annoyed. While I hadn't planned to start the morning this way, I might as well be honest. I pull in a deep breath and let it out slowly. "Pipes, I am excited to take them, and I promise I eat them."

That I need to keep my eyes on the road as we're talking is a small mercy. I clear my throat.

"My mom used to make them when I was a kid. I hadn't thought about them in years until I saw you eating one on the train."

She leans in earnestly, her hand propping up her head as she rests her arm on her raised knee.

"She, uh, she died last year—my mom—and in a way, seeing you eating those sausage balls felt like a nudge from her. A sort of encouragement that maybe I should pay attention, that this mystery woman on the train shouldn't be a stranger.

"I don't know, it sounds weird and I'm not explaining it well, but every morning when you toss these to me," I fumble with the bag in the console, "it's like getting a piece of home I thought I'd never have again."

I glance her way, nervous I've said too much with the whole day still ahead of us. She's looking at me intently, her eyes misty, and it's not pity or sympathy on her face but compassion. I didn't know how much I needed it.

"Sorry to make things heavy by dumping that on you, but I wanted you to have context and to say thank you. For the breakfast and for everything else." I leave the rest purposefully vague, keeping my eyes straight ahead. "And, for what it's worth, I'm glad you're not a stranger. Turns out my mom is still right even when she's not physically here to hound me anymore."

I let out a soft laugh, almost silent.

Piper reaches over and wraps her hand behind my neck, drawing circles with her thumb and pressing her fingers into muscle that's been tense for a decade. It's a reversal of our typical pattern, this moment in the car, with me baring my feelings and her comforting me with touch.

The house of straw I built around my heart starts blowing down without my consent, every pass of her thumb a puff of air that shakes the foundation.

"Your mom sounds lovely," she says softly, turning further toward me as I move my right hand to the gear shift. "I'm sorry she's not here. You must miss her a lot."

There is no bigger understatement. The ache of losing Mom has claimed permanent residency in my chest for the last year and a half. At this point, the pain is almost welcome—it's the thing still tying me to her. I sniffle up the moisture that accompanies the thought.

"I do miss her," I say quietly. "Though the hardest thing has been watching my dad try to move forward. They got married when they were twenty; he's never been an adult without her. I visit him when I can, keep him company, help him get organized—he wants to sell the house—but it's difficult with work and everything."

"I'm sure." She nods, moving her hand from my neck and placing it on top of mine, gripping my fingers. "Thanks for telling me."

She doesn't try to make things better, doesn't give suggestions about how to help my dad, doesn't spout platitudes about grief. I've had enough of that shit for a lifetime. Piper just sits here with me in the heaviness, letting it hang in the air like she knows it's the only way hard feelings can pass.

"Thank you for listening," I reply.

We ride in comfortable silence, the heaviness dissipating just like Piper knew it would until we pull up to the address on Piper's list. I can't say I've been to a place like Shindigs before, but now's as good a time as any.

"What are we picking up, P?" I ask, though it's obvious from the window display that the answer is party supplies. She circles the front of the car before throwing open the shop door, too excited to answer my question.

"Mr. Ellis!" She squeals as an elderly man peeks up from behind the balloon counter, smiling like he's won the lottery.

"Piper! How are you, darlin'?" The man comes around the corner and gives her a hug, her head towering over his—a wild sight since she can't be more than five foot four. "And who might this young man be?"

He wiggles a finger in my direction before looking at Piper with curious eyes.

"This is James. He's my muscle for the day." She nudges me

in the ribs before looping her arm through mine as we follow Mr. Ellis to the back room.

Her phrase, "my muscle," has me tripping over my feet. I like the sound of being *hers*. I think I'd like to be hers in any way she'd have me.

Mr. Ellis points us to a stack of boxes piled neatly in the corner and we scoop them up, Piper carrying two boxes and me with the last three. We load them in the backseat of my car before waving goodbye and backing out of the parking lot.

The whole thing took three minutes tops, and I have no idea how Piper would have managed to haul five boxes by herself on a multi-stop train ride.

"So, I'm the muscle?" I glance at her slyly as I steer the car toward the highway ramp to head back to her house.

"Don't let it go to your head," she replies, pushing at my shoulder with a gentle shove. "What was I supposed to say, that you're my fake husband? I suppose I could have called you my partner-in-crime, though that might've invited just as many questions."

"I'm happy to do the heavy lifting. So tell me, what's the story with Mr. Ellis? He seemed excited to see you."

"Ooooh, he's just the best. I used to visit his store each week to pick up stuff for my mom when I was unemployed." Piper shifts uncomfortably like she's worried I'll think less of her after this story. I can't imagine I will.

"Last year, I, um, spent a few months living at home, and I filled my time helping my mom with materials for her classroom. She's been teaching first grade for twenty-three years.

As a consolation when I moved back to the city, I'd get trinkets and craft supplies from Shindigs to send her for the kids. You'd be surprised by how much crossover exists between party favors and craft project materials."

She beams as she continues like the memories of those days are warm and sunny.

"After I got my job, I had to tell Mr. Ellis I wouldn't be coming in as much. He acted as proud as my own parents and made me promise to call him if I ever needed anything. When I started planning the fundraising gala and securing in-kind donations, I called him first. He was elated to donate all the stuff in the back."

I steal a glance to take her in, all wild hair and tucked-up limbs in my passenger seat. Piper is the kind of woman who gets what she wants—not because she's demanding or entitled, but because she's so goddamn sweet no one would think to say no to her.

It's a special kind of gift, this ability to disarm people and make them comfortable enough to engage deeply. She's certainly had that effect on me.

"Can I ask you about living at home?" I'm curious, of course, but I want to be respectful if she doesn't want to talk about it. "How'd you end up back there?"

I glance over to her but she's staring ahead, her right hand resting on her chin as she picks at a fray on her pants with the left. She briefly catches my gaze before turning back to her jeans.

"You can ask as long as you're okay with making things

heavy again.”

She forces a laugh, but it's guarded, like she could share more but is worried about my reaction. I stretch a hand to her thigh and linger, my signal to her that she's safe with me. It's becoming habitual, this casual gesture, and far too comfortable.

Piper relaxes under the pressure. The way she responds so physically to so little of my touch is exhilarating. I push down the desire for more—to inch my hand higher, to keep drifting up her thigh until her breath catches, to watch her arch into my seat and grip the armrest, her head falling languidly against the window.

*Stop. Stop. Stop.*

I can't continue the thought. It takes every ounce of strength to pull my thoughts back in the right direction, to win the tug-of-war between my head and my dick.

“I'm okay with that,” I reply, prompting her to continue.

“I used to work at a bank downtown. I was part of their internal accounting department, which, admittedly, wasn't the dream, but Kent helped me get a foot in the door. The salary was great too.”

She sucks in a breath, miffed at the memory of making a livable wage for a job she didn't like.

“For four years I did the whole corporate thing—long hours and designer shoes and constant crises that didn't have to be crises.”

I nod, understanding exactly what she's saying because it's been my life for ten years.

“No offense, though!” she adds.

"None taken." My chuckle acknowledges how soul-sucking finance can be.

"Things were fine enough. My life was on the path I thought it should be. I got promoted, felt like I was valuable to the team, and was making enough money to do the things I wanted to do—had I had the time to do them."

She rolls her eyes.

"I dated a guy for a little over three years who worked in wealth management. He was the kind of man I thought I wanted. Or maybe he was who I thought I *should* want. I was happy enough."

I stiffen at the words, the image of Piper being with someone else, even in the past, prompting a defensiveness it shouldn't.

"Then one day I caught an error when I was running numbers, so I brought it up to management. Turns out it wasn't an error at all but a purposeful fudging to hide the fact that my boss and my boyfriend were siphoning money from the accounts."

Holy shit. This was major news in the industry about two years ago. My brain searches frantically through the details before landing on the one I want—she must've been seeing Henry Sierra.

That smarmy fucking asshole. My anger builds, rage growing red hot behind my sternum. Piper must notice—she grips my hand tightly before calling me back to her.

"James, it's fine."

I shake my head, the knuckles of my other hand clenching white against the steering wheel.

"I mean, it wasn't fine—my entire life fell apart in the span of an afternoon, and it's taken two years and a stint back in my childhood bedroom to put it back together—but I'm fine now. I'm here. I have a job I love, my apartment with Sami, my flea markets, painting classes, and sausage balls, and you."

The word tumbles out of her mouth like an afterthought, like somehow I belong in the category of things that make her life meaningful. Piper clears her throat when she realizes the word slipped past her lips.

She'll want to say, "Wow," and to start talking her way out of it... but she doesn't. We let it hang in the air, just like the heaviness from before, and we sit with it. Or, at least, I sit with it, this realization that we're starting to mean something to each other.

Is Piper thinking the same thing?

The thought buries itself in my brain, and I loosen my grip on the wheel, bringing my right hand over my left as I ease into a turn. A few deep breaths, either to offload my anger at Sierra or calm my nerves about Piper (or both) help me think clearly again.

We have twenty-five minutes until we're back at Piper's house. I want to use this time wisely. I don't know if I'll see her again outside of our commute, and I don't want her lasting memory of us to be what just happened—her sharing her dating history, letting it slip that she might like me, and me unable to form a response.

*How has the morning gone by so quickly?*

"So, Pipes," she glares at me for calling her that but can't hide the smile creeping up her cheeks, "I never asked you about giving your statement on Monday. Obviously you did great, but how did you feel about it?"

She gives me a look that says whatever I'm envisioning is not quite right.

"Glad it's done," she replies. "I'm not sure anything I said will be helpful for the case. The details from the morning, at least after the bomb went off, are incredibly fuzzy for me. You may recall that I curled up into a catatonic ball for the remainder of the ride." Piper pulls her lips together, rubbing them back and forth as she thinks.

"Hmm, I don't remember it like that," I explain, willing my eyes to leave her lips and meet her gaze for a brief second. "My memory is of you being a very brave, concerned, and cozy ball."

I reach back over to rest my hand on her thigh, deciding I should keep it there because it doesn't want to be anywhere else.

"Ahh yes, and that's the account you gave the officer? That you didn't notice anything either because you were busy wrapping me up so I didn't hyperventilate?"

My head rocks from side to side, considering. "I told the officer we were huddled together, but I left out the part about keeping you cozy. Figured that wasn't totally relevant for their purposes."

She chuckles and I grin, high off the ability to make her laugh.

"The officer did circle back on the possibility of the case

going to trial," I add, "and that I could be called to testify. Did they talk to you about that?"

The color drains from Piper's face immediately and it's obvious the answer is no, the officer did not speak to her about that.

"P, hey, look at me." She is slow to meet my gaze but comes around eventually, the white of her eyes more pronounced than usual. "A trial might not happen, and even if it does, I know you'll be fine. It's just another forum for telling the truth about what happened. That's all."

"You mean another day when I'm on the spot but this time in front of a room full of people with a trained lawyer asking questions with the expressed purpose of poking holes in my story and getting me to say something I don't mean?"

She brings her hands to her face, the tips of her fingers pressing near her hairline as she continues. "Not to mention these folks think we're married because we let them believe we are to cover our asses. I could play along for a morning at the station, James, but I don't think I could handle being on the stand. I'd probably break down and confess this whole ruse when they're asking me my name and age or something stupid."

Piper is spiraling quickly as she considers the possibility that she may be subpoenaed, that she could be called to testify whether she wants to or not. I slow down my breathing, taking obnoxiously loud inhales and releasing obnoxiously loud exhales in the hope she'll follow.

"Ugh, I'm sorry, P. I didn't mean to make you anxious." I hope I look as sheepish as I feel. "I was actually trying to keep this part of the trip light, if you can believe it. I didn't realize the officers hadn't talked to you about next steps."

"You had no way of knowing because *we* hadn't talked about it. That's not your fault, and it's also not your fault I'm incapable of keeping my shit together when I'm under pressure."

She sighs, sounding defeated, as though whatever confidence she gained from Monday's success has gone straight out with her breath.

"How about this," I offer, trying to right the ship after being the one who capsized it. "We can do a practice run. Even if we don't know whether you'll have to testify, we can practice, and you can work out your nerves. Maybe it would make you feel better while we wait to find out if we'll be called?"

It sounds like a good idea coming out of my mouth until I remember I'm not a lawyer and have absolutely no idea what happens in a hearing. I'll need to figure that out.

"It doesn't have to be a big deal," I continue, using the same phrase that taunts me every time I say it, stepping further down this road I won't be able to come back from. "I'll ask you questions and you can answer. You'll realize you do know what to say, and it'll give you some peace of mind. We could do it before the gala or after, whatever feels better to you."

I'm not ignorant of the fact that we keep proposing reasons to see each other even though we don't need to. We were convincing enough at the station that no one suspected our ruse, and we could be as convincing during a trial.

But I want to keep seeing Piper, and it's easier to suggest this is part of our game than to admit I'm starting to really fucking like her.

She mulls it over, her fingers still massaging her temples as she processes the idea and decides what to do. "How about Monday evening?" she asks. "We could get it out of the way so it's not hanging over my head during the event next weekend. Is that doable?"

"Of course." I try to think through my calendar, but the fact is I'll make Monday work regardless. "Given that you live with Sami and this isn't something you'd want to do in public—because the idea of testifying in front of people is what's making you nervous—it likely makes sense to practice at my place."

The suggestion sounds *suggestive* and I don't mean it to be. Well, I don't NOT mean it to be, but my house is objectively the most practical space for this sort of thing. I want this practice run to feel helpful because I want to be helpful for her... even if I also want to have her in my space.

One doesn't negate the other.

Her breathing settles back into a normal rhythm which tells me it's time for the last step in the Comforting-Piper-Pipeline. First touch, then encouragement, and then humor. There's not much about her that fits my tendency to find and claim A+B=C patterns, but this one certainly does.

"If it helps, I can promise Sami I won't murder you. She's welcome to stake out the bushes if it would make you more comfortable. I can set out a chair and some coffee, and she can make a night of it. Though you both should know that I'm not interested in committing a crime... while trying to hide a crime... as a victim of a crime."

Now that's a series of words I could've never imagined my-self saying. Frankly, a lot is happening lately I wouldn't have imagined.

"Okay fine," Piper says, a hint of amusement in her eyes showing I've been successful in my effort to lift her spirits. "But I'm not showing up to some random address in the dark. Can I meet you at your office? We could take the train together."

"You know I would never miss an opportunity to take the train with you." It's sarcasm, on the surface, but it's also the truth. "I'll text you the address; just let me know at some point when you think you'll come by."

She nods with a soft smile and some of the tension releases from my chest.

*I'm going to see Piper again, and not just on the train.*

The last few minutes of the drive are comfortable. My hand lingers on her knee as we pull onto her street and slow to a stop in front of her house. The question of how we wrap up the morning lingers between us—it no longer feels like our usual waves are appropriate.

"Well, you were right, Piper Paulson," I turn to face her.

"I'm always right!" she blurts before I can finish my thought.

I shush her with a grin and continue, "I don't regret being your errand boy for the day."

She bites at the corner of her lip, and I wish it were my teeth there instead of hers. My car is off but neither one of us makes a move to leave. Her eyes glance to mine.

"That's great to hear because I don't regret having you. In fact, I may ask you to help again sometime. You set the bar too high, Mr. Newhouse. Made yourself invaluable. Laid your own trap if you will. Had you been insufferable it would've been easy to leave you alone the next time I need something."

Piper offers a coy smile, rubbing her hands down her thighs like she does when she's nervous. It makes the hair on the back of my neck stand up. It would be wise to end our time here, to say thank you and goodbye and "I'll see you on the train."

But my curiosity turns bold, a surprising need to find out what could happen if I lean into the feeling pulsing in my heart instead of out.

"Good thing I don't want you to leave me alone."

"Guess I won't, then," she replies, tiptoeing her fingers up my arm before resting her hand between my shoulders. Her head cocks to the side as she studies my face. I swallow hard as Piper's eyes travel to my lips.

"Is that what you want?" *It's what I want.* My pulse throbs wildly as she nods.

"Are you asking if I want to keep pretending you're my husband so I can ask things of you?" Her pupils expand, her face flushed. "I do."

I lean in further, pressing dangerously against some imaginary line, the one supposed to keep us safe.

"What if I don't want to pretend?"

Piper pauses, holding her breath as she pieces apart what I just said and considers whether to push the line further. Her fingers tense into the muscle at the base of my neck.

"Then you should kiss me."

Adrenaline courses through my veins as Piper waits for my

reaction.

I take off my glasses, set them on the dash, and then reach for her jaw, gently but with authority. My eyes search hers for a second, looking for doubt or nerves but instead finding an eagerness that makes my stomach drop to my knees.

With a thumb on her chin, I angle her mouth the way I want it before leaning in and brushing my lips below her ear. I drag my mouth across her jaw, trailing a warm path before I pull her bottom lip between mine.

*Fuck, it's a good kiss.*

A soft sigh escapes her as I stretch my fingers through her hair, relief washing through me as tension melts before immediately building again. I keep Piper with me, my mouth on hers, as we learn each other.

We move slowly at first, with purpose, savoring each kiss, breath hovering between us when we break before coming back together. I nudge her lips open and our tongues find each other like magnets, deepening the kiss and increasing the urgency.

I've never had a kiss like this, the kind born from weeks of emotional and physical build-up. This is a kiss more intimate than much of the sex I've had, more intentional and effusive, and the thought—of what sex with Piper would be like if kissing her is like *this*—awakens a desire that's been buried for years.

She wraps a hand in my hair and pulls as her mouth moves with mine, making a noise I'll chase for the rest of my life if she'll let me.

I want more of it, all of it, her sounds and her tongue, my hands on her back, my mouth on every inch of her skin.

She pulls away too quickly, resting her forehead against mine. Her breath is fast and heavy, our heart rates matching as I slide my hands down her arms to her thighs, closing my eyes against hers, her eyelashes tickling my cheek.

I'm desperate for another kiss, to continue what we started, but I want her to feel in control here, to be in control here.

"James?" she whispers, and the sound of my name on her lips makes me question my resolve.

"P?" I return, settling my nose under her cheekbone and pressing a peck just below.

"That was A-plus husband behavior." Piper chuckles and I sigh, turning to drop my head to the back of my seat. I don't know if this is real for her, whether this kiss was an extension of our game or a foray into how we could exist outside of it.

I'm too scared to ask.

"Happy to be your husband any time you need one." I laugh, scrubbing my hand through my hair as I exhale, trying to redirect the blood from my groin to my brain.

"Thank you for doing this today. For helping me. For all of it." She glances around the car, her eyes lingering on the items in the backseat before coming to rest at my mouth.

"Can I help you bring these inside?" I gesture to the pile of boxes in back. She seems to consider the offer, and while I didn't mean to ask if we could *take this inside,* the suggestion is there.

"To be honest, I'm not sure how I'd get this stuff from my

house to the event space next week. Any chance I could get you to drop the boxes there next Saturday? During the day, not when a bunch of guests are there. If not, I'm sure I can figure something out."

She's trying not to cringe, like asking for another favor makes her uncomfortable. Piper wants me to know she's not using me, which is ironic because I'm finding I'm thrilled to be used. Any day, any way.

"Absolutely, just tell me the time and I'll be there. Promise I'll keep these things safe in the meantime—wouldn't want anyone smashing my window to steal the placemats." I give her a soft smile and she returns her own.

"Thank you, thank you. I guess I'll see you Monday night, then? For the trial practice?"

I forgot all about that. Piper's going to be at my house on Monday.

"Well, I guess I'll see you Monday morning on the train too, but also Monday after work." She steps out of the car, smoothing her pants and brushing a rogue curl behind her ear. She gives her usual wave before turning and scampering to the coach house without looking back.

When she's gone, I rest my head on the steering wheel to collect myself before putting the car in drive and starting down the street.

I have no idea what I'm doing with Piper, and it's reckless in a way that should feel scary. Except this time, it doesn't, not the possibility of being with her; only the possibility I may not get the chance.

I need to get my head on straight before Monday. I drive to the office to pour myself into work—even though I'm supposed to be off today—because it's the only thing that will help.

## 11

## *Piper*

I CLOSE THE DOOR behind me and turn to collapse against it, sliding down until my butt is on the floor and my head is between my knees. My brain is a jumble of questions, my heart a tangle of emotions.

I don't know how to make sense of this morning, of James opening up, existing outside of the parameters I'd created for him, kissing me like a man who wants something.

Even more, how do I process the fact that I liked it? And not just the kiss, although it was a hell of a kiss, the best kiss of my life... but also his hand on my leg, his playfulness, and the way he looked at me while talking about his mom?

A few weeks ago, I would've sworn I knew the kind of guy he must be. I was certain James Newhouse was a means to an end, a way to Robin Hood from Big Finance for the sake of my budget. The plan was to save a little money and make the morning commute more fun.

It wasn't to end up in a legal proceeding and then start falling for a guy who is exactly the type I swore I'd stay away from.

Except maybe James isn't that type, and the possibility is scaring the shit out of me. I grab my phone and open my text thread with Sami.

> **Piper**
>
> SAM. We have a problem.

> **Sami**
>
> You slept with him, didn't you? 🍆

God, I love her and hate her.

> **Piper**
>
> Why do you think I'm talking about James? This could be a work thing for all you know. And also, no, I did NOT sleep with him.

I won't mention I might have if I'd let him come inside. Shit—there's another phrase, "come inside," I need to *not think* while thinking about him.

> **Sami**
>
> So this problem IS about James?

Piper

Of course, it's about James. We kissed in his car after running the errand for the gala and it was goooood. It was too, too good and I need you to talk me out of this. Tell me I'm an idiot and that James is a bad idea and no ass in the world, not even his, is worth messing up my life again. Pleaseeeeee be the voice of reason here.

Sami

You're right. You are an idiot and he probably is a bad idea and while his ass is fine as hell, it's not worth wrecking your life over.

I take a breath, her words settling into my bones as I read them. Then the three dots appear: Sami's still typing.

Sami

You should totally let him wreck you for a night though... 😏💦 I mean seriously, it's been how long? Almost two years? You could hit it and quit it as the youths say.

Piper

Do the youths say that? Certainly, they don't. 💀 Remind me to never text you ever again with any problem I ever have going forward. Have a great life!

Sami

You're welcome for the advice!! Always here to help!! 🫶 😊 But seriously, Piper, you should consider it. One night won't hurt.

Piper

Yeah, I'm pretty sure that is NOT true, especially with the gala next weekend. Hitting and quitting isn't on the to-do list. 😬

I'm back at my desk, typing up an event flow to stay busy while I wait for five o'clock. I've gotta give it to James for one thing—I've never been as productive in my life as I have these past few days, if only to keep my brain from lingering on our kiss.

If this event is a success, he'll be responsible for most of it and Sami for the rest. We spent the weekend making table cards and centerpieces, incorporating prints of her watercolors throughout the decor. The ballroom will be stunning when the place is decorated.

My fingers tap fervently on my keyboard while I work myself up for what's coming next. The gala, of course, but not until Saturday. I need to make it through the practice session with James first.

Which happens tonight.

At his house.

Just the two of us.

Alone.

The clock strikes five. I slam my computer shut and retrieve the pieces of myself that I've scattered across my desk. My water bottle, my notebook, my collection of rollerball pens, and the remains of my half-eaten snacks. I don't think we're getting dinner tonight, James and I, so I might need those snacks later.

I stop by Sadye's desk on my way out to check on the gala's setlist, pleased with myself for assigning the task to our Gen Z intern who knows the current songs from TikTok. I couldn't name them if you paid me.

It's not too far of a walk from my office to James's, which makes sense given that we get off at the same train stop even though we work in opposite directions. Unease creeps into my throat as I enter the financial district. It's a lingering side effect of my past that I typically avoid by never coming down here.

I slip through the revolving door of James's building and am dropped into the lobby like an alien to Planet Corporate, complete with a band tee and pleated skirt.

"I'm here for James Newhouse at Trion."

The security guard at the desk waves me through quickly without stopping to question what I'm doing here. The elevator opens on the twelfth floor, directly into Trion's office space.

Turns out finance has a smell, and it greets me immediately

as I step into the foyer. It's something like printers burning through paper mixed with cologne and the high-end leather of conference room chairs.

It's achingly familiar.

A man strides around the corner and stops, taking me in and trying to place why I'm here. A smile creeps up his face. "Yo, Newhouse!" He swings his head around with a shout, "I think someone's here for you."

I don't know who this man is, but he must know who I am... or at least he knows James is expecting someone. By the look on his face, the same subtle glee sweeping across it I recognize from Sami lately, James has told him plenty about me.

"I'm Piper," I say with fake confidence, extending my hand which he shakes with a firm grasp.

"Oh, I know," he says with a smirk before putting on a professional smile as James turns the corner. He punches James in the shoulder which prompts an immediate eye roll before he shoots me a look. "I'm Kyle, I work with this guy."

"Kyle and I go way back," James says apologetically. "We were in the same investment banking analyst class almost ten years ago."

"And we had fun, didn't we?" Kyle is ribbing on him and it's making him flustered; I get the sense he wanted to sneak out unnoticed.

"Yeah... I wouldn't call it *fun*," he says with a sigh, rocking back on his heels, "but it was something."

"That it was, my man. That. it. was." Kyle turns back to me, leaning in like he has a secret, his hand cupping his mouth.

"You see, Old James here," he points at him with his thumb, "it might seem like he's a hard-ass but I can tell you with confidence, he only *has* a hard ass, he really isn't one."

With that, James grabs my arm and pushes past Kyle, shepherding us to the elevator and jamming the down button at least eight times.

"Have a great time! Make good choices!" Kyle taunts with a laugh as we wait for the doors to open. James slides his hand down his face and takes a deep breath before shaking out his arms.

"Sorry about that," he says sheepishly as we enter the elevator and head down to G. "Kyle is... he's something else."

"I gathered that." My words come out with a lilt of amusement; I'm not bothered by the interaction with Kyle, even if he is.

"I should've met you in the lobby. Sorry, I lost track of time; I didn't realize it was already 5:20." He shrugs with regret.

"James, I'm telling you, that conversation was the most fun I've had all day. Give Kyle my regards and thank him for the extra serotonin." My shoulder nudges his side, and he ekes out a small smile. We walk through the lobby, and he waves at the guard before we enter the revolving door, both of us in the same bay.

It's brief, of course, but it's tight, his front against my back as he reaches around me to push the door forward. *God, he smells good*. It sends a shiver down the back of my neck to have him pressed against me, even for five seconds.

I let him lead the way to the station, and just like a week ago, there's something lovely about boarding the train together, stepping into a space that is ours versus his or mine. We find our seats on the left and crash, my leg rolling into his as we settle. It stays there, my knee pressed against his thigh as we ride.

"So, tell me," I turn toward him with a grin, "what do you have planned for this evening of ours? It can't be murder because Sami is busy tonight." Making a joke about homicide is not the right move, but my words spill out before my brain stops them. He already knows this about me.

"To be honest, murder sounds like way more of a mess than I could handle, and frankly, I'd miss you too much to go through with it."

"Don't lie, you'd just miss my sausage balls. The recipe is online and it's literally four ingredients that you—"

James shoots me a look before cutting me off. "I'd miss a lot of things about you, Pipes. The sausage balls wouldn't make the top ten." He says this with a gruff laugh.

What would be on his top ten list? I'm desperate to know, but I don't push him.

"I don't have anything planned, to be honest," he says, both of us thankful to move away from murder talk. "I figured we'd talk through some questions, get to the bottom of what you're nervous about, and sort through it."

"I can do that," I reply.

He slides his hand to my leg before adding, "I know you can."

His fingers press into the fabric of my skirt, and it feels different after our kiss on Friday. Before, this touch felt friendly, comforting. Now, it's a trap door, a pit of decisions we might regret lying below it.

The seven-minute walk from the station to James's house goes by quickly. I follow him up the steps to the porch, James jostling the key in the lock as I wait behind him.

This is a bad idea, being together at his house, but I'm not sure where else we could do this—practice a cross-examination and allow me to work out my nerves. He holds the door open, ushering me in.

It's shocking how sterile his home is, though perhaps it shouldn't be. There are no signs of life other than the shoes James just kicked off behind me and the keys he hangs on a hook just above. I follow the hall until it drops into the main living area. Beautifully open concept, he has a white, modern kitchen with barstools lining a granite counter, an adjacent dining area, and a family room separated from the kitchen with a stand-alone, two-way fireplace.

I glance around, looking for crumbs (literally and figuratively) to inform who this man is and how he lives. Does he keep any food in the fridge? Probably not. There isn't a single magnet on either door, no invitations or announcements covering the stainless steel like the patchwork of friends and family Sami and I display in our kitchen.

I can't imagine what he's paying each month to only sleep here.

My eyes catch a flier tucked near an empty fruit bowl on the counter and I recognize it instantly. Heat rises to my face, reddening the tips of my ears as I stare at the donation drive postcard Hope First mailed last month. Of course he received one; his address is well within our target region for promotions like this.

But why did James keep it?

A quick glance around confirms there's barely enough stuff in this house for one person to survive—certainly nothing extra to donate. I rifle through memories of our prior conversations, looking for any mention of the name of the organization where I work.

*Does he know I work for Hope First?* I can't imagine that he is holding onto the flier because it's tied to me... but I also can't ignore the possibility. I push the thought away as he comes up behind me, taking my coat and pointing me to the couch.

"It's uh... a work in progress, as you can see." He gestures to the space, all clean lines and empty shelves.

"Did you move in here recently?" I ask, trying to keep things light as we settle into our respective sides of the sofa, the leather dipping under each of us.

"About five years ago, actually." He confesses this with a wince like he's embarrassed for me to see him here. He can't hide behind his usual armor of a put-together appearance. I delight in the knowledge that he is, in fact, human.

"It's a wonderful home! I mean it. This place has loads of potential. If you want, I could connect you to Sami, or rather, re-connect you. She's an artist and specializes in home decor. She's the one who got me into painting, actually."

He adjusts his position, his legs spilling wide as he settles deep into the seat of the couch, turning towards me. "I appreciate the offer, but I don't need you to blow smoke up my ass about how lovely and homey my house is when we both know it's not. It's fine for now. For me, I mean. Let's start with the task at hand, yeah?"

James is flustered having me here on his couch, and I can't help but take the opportunity to make it worse. "Noted. No kindness for the rest of the night, and I'll keep myself away from your ass as well."

This might be my new favorite thing, poking James with something suggestive to see how he responds. He runs his hand down his face and gives his head a slight shake like he can't believe this is his life right now.

It's a good look for him.

Gathering his resolve, he stands. His energy shifts as he heads toward the kitchen, losing the nerves and picking up something authoritative. He returns with a stool and sets it opposite his spot on the sofa. A mischievous new gleam sparks in his eyes.

"So, she's here to play." He smirks as he settles himself back into the divot in the leather he left a minute before. Gesturing to the stool, he doesn't break eye contact. "Sit."

"Why do I get the stool and you get the couch? The stool is hard and cold! You could at least grab me a pillow," I say in protest, while still uncrossing my legs as I prepare to change locations.

"Being on the stand won't be comfortable and the purpose of this exercise is to let you practice. Like I said, sit."

The confidence in his voice makes me suddenly aware of the pressure gathering between my legs.

I do as I'm told and now we're facing each other, two feet between my shins and his, our eyes locked.

"Atta girl," he praises with a nod.

*So, he's here to play too.*

My skin prickles with a heat I try to ignore.

I study this Bossy James with purpose, certain this is my new favorite iteration of him. I've met Corporate James, Gracious James, Protective James, even Angry James. But Bossy James is something else entirely.

So much of the time, James seems to slip into roles, putting on the persona someone needs at the moment, his behavior informed from the outside in. This though, whatever this is, is coming from the inside out.

"And now we do what, exactly? You ask me questions and I answer them?" This was the plan, after all, to do a practice examination before a possible trial. James and I both know that banking on me being an articulate person in real time is too much of a risk.

"I'll ask you some questions, yes. The lawyer could ask you all sorts of things on the stand, but I don't think the specific questions matter. The goal isn't to flesh out your answers, it's to practice managing your nerves."

He looks determined, a glint in his blue eyes that makes my heart flutter.

I wish he was closer.

"Gotcha. You must assume, then, that you can make me

nervous?" The line I'm walking is paper-thin and we both know it.

"I don't assume." James gives a cocky smile. "I'm sure of it." His eyes dart down to my mouth and linger a second before meeting up with mine. "What's your name?"

"Piper Paulson."

"Good. And where were you at 7:26 a.m. on September 28th?"

"I boarded the B Line at Roosevelt, heading toward downtown, in the third car. I always enter the third car."

"Great. Did anything seem amiss when you boarded the train?"

"No, though I wasn't paying much attention to my surroundings. I saw an open seat and made my way to it."

"Why did you choose that seat?" The smirk returns to James's face, and I lean forward to shove at his knees.

"They're not going to ask me that, James!" I huff as he breaks out in a laugh. He must be tallying a point for J on his mental scoreboard.

"Your reaction is why we're doing this, Pipes. You tried to talk a big game a second ago about me not being able to fluster you. Show me that you can control yourself."

"You're trouble," I muse. He doesn't understand just how much.

"Answer the question."

"I chose the seat because I wanted to sit next to you."

"Uh-huh. And why was that?" James pitches forward, his hands dropping between his knees, stony blue eyes stuck on mine. *Why did I agree to this exercise, again?*

"I sat next to you because I had something to give you."

"Was that the only reason? You're under oath, remember."

"But I'm not!" Thrusting my arms out in front of me, I wave maniacally. "We're in your living room, James. These questions aren't going to help when I get on the stand, and you know it. You're just messing with me."

"Am I?" He slides closer to me, sitting on the very edge of the cushion with his forearms resting on his thighs. Our knees almost touch. "Because when we decided to see this agreement through you told me your concerns. You knew that managing your anxiety could be a problem. I told you then and I'm telling you now that I can handle you, but you have to let me. I'm doing my job here—focus on yours."

I settle my butt on the stool, accepting that I can't worm my way out of this exercise. He has a point. James *is* making me nervous, and I am *not* managing it well.

"Fine. I sat next to you because I had something to give you *and* I wanted to talk to you."

"That wasn't so hard, yeah?" I roll my eyes for dramatic effect. "And what happened next?"

"You offended me by suggesting I wouldn't hold up my end of our bargain."

"I did." He nods.

"And then you put your hand on my leg and apologized."

"I did." A stark pause hangs between us. "I'm surprised you remember that. It was only for a second."

Breaking character, a pleased expression warms his face, as

though his memory of that fleeting moment cracks something open within him... just like it does for me.

"And after that?"

"There was a loud noise, a pop or a bang, and I thought it was a bomb or maybe a gun. I dove for cover between the seats."

"Of course. Were you alone?" He pulls his bottom lip between his teeth as he holds eye contact.

"No. I was with you."

He rolls up the sleeves of his button-down shirt, exposing his forearms as he folds the fabric to his elbows. I try not to look. The tension between us is like a guitar string pulled taut, one that would snap with one more turn of the knob.

With every question, James twists the string tighter.

I won't be the one to break, even though I *want to*. Letting go of control, letting James get me all riled up to bring me back down again... it's an inviting idea. The building ache between my legs is at war with my brain about tonight's preferred outcome, and I realize I'm not just sparring with James. I'm also fighting myself.

"Can you describe your position?"

My attention snaps back to James's face, his eyes darker, intent, his eyebrows furrowed.

"You were sitting on the floor, your back facing the aisle of the train car. I curled myself into a ball, tucking up my knees and settling between your hips. My head was under your collarbone, and you wrapped your arms around my back."

He stands, and I watch him walk a half circle until he's

directly behind the stool. My heart leaps into my throat as he stops there, draping his arms over my shoulders and hugging me tightly from behind.

"Like this?"

The warmth of his breath on my neck makes my blood hum. "Not quite," I whisper, turning my face into the crook of his arm. "We were chest-to-chest; I was facing you. Right now, we're back-to-chest."

"Is that a problem?"

A whimper escapes my throat as he nudges back my hair and presses his mouth to the delicate skin under my jaw.

"No. It's... goodness, James..."

He kisses a line from my ear to my collarbone, my head stretching in response to give him more access. It makes me light-headed.

"Focus, Piper. You need to control yourself."

I strain to remember the question, his body pressed against mine and the words coming out of his mouth an impressive distraction. "No...it's... not a problem."

"Good." His voice is soft in my ear, quiet and familiar, before he gives the lobe a gentle bite. "What else do you remember?"

"You held me there on the train, tracing circles on my back, gripping my sides, encouraging me to breathe, reminding me I'm safe."

James's hands echo his movements from that morning, holding my arms tightly within his, his fingers splayed across my ribs.

"You *are* safe." Breathing deeply, he nuzzles his face into my hair before releasing a contented sigh. "You're safe with me." His hands move slowly to the curve of my waist, pressing in gently. "You can be fine or not fine, okay or not okay, but you'll never be unsafe. Not with me."

A shaky exhale is all I can muster.

With all the pushing and pulling, teasing and bartering, disagreements and compromises and *compromising situations*, I've felt a lot of things for and with James Newhouse.

But never once have I felt like he's reckless with me. He makes me feel like I could collapse into a puddle or explode like a geyser, my heart seeping in every possible direction, and that he'd wait patiently to dam me in.

"Can I touch you?" He says it in a whisper, his tone a mix of tenderness and hunger as he strokes up my sides, slipping under the hem of my shirt. I nod, hoping it's enough encouragement for his hands to move where I want them.

"I need you to say it." It's both dominance and deference, this demand, and it turns my insides molten.

"Yes. Please, James."

He groans at the sound of his name on my lips, his hands drawing up to my breasts as he sucks gently behind my ear. I'm impatient to bring my mouth to his and my hands to his chest, returning the favor. "Do you want me to turn around? I can turn around."

"No, I want you right here, exactly like this." He slips a hand under my bra, twisting my nipple and making it hard, pulling a moan from my throat as he tugs. His head is tucked into the crook of my neck, the stubble on his chin grazing my shoulder every time he exhales, lightly tickling.

He peels off my shirt and then my bra, and both land at my feet. Somehow, he manages to do this while keeping his lips on my skin.

He moves achingly slow, touching and tasting like he's cataloging my body and my response to his touch. We're working in tandem this way, the arching of my back and my whimpering sighs charting a path he attentively follows.

"Please, James..."

I want all of him—his hands, his mouth, his abs, and what lies lower. I'm frenzied by the need building in my center. If he senses my growing urgency, he doesn't match it.

His left hand is on my breast, pinching my nipple and rolling it between his fingers as I squirm within his arms. His right hand traces my stomach before ducking beneath the waistband of my skirt and resting on the lace of my panties.

I need him to touch me, to diffuse the tension that's pulsing through every inch of my body.

"Please what?" he whispers, tapping his thumb once to the most sensitive part of me and sending electricity crackling through my limbs.

"Please touch me," I whine, sliding forward on the stool to press myself into his hand. He tightens his grip on my breast, pulling me back against him.

"Here?" He moves his fingers along the front of me, stopping where I'm wet—he can feel it through the layer between us. "Shit," he says with a groan, and I can feel his hand trembling. He wants this as much as I do.

James brings his hand back to the top of the lace and then slips under, his palm cupping me briefly as he takes a composing breath. He puts his mouth to my ear, and I swear I might die if he doesn't start moving.

"I want you to focus, Piper, on my thumb moving against you, my fingers parting you and slipping inside, my hand on your tit, my mouth on your neck. I want you to feel every bit of it."

There's no time for shock at James's words because his hand starts moving in rhythm, pulsing right where I need it, making me gasp. He works slowly at first, building momentum to match the rise and fall of my breath. He sucks on my neck between whispers of encouragement, each praise pushing me higher.

*That's it.*

*You're perfect, you know that?*

*I've got you.*

*Shit, Piper, you feel so good.*

*Go on, come for me.*

I break apart as soon as those last words hit my ear, waves of pleasure crashing down as I collapse into him. James sweeps his left arm across my chest to steady me, his right hand drawing out every bit of my orgasm.

We breathe heavily in unison, stuttering inhales and exhales as I come back down. He wraps me up in his arms, keeping me tight to him as he dots kisses along my hairline.

I gasp out a laugh, startling him as I straighten.

"That bad?" He comes around to my front, his eyes glinting brightly as a smile creeps up his cheeks.

"*That good.*" I chuckle, my face flushed and my hands trembling as he takes them in his, walking backward toward the couch and pulling me off the stool to follow. "I never imagined you'd make me come before I've even seen you shirtless."

It feels like it should be awkward, this acknowledgment that I've bared more of myself than he has. However, on second thought, he didn't hold back from giving me so much of himself just a moment ago.

"Let me fix that." Slowly, James unbuttons and then peels off his shirt. This man is something else—defined muscles typically tucked away behind starched cotton; brazen sexiness hidden under unassuming sweetness.

I don't take for granted he's offered me both sides of himself. As if to prove the point, he draws me onto his lap, taking my face in his hands as he finds my mouth for a kiss that's equal parts hungry and reverent.

# 12

## James

PIPER IS ON TOP of me, straddling my legs. Her weight provides the pressure I desperately need on my dick, which is acting more eager than I'd like. She kisses me sweetly like she's still lingering in a post-orgasm haze and doesn't want to see clearly just yet.

"God, you are so beautiful like this," I murmur, enjoying everything about this soft and satisfied woman who is mine, at least for tonight.

"Half-naked on your lap?" She giggles, nicking at my collarbone before kissing the spot with a tender brush of her lips.

"Absolutely my favorite version of you to date. Ten out of ten, no notes." Even in this moment, this potentially awkward moment, we default to being playful.

I take Piper's chin in my hand and guide her lips to mine, pressing a deep kiss to her mouth. Sinking back into the leather, her body sinks into me. The kiss starts slowly, like she's searching for something. It's not tentative, but it's also not rushed.

She takes my bottom lip between hers as her hands roam

freely, first grazing my chest, then weaving through my hair, then wrapping around my neck and gently playing with my ear. It's like she's getting to know these pieces of me, and she wants to honor each one.

I tease her lips with my tongue and she opens for me, our tongues finding one another as we deepen the kiss. Tilting her head, I find an angle that works to increase her urgency. Her hips roll across my lap, making me groan.

"What do you want, P?" I pull away for a second, meeting her eyes and enjoying the small pout she puts on at the loss of my lips.

"What do you mean, *what do I want*?" She presses her mouth to the end of my eyebrow, again to the apple of my cheek. "I should be asking what *you* want. You've done plenty already."

Piper smirks with appreciation like the fresh memory of her orgasm is a secret she can't contain. That naughty little grin brands my heart, claiming it for her.

*I'm in so much fucking trouble.*

"Let me be clear, what happened a few minutes ago—making you come on my fingers while you gasped my name—that was for *me*. This next round is for you."

She grinds into me as she restarts our kiss, her naked chest grazing my pecs.

"Okay," she replies, looking the tiniest bit smug. "I want you to lose the pants." Piper reaches down between us, and my dick jumps at the contact. She settles back on her heels as she undoes my belt, slides out the button, and pulls down the zipper.

"Off, please," she says.

She seems to forget that she's sitting on me, thereby keeping my pants pinned to my legs. I grab her by the waist and toss her to my left, careful that she lands on a cushion, but not so careful that she thinks I can only be gentle with her.

I strip off my pants, dropping them in the pile with our shirts and her bra. My boxer briefs are still on, and she's not thrilled.

"Yeah, that's not what I want," she says, eyeing my frame, her gaze trained on my lower half. I like this Piper—self-assured and demanding. I peel off my briefs, watching her expression change as reaches for me and pulls me to the couch to sit, standing to take my place.

"It's only fair," she shrugs as she drops her skirt, her lace panties a treat before she pulls her legs out of them one at a time. Standing naked in front of me, Piper is a masterpiece.

The swell of her breasts, the dip of her waist, her wild hair framing the face that is quickly becoming my favorite—it sucks the breath out of my lungs.

She makes her way to the couch and lays down on her back, draping her legs over my lap as I take her in up close.

I want to memorize this moment, to capture the landscape of her body with my mind and then with my mouth: the way her chest dips under her collarbone, the tiny birthmark that lives on her lower belly, the scar on the back of her arm.

"I want you to kiss me," she says, and it's as much an ask as a direction.

I pick up her right leg, smooth and soft and warm, running my fingers across the skin of her ankle before kissing behind the bone. I press my lips against her shin and then again, inching myself closer to her knee. I spread my thumbs behind the back of it, kneading the muscle at the top of her calf as I press my teeth to her kneecap gently before closing my mouth around it.

She releases a whispered moan at the contact.

Shifting myself to kneeling, I perch her legs on either side of my hips as I continue my ascent up her body. Hovering over her, I mark the curve of her waist, the jut of her ribs, and the soft warmth of her stomach with my lips. She sucks in a fast breath as I approach her breasts, nudging between them with my nose as I drag a hand between her legs, my other hand propping me up as I inch forward.

I've imagined this scenario since I first saw Piper and I've wondered what it would be like to have her writhing under me and desperate for my touch—how she'd taste and how her skin would feel, the sounds she'd make, the look on her face when I'd make her come.

It was all wrong. The image in my mind was an arts and crafts project; being with her tonight is Michaelangelo sculpting the David. It's infinitely better, more evocative, so awe-inducing there aren't words to describe it. Just the feeling deep down that you're a witness to something profound.

I take her nipple in my mouth, a groan vibrating from my lungs when she arches into me, her hand raking through my hair. I swirl the tip of her breast with my tongue, tugging occasionally with my teeth, as my thumb mirrors the motion on the sensitive spot between her legs.

"Holy shit, James." Piper whimpers my name into my skin, her breath becoming erratic as I slide two fingers inside her, moving my mouth to her other breast. I drag her wetness back and forth, creating friction where she needs it before dipping back inside in rhythm.

She clenches around me, digging her nails into my back, scraping up to my shoulders and down again as I tease her nipple with my mouth. She's leaving marks for me to remember her by tomorrow.

As though I could forget.

"I need to feel you," she begs, and I move my mouth to hers, slipping into a wet kiss as I position myself above her, my tip trailing down the front of her to where we both want it.

"I'm not going to last," I warn. The sight of her, the feel of her, has been nearly enough already.

"I don't care. I want you closer. Do you have a condom?"

"Absolutely."

If only one would materialize beneath the cushions like spare change you find the moment you need it.

Rolling off Piper, my hand lingers until I can no longer reach her on my path to the kitchen. I yank open a drawer and grab the foil packet, tearing it open with my teeth as I walk back to her, her chocolate eyes watching me intently as I stop, slip it on, and roll the latex up my shaft.

"Thank you," she whispers, "for not making that a big deal."

I can't stand that the request may have been difficult for her to make. "I meant what I said. You will never be unsafe with me."

I climb back on top of her, and she melts into the leather of the couch beneath me. I take her mouth in mine, sweeping my tongue through the space and feeling her moan when my tip finds her opening.

"Is this what you want?" I ask, nuzzling my lips against the side of her neck as she palms my ass.

"Yes," she whispers, and I push in slowly, her hands gripping me as she inhales and holds her breath.

"Breathe, Piper." I smile into her skin as this refrain I've said so often comes to life in a new context. She adjusts beneath me, changing her angle to let me in fully.

"It's so good," she chokes out, and now I'm the one who can't breathe, the sounds of her pleasure short-circuiting my brain as I fill her.

"So good," I echo. It would take fifty thousand words to describe how incredible she feels, a tome dedicated to Piper and the experience of being inside her. I can only manage two, so I say them again. "*So good.*"

We settle into a rhythm, our mouths in sync with our hips as we push and pull. *I could die doing this*, I think to myself. Maybe it's because this level of pleasure could kill me, or that I would be happy to do nothing else for the rest of my life.

It's both.

"What do you need?" My words come out as a whisper, goosebumps erupting down the side of Piper's neck where my mouth is lingering.

"Can you go faster?"

I'm there in a heartbeat, increasing the pace until her breath catches, her fingers clench against my skin, and I keep it there, steady.

My control is slipping, and I tell her as much. She grips my neck with one hand and slides her other between us, adding pressure where she wants it. We're breathing in unison, our hips anchored together as we push each other higher.

"Please, please, James, I'm so close." She comes undone a moment later, her body pulsing around me as she shudders beneath my chest. I let myself go as she starts coming down, jerking through a last thrust until I'm empty inside her.

I collapse onto her, cradling my hand behind her head as we lay there together, my heart flying against my ribs and hers doing the same.

"That was...," Piper says hoarsely, turning her head to look at me as she tangles her fingers in my hair, a smile curling her lips, "*Exactly* what I wanted."

"Happy to oblige." I chuckle before noting the opportunity to meet her vulnerability with my own. It's not a skill I have much experience with. Piper makes me want to try.

"Giving you what you want will always be what I want," I reply.

My fingers tuck a strand of strawberry blonde hair behind her ear before giving her another slow, lingering kiss. She greets it with a soft giggle.

"Well, Mr. Newhouse, I've gotta believe an examination

won't go down like this in court," Piper jokes, burying her face in my neck.

"What's that about going down? Because, believe me, I'm up for another round..." I laugh and she bites at my collarbone lightly before digging her nose into the divot where it meets my shoulder. Piper's head fits there like the spot was made for her.

"I'm just saying, I'm not sure I'm any more prepared for a hearing than I was before. Which is not to say that this night was a bust..."

The cackle that splits her open tells me she's noted the innuendo. My own chuckle joins hers and soon we're both laughing, trying to catch our breath like we did the day of the smoke bomb and only making it worse.

It's full circle, holding her now and laughing this way, just like I held her that day and we laughed just like this, except now everything is different.

Because this time I know her, and if I'm willing to be honest, I think I could love her if I let myself. And while I don't know for sure, I'm starting to believe that she could love me too.

After spending a minute cleaning up—a towel for her and a bathroom visit for us both—I roll onto my side and pull her into my arms, wanting her as close as she can possibly be and thankful the width of the sofa leaves her no other option.

We become a tangle of arms and legs as we talk and then doze, adjusting occasionally due to tangled limbs or trapped shoulders. The thought I failed to catch once before runs across my mind, but this time instead of fear, it prompts hope.

*Piper fits here.*

Light pours into the room, and I'm aware of two things upon waking. One, I can barely rotate my neck after sleeping on this couch, and two, Piper is still here, curled up between my arms and legs, the two of us sharing a space smaller than a twin bed and touching absolutely everywhere.

I also realize I'm hard, which isn't surprising and shouldn't be embarrassing after last night... but it still feels awkward given the zero centimeters of space between us.

I extricate myself from her—a herculean effort both physically and emotionally—and pull on my pants before heading to the kitchen for a drink. Glancing back to the living room, Piper looks so small and so peaceful, like everything in the world is exactly right.

Maybe it is.

Scanning the counter, I find my phone, which was happily abandoned to die overnight. It's so bright, too bright as it powers up; 8:17 a.m. flashes on the home screen before I can even swipe in. I blink and then blink again. No, that can't be right. The microwave reads 8:18.

Whatever bubble of oxytocin I'd been living in breaks open.

"Shit! Ahhh. Shit, okay. Okay." I rush over to Piper, pushing gently on her shoulder in an attempt to wake her up before I move on to saying her name and then shouting it. She comes alive with a jolt, and it's clear that she has no idea where she is or what's happening.

"P, hey, it's me. You've gotta get up. We overslept. I'm so sorry. It's 8:20."

Her eyes grow wide and she sits straight up before diving to grab her clothes and throwing them on.

"No, no, no... it's not... it can't be, right?" She stares at me wildly as she hauls her skirt up to her waist, desperate for me to change the answer to the question, to tell her what she knows isn't true.

"It is. I'm so sorry. What can I do? Can I bring you to your house to change? Drive you to work? What do you need?"

*I liked that question a hell of a lot more last night.*

"Shit, is it Tuesday? I think it's Tuesday. *Damn it.*" Piper starts palming at her clothes, at the couch, lifting the cushions to look for her phone. "I have a donor meeting on Tuesday at 8:30. It's a referral from the man who committed to the scholarship fund. I should've been at the office ten minutes ago."

She's a tornado as she moves, hopping on one foot as she puts on a shoe, wrapping her hair up in a bun with the tie she keeps on her wrist, locating her things and throwing them in her bag before sprinting for the door.

"Please, let me drop you off." I hobble after Piper, ignoring the guilt seeping into my chest and my rational desire to grab shoes before leaving. "I can get there quickly; I'll speed if I have to."

I grab my keys from the hook and we race to the car, throwing open the doors and peeling out before we even pull them closed.

Apology after apology spills out of my mouth. I didn't know Piper had a meeting, much less that she'd be spending the night, but it doesn't matter. All I can think about is how important this job is to her and that I'm the reason she's not at her best this morning. The knowledge twists painfully in my chest.

We arrive at her building at 8:32, Piper rushing inside with an "I'll text you" and a frantic wave as she disappears behind the door.

My life, and whatever is growing between Piper and me, went from perfectly right to horribly wrong in the span of fifteen minutes. Reality crashes down like thunder, splitting apart whatever dream state made me believe, even for a night, that I wouldn't ruin her.

I head back to my place, dying to take a shower to try and rinse away the unease that's sitting like a brick in my stomach. For the first time since we started this ruse, I don't know when I'll see Piper again outside of our commute.

While I have to drop off the boxes for the event on Saturday, she could send out an intern to greet me.

"Just wait for her to text," I tell myself out loud as I put the car in park in front of my house. Hesitant to go inside and see the evidence of the best night and the worst morning, I sit for too long and stare aimlessly. "Wait for her to text."

## 13

*Piper*

I BURST INTO THE building and take the stairs two at a time to the second floor. I'm late, of course, but I'm also disheveled. Yesterday's clothes hang on my body, my tangled hair is in a messy bun, and the remnants of last night's mascara are smudged beneath my eyes.

This is not how I'd like to present myself for work any day, but today? This is the worst-case scenario. Byron Cargill of *the* Cargills, one of the city's wealthiest families, has an appointment with me for 8:30 a.m.

He's already seated at the table when I swing open the conference room door.

"Mr. Cargill! Thank you for being here. Piper Paulson, great to meet you." I stick out my hand, hoping it's not sweaty from running up the stairs or from my nerves. Of course, it is.

He rises to take it and gives me a quick shake before sitting back down in his seat. His eyes scan me curiously as he raps a pen on the table.

"So sorry I'm late, I'm normally more organized. I appreciate your patience." I smile weakly as I grab my notebook from my bag, desperately wishing it was my laptop but unwilling to waste the time it would take to retrieve it from my office. "I heard from your assistant that you're interested in learning more about the scholarship program?" I finally sit my butt in a chair.

He nods, leaning back in his seat. "I am," he says, his mustache rustling as he talks. He looks to be mid-sixties, and he'd remind me of my dad if my dad was frivolously wealthy and incredibly intimidating.

"Honestly, though," he pauses briefly, "I'd like to get to know you first. There are thousands of organizations that have ideas about how to use my money, and the *how* is less important to me than the *who*."

I take a big inhale. I could talk about the scholarship fund and why it's important for hours. But to talk about myself? I've never been overly articulate that way.

"Of course," I start, trying to keep my voice steady. "We always want our donors to feel like a partner in this work. It's natural to want to know the kind of partner you'd be getting in bed with."

The second the words are out of my mouth I want to stuff them back in. This is a business meeting, for God's sake. Plus, the unfortunate phrasing brings up memories of last night. I push them out of my brain with superhuman strength.

*Get it together, Piper.*

Mr. Cargill shifts in his seat. I'm not sure if he wants to ask questions or if I should offer up information. I decide on the latter.

"As I mentioned, my name is Piper Paulson. I work at Hope First as the program director overseeing after-school classes, events—like our upcoming gala—and our new scholarship fund.

"I have a corporate background but began working here six months ago after starting as a volunteer with the lower and middle-grades painting classes. We use a lot of art therapy techniques to help the kids we work with. I'd like to complete a master's degree in social work someday so I can counsel our clients directly."

The words are coming a mile a minute. I need to cool it, but I can't seem to cut the gas to my mouth.

"We work with roughly a hundred and fifty single-parent families in the city right now, though we're hoping to increase this number to two hundred by year's end. Our funding comes primarily through individual donors like yourself... if you're interested, of course... and via grants from local foundations. We help families with financial management, accessing available government support programs, getting their GED or associate degree, and with childcare expenses. It's really life-changing for them."

I suck in a breath, and he continues to sit silently, tapping his pen and squinting at me.

"Is there anything in particular I can answer for you?" Giving him the floor allows me a moment to compose myself.

"This is all very interesting, Ms. Paulson. Can I ask what you know about our family and the types of programs we support?"

*Shit. Shit. Shit.* The answer is in his prospective donor file—the one I planned to review meticulously before this meeting and which is sitting, unread, in the bottom left drawer of my desk.

"I'm aware you support a variety of programs throughout the city, as well as nationally, and your family has been instrumental in funding..." I think carefully as I have no idea what I'm about to say but it needs to sound legitimate, "... organizations that serve vulnerable populations."

I rest my chin on my fist, my elbow on the table as he takes in my words. It was a vague statement, certainly, but it wasn't incorrect. It could be true of any donor in the world, but that doesn't mean it's untrue of Mr. Cargill.

He nods before rising to stand. We're only ten minutes into our thirty-minute meeting, and that's counting the three I made him wait before I arrived.

"Thank you so much, Ms. Paulson, but I'm going to pass at this time. Please reach out in the future when you have a better sense of our family's values and how they may fit with your programming. I'd also consider another appointment if I could speak with someone better able to articulate how our financial partnership with Hope First would benefit all parties."

Mr. Cargill doesn't look stern or disappointed, just matter of fact. He nods in my direction like he's tipping an imaginary hat. I sit frozen at the table, dumbfounded.

"Of course, thank you for your time. Have a wonderful rest of your day." The words eke out of my mouth as I watch him slip through the door and down the stairs to the lobby.

He's out of sight when my body moves without conscious thought, slithering down my chair until I land with a thud on the scratchy jute rug beneath the table. I may spend the rest of the day here. Maybe the rest of my life.

How can I show my face to the team after fumbling the biggest donor in the city? Tears breach the barricade of my closed eyes and spill down my cheeks, dripping onto the fabric of yesterday's skirt.

I'm still wearing yesterday's skirt.

Air enters my lungs in short and shallow gasps as the thoughts that have haunted me for years, the ones I've tried so hard to replace with positive self-talk and therapy, come flooding through my brain.

*You're the world's biggest idiot. The idiots of all idiots. Purveyor of the most idiotic idiocy that ever was and ever will be.*

*You can't do anything right.*

*Of course, this would be the result of opening yourself up. You should've known better.*

*You're always a disappointment.*

I can't even argue with them. Here I am, twenty-eight years old, crying under a conference table to avoid a walk of shame to my desk.

If there was a literal hole I could crawl into to die right now, I would.

The fact that I let this happen, that I let myself be distracted by a man who I knew from the start I shouldn't get involved with? It's proof I'm no better than I was two years ago. Two entire years I've dedicated to putting my life back together—blood, sweat, and tears shed to dig myself out of a Fundament-shaped hole—only to risk it all for another banker.

All because he was nice to me and I liked the weight of his hand on my leg.

The worst is that it's not just my life I put on the line. There are women with kids who won't receive scholarship money because I fucked up this meeting on account of fucking James.

*I'm the most terrible person alive.*

The list of my sins yesterday plays on loop in my mind, stopping only to let me beat myself up over each one:

I let the chance of a trial (which may or may not happen weeks in the future) make me stressed.

I went over to James's house on a work night.

I told him to touch me.

I fell asleep on his couch.

I forgot to set my alarm.

I let myself believe I was different, that James was different, that this thing growing between us could be something special.

Stupid. Stupid. Stupid.

I consider everything before last night too, namely, the foolishness to accept his asinine Family Fares offer to save a few bucks. A few bucks which cost Hope First ten thousand this morning. Likely more.

The heels of my palms press into my cheeks in an attempt to stop more tears while I take out my phone to text James. Boundaries are needed *now* so this never happens again. It can *never* happen again.

And while I'm pissed at James for being charming and persuasive and so handsome I want to eat him whole, I also want him to know this shitshow of a morning isn't his fault. This is on me, not him.

My fingers tap open the thread and I wince at our last exchange, playful and light with no hint of the ache that's squeezing my heart like a vice.

I'm not sure what to type that will communicate, "Hey, really grateful for the amazing sex last night, but it turns out I cannot have both you and a job, so I'm picking my job, no hard feelings! (And also I'm dying inside.) (But that's not your fault.)"

I decide to go with something more understated.

Piper

Hey, thanks for dropping me off this morning. Sorry you had to speed here.

The desire to add a grimacing emoji itches under my thumbs but I ignore it. I wait for his reply but continue when none comes.

Piper

Just a heads up, I probably won't see you on the train the rest of the week. I'm going to come to work early to do gala prep. Didn't want you to think that I was avoiding you! I'll text you details about when and where to drop off the items on Saturday. Thanks for keeping them for me this week. 😊

I know the exclamation point I used is too much, but I don't have the energy to edit myself. The traditional smiley face at the end stands in stark contrast to my crying face still tucked under this table.

His message comes ten seconds later, and I hate how it makes my heart leap to feel the vibration in my hand and see the message from James.

James

Of course, happy to drop you off and happy to keep your gala items company. 😊 How did the meeting go? I'm sorry I couldn't get you there any sooner.

My head falls between my knees, a sniffle escaping my nose as I think about what to say. I don't want to lie to him. I can't tell him the truth.

Is it because I don't want him to feel bad? Or because I don't want him to know I'm a failure? I'm sure it's both.

> **Piper**
>
> It was a meeting!

I hope he reads into a lightheartedness that I don't currently feel.

> **James**
>
> I'd love to hear more about it soon. Are you sure I can't help with anything before Saturday? You don't have any heavy boxes for me to lift or tables I could drag across a ballroom for you?

He sends a gif of Shia LeBeouf flexing and it makes me smile for a brief second.

> **Piper**
>
> No, I'm fine.

(I am decidedly not fine.)

> **Piper**
>
> I'll see you Saturday when you stop by the space. I'm going to keep my head down this week.

James

> Sounds good, P. Text me if you need anything though. Like I said before, I am happy to be your fake husband any time.

The screen goes dark and I turn my phone over on the carpet. James's words are tumbling through my mind like my stomach is tumbling to my toes. *Fake husband.* Not real. Bogus. An imitation, a counterfeit, a sham. F-A-K-E.

I should remind myself of this constantly, have it tattooed on my forearm or maybe my forehead. A fake relationship can't mess up my very real life; I won't allow it.

I grip the skin at my cheeks and pull, hoping it brings some color there to distract from the pink in my eyes. Lifting my head out from under the table, I sneak a glance to ensure no one is around before I heave myself back into the chair, sitting for a few seconds to gather my composure.

Swiveling toward the door, I stand, throwing my shoulders back as I head toward my desk. It's an act I put on for everyone in the office, but it's also for me, to distract from my nausea—undoubtedly the result of skipping dinner last night and having no time for breakfast this morning.

It's not from the gnawing ache of having to pull back from James.

I wave at Sadye and Jenny, both of whom are pouring over a guest list or a vendor contract and I retreat into my space with a sigh. It's barely 9 a.m. and the whole day is still ahead of me. If I can knock out a bunch of tasks for Saturday maybe I won't be so stressed. At the very least, it'll keep me from thinking about James.

## 14

## James

MY PHONE BUZZES, AND I pick it up to see a text from Piper—an address for today's event, a note that she'll meet me at four, and the prayer hands emoji. My exhale comes without conscious thought, the stale air escaping my mouth after building in my lungs each day since I last heard from her.

I tried to convince myself she's busy, that she needs to focus on the gala, that her priorities don't include me, and that I can't expect them to because this isn't a real relationship.

My brain didn't get the memo though. I've been relentlessly bombarded with the thought that things went too far on Monday and that's why Piper has backed off. I'm surprised you can't see shrapnel wounds on my skin.

My thumb drags along the cool glass screen to heart the message before I slide the phone into the pocket of my sweats, the rap of my fingertips on the kitchen counter acting as the soundtrack of my nerves. I wander to my bedroom and flop face-first onto the mattress, the frame groaning under my weight as I sink into the blue comforter Mom bought when I moved in here.

If only she could see me now, completely destroyed by a woman who I swore not to mess with lest I end up just like this. She'd be smug—delighted to see that I do have a heart—and then she'd tell me to buck up and go get the girl.

She'd be right.

Sliding my feet to the floor, I push myself up until my legs support my body. I know I should get dressed, but that means confronting the question I can't seem to answer. *How do I show up tonight and be helpful but not desperate, interested but not infatuated?*

Our relationship is a spinning plate, and an accidental nudge could crash it. I don't want to be the one who knocks it down.

I settle on a suit, telling myself it's because I have so few casual clothes and not because I hope to stay for the gala. I peel off the T-shirt I've been wearing since last night and roll it into a warm ball that I sink into the hamper before grabbing a white button-down.

The starchy fabric of the dress shirt grazes my arms as I stretch them through the sleeves. The buttons are done by feel, my fingers aching with the memory of this action in reverse when Piper was here, each round button a gatekeeper we excused for the night.

A pressed navy blazer with matching slacks completes the look, a sharp crease standing at attention on the front of each leg. I spread the collar of the shirt and leave the top two buttons undone. The outfit is relaxed—unpretentious—which is the vibe I'm hoping to project. A tie bulges in my pocket just in case.

My phone alerts at 3:15, so I pick up the pace. Tossing rolls of socks within the drawer, I find the ones with the navy and green stripes, sliding them on before reaching for my loafers—the ones with the scuff from Piper's nail.

I roll some sticky pomade between my hands before roughing up my hair to create a looser style than I typically wear. Let's hope the look says "I'm not trying too hard" even though I've never tried harder in my life.

I pull up at 3:58 p.m. to what looks like an abandoned warehouse, and while it's not in a bad part of town, it doesn't scream "event space." Not that I have much experience with event spaces. I grab three of the boxes from my backseat and make my way to the loading dock.

Piper said she'd meet me here, so I wait, the cigarette butts and gasoline stains that line the concrete distracting me from the question of what I'll say when she shows up.

A whistle comes from behind a half-wall as Piper rounds the corner, looking me up and down.

"*Damn, Banker Man,*" she says with a smile. "This was an Errand Boy task; you didn't need to get fancy." My teeth find the inside of my cheek and bite as I wonder if I should've skipped the blazer.

"The details online made it sound like a dressy event. Didn't want to be unprepared."

Piper gestures to herself, an old t-shirt and a pair of ripped jeans hugging her body, with a bandana tied around her hair. "Well, you're certainly showing me up!"

She says it with a self-deprecating laugh, and I think about telling her she's never looked better, but I restrain myself. It feels easy between us right now, normal even, like maybe she truly was busy this week. I don't want to push it.

She turns back to enter the building, and I follow her through a long hallway, past the lobby, and into an expansive room to the left. Lights are strung across the ceiling, casting a warm and inviting glow, and round tables surround a dance floor at the base of a stage with a few high tops at the perimeter.

The room is still a work in progress, as evidenced by the people who are scurrying around like ants pinning tablecloths and setting up centerpieces.

"So, how does it look?" Piper asks, wiping her forearm across her brow.

"It looks incredible, Pipes. Really well done. Your guests are going to have a great time tonight." The boxes shift in my arms, awkward but not heavy, and she notices as I try to balance them on my hip.

"Let's put those over there." She leans in the direction of a younger woman near a high top. "I'll have Sadye unload them and start doing place settings. Can you grab the other boxes and bring them here?"

A quick gesture to the left proceeds her next thought. "The auction items need my attention; they aren't going to set up themselves!"

Piper walks over to a collection of rectangular tables where she drops a bag from her shoulder and starts unloading autographed posters. There are a variety of items lined up already, each with a sign describing the item, its market value, and a suggested starting bid. Bid sheets live neatly in front, a capped pen resting diagonally across each one.

There won't be an empty sheet at the end of the night if I can help it—anything that doesn't get a bid will come home with me.

"Absolutely. I'll be back in a few," I reply. I know she's not asking for anything new, just the fulfillment of the agreement I made to drop everything off, but it still makes me happy to be needed by Piper.

Five minutes later, I'm back with the boxes and headed toward Sadye who is making quick work of her task. Who knew it was possible to fold napkins so efficiently? She is folding and placing and setting each table in a matter of minutes. It's impressive.

Meanwhile, Piper's hands are working furiously as I head over to the auction staging area, boxes and bags spilling out from underneath the tables, each one containing something else to unpack. I grab a bag, gently lifting a ceramic vase out the top and carefully unwrapping the packing paper that surrounds it.

"What are you doing?" She glances up and catches me there, and I wonder for a second if she thinks I'm trying to steal this.

"Unpacking this vase?" I say, speaking slowly and deliberately. "You said you needed to keep working on the auction set-up. I'm helping." My shoulders shrug, tape sticking to my fingers as we talk.

"You really don't need to," she says, her eyebrows pulled

together in question. A small grin betrays that she's grateful for the extra hands.

"I know I don't," I reply. "I want to."

We find a rhythm as we work for the next forty-five minutes. I untie bags and break down boxes, she places the items and sets up the detail cards, I lay out the bid sheets and she distributes the pens.

We don't talk much, but it's familiar nonetheless, like our bodies have a sense of what the other will do and accommodate for it without thinking. When the set-up is complete, Piper steps back to take it in, cocking her head and narrowing her eyes to appraise our handiwork.

"It looks good!" My palm extends toward her for a high five, which seems like the lowest-stakes suggestion that I'm dying for her to touch me.

"It looks good," she agrees, weaving her fingers through mine and giving a brief squeeze. She leans her weight into my side with a sigh, the rhythm of her breath slowing. It feels indulgent, this fleeting bit of contact, like she's giving herself a single moment of rest before the madness of the gala starts in full.

I want to linger like this, to continue to have the weight of her body pressed to the side of my stomach, but Piper straightens quickly, pulling her hand away to smooth it down her thigh.

"Sorry, I... I need to change before people arrive in thirty," she says, her lips pulling to the left to blow a piece of stray hair out of her eyes. "Thanks again for being here and for helping out." Her body twists away from me as she scurries toward a corner door, throwing up a wave on the way.

This is my cue to leave. I know I should leave. Leaving is the smart thing to do.

I don't leave.

Instead, I scan the room for another task. Chairs bang and clank as they are pulled from a stack, their metal legs dragging across the floor behind two women who place them around tables. No one asks who I am or why I'm here when I grab three chairs from the top and slide them into place, nor when I repeat the motion until every table is full.

I fill the time by filling needs, joining Hope First employees as they scamper to get everything finished. By 5:20 p.m. the place is shimmering, reshaped from a warehouse into a ballroom, lights glinting off cutlery and centerpieces with easy jazz wafting through the air.

It's incredible.

Piper tears into the room five minutes later, and her transformation rips the breath out of my lungs. A short black dress has replaced her tee and jeans, and it hugs her curves effortlessly, highlighting the spot at her waist where my palm, now damp at the sight of her, fits just right.

Her hair drapes loosely over one shoulder and my heart bumps against my sternum every time it brushes over the jut of her collarbone. She moves with an authority I have never seen from her; she's confident, almost aggressively so, as she directs folks to their places, her red heels showing off the cut of her calves with each step.

I'm trying not to stare, but it's difficult. This dress makes me want to corner her—to wrap my hands around her wrists and pin her to the wall to steal the lipstick from her mouth.

She catches me out of the corner of her eye and stops mid-stride. I never made it clear that I planned to stay, though she never explicitly asked me to leave. My arm lifts my sweaty hand for a wave since that's what we do, and she rushes over to me in ten seconds flat.

"James, I..." Her brown eyes are wild, as though she has one hundred open tabs in her brain and seeing me has caused the machine to freeze.

My fingers find her shoulders and give them a gentle squeeze.

"P, this dress... you look incredible."

She blinks and comes to life again, giving me a grin. "Of course I do." Her eyes dart around the room to make sure everyone is still playing their parts before returning to my gaze. "I didn't expect you to still be here."

"Like I said, I came prepared for a fancy evening." I grab my lapels and tug. A chuckle slips between her lips before her expression changes, her eyebrows furrowing as catches sight of the empty bar behind me.

"Hey, actually, could you do something for me?" Her face transforms from concerned to pleading as she gives me the expression I recognize from each prior request—puppy dog eyes with an earnest glint and a soft smile.

It works on me now just like it always has. I nod and shoot her a curious glance.

"The bartender we hired isn't here yet, and I don't want to panic. Can you hang by the bar and pour some wine until he arrives? It shouldn't be long."

"Pipes, of all of the requests you've ever made, this is... *almost* my favorite one." A grin stretches across my cheeks, heat lapping up my neck as the memory of Monday night—the way she asked me to touch her—floods my brain. She whacks me lightly on the arm before pointing me to the bar.

By 5:30 the room is buzzing with chatter and I'm the most popular person here as a line forms for drinks. Even better, my view of Piper is unobstructed as she navigates the crowd, schmoozing with donors, talking about auction items, and intermittently lifting a radio to her red lips to message her teammates.

She is effortless in this environment, floating between roles, and it's remarkable to see. The nervous, unsure, stressed Piper I see on the train most mornings is gone.

This Piper is a handler and it's sexy as hell.

An hour and a half goes by quickly as the meal is served and several clients share their stories from the stage, each one heartbreaking and galvanizing. Soon, Piper takes the mic, leading the crowd in a round of applause for the clients and sharing how the money raised will go toward bettering the lives of women and children in our city.

I'm biased, of course, but I would give this woman anything. By the look of the crowd, I'm not the only one. People are dropping checks in baskets at the center of their tables while others are pulling out their phones to scan QR codes to donate. The money is flowing as easily as the drinks.

The space transitions for music and dancing and Piper mingles, giving hugs and handshakes and pointing folks to the auction before it closes at 8:30. After a while—too long, in my opinion—she makes her way over to me at the bar.

"Need a drink?" I ask, cocking my head and lifting my eyebrow to accompany a smirk.

"Can't drink on the job, sorry." She shrugs but there's nothing sorry about it. She's glowing, a mix of pride and sweat from working the room clinging to her skin.

I hand her a glass of water and watch as she finds my cup behind the bar and gives it an intentional tink, holding eye contact as she takes a long sip before setting it down with a smile.

"The bartender officially bailed, I guess," she laments while scanning the room as though she'd find him here now if she looked hard enough. "Thank you for stepping in. No one has complained about the drinks, so you must be doing a decent job." Her eyelashes flutter along with her grin.

"Decent is what I'm known for," I say while pouring a glass of cab for a waiting patron. "At least, I hope *you* think I'm decent."

"You are satisfactory *and* respectable. Truly decent in all ways," she replies with a small curtsy and a chuckle. "Seriously, though. Thank you. I'm not sure what we would've done without you here."

Piper reaches up to gently grasp my cheek as she says it, making sure to hold my gaze. It sparks a fire in my chest that'll stay the rest of the night.

"Time to check on the auction. Keep up the good work, Mr. Newhouse." The wink she gives me before sauntering over to the rectangular tables damn near makes my knees buckle.

I redirect my focus to pouring drinks, some wine and some liquor with a few cocktails thrown in, and on singing Piper's praises with every guest I serve. No one should leave here without knowing she's behind this incredible event.

For someone who likes order, routine, and near-guaranteed results, I am having too much fun tonight. I'm making things up as I go and it's working. It's freeing to be here in this environment, to have to wing it, and to be successful doing it.

Maybe it's okay to let go of the plan sometimes after all. Maybe things work out when they are meant to.

The night wraps up with a last call for bids and drinks and folks are happy, carrying newly won items in their arms and leaving tips on their way out. The staff starts to clean up as Piper finds me again, giddy from the compliments she received from donors as they leave.

I'm almost as proud as she is as I wrap my arms around her and lift her off the ground, kissing her gently under her ear before setting her back down.

A man clears his throat behind us, and I'm reminded that we're not alone.

"So sorry to interrupt," he says apologetically, "but I just wanted to tell you, Piper, what a wonderful night this was and how thrilled we are to partner with Hope First." Turning to me, he raises his empty glass. "And I didn't know you were with this fine young man. Best Old Fashioned I've had in years thanks to you."

He smiles and Piper grabs my hand, pressing her fingers between mine.

"Thank you so much, Mr. Goldstone," she replies. "I'm so glad you and Ginny could make it. It's always a joy to see you both." Her shoulder tucks under my arm as she continues, "And yes, James does make a good drink."

Mr. Goldstone watches us for a moment before adding a final thought, as though it's a postscript and not a bomb. "You know, I'm so thrilled these single women have you to look up to, Piper. It's important for them to have an example of a healthy relationship."

While it's too dim to confirm, I am positive every ounce of color drains from my face at this exact moment. Piper keeps her hand in mine, gripping tightly, as she gives Mr. Goldstone a loose one-armed hug, thanking him again before he turns to find his wife.

Our gazes catch as we stand there, hands linked, feeling the weight of his words.

But after a moment, Piper turns and drags me to the floor to join the clean-up effort, effectively making the call that we shouldn't talk about the exchange with Mr. Goldstone... or at least not right now. I follow her lead, tidying and organizing and ignoring the elephant in the room.

If she wants to bask in the afterglow of a successful fundraiser, I won't stop her.

"So, Piper," a woman pauses with a trash bag in hand as she cocks her hip, "are you gonna tell us who this man is? Or do you want us to nag you incessantly until you relent? Totally your call!"

A shit-eating grin commands the lower half of her face as she bends down to retrieve a bent program from the floor.

"Wow, Jenny, how gracious of you!" Piper replies with an eye roll. "This is James." She places a hand on my arm with a pat. "You all should be grateful for his help."

Jenny makes a show of an exaggerated bow as though I'm the king of England and she's a loyal subject. I tip my head back to her.

I'm acutely aware Piper didn't define our relationship or explain how we know each other. The only reason I wanted her to was to give me a clue about the way she views me. It would be easier to keep my distance if she called me a friend.

Instead of keeping my distance, I pull closer to her and watch her as she works. It's striking how content she looks even as she's sweeping pieces of sticky confetti into a dustpan. Like she's had her fill of something delicious, or her pumpkin pie won first prize at the fair.

I recognize it as the same satisfied look she had when I pulled her onto my lap on Monday.

I want it there all the time.

We continue our cleaning for about an hour, me stacking

chairs and Piper organizing donation envelopes while varying members of the team clear plates and strip tablecloths, collect signage, and finagle a standing banner back into its case.

When everything is in good shape, she starts giving hugs and thanks, picking out specific ways that each member of the team was instrumental tonight and expressing her gratitude for it. She is nothing but heart, this one.

We make our way through the maze of the building to my car sitting alone in the back lot. Piper replays the night's events aloud as we walk, giving context and sharing tidbits about her conversations and what they could mean for Hope First.

She's practically skipping—the phrase "a pep in your step" comes to life in front of me as she moves—like a girl at Christmas who got everything she wanted and can't keep her excitement contained. The perma-smile it puts on my face has my cheeks aching.

Piper turns in front of me as we approach my car, blocking me from opening the passenger side door. "What was *your* favorite part of the night, Mr. Bartender?"

She eyes me eagerly as she waits for me to give her another moment to relive. I reach for the handle of the door and find my hand on her waist instead.

"My favorite part," I say, keeping my hand planted firmly and my eyes locked on hers, "was watching you pull the whole thing off. This night and all the good that will come from it happened because of *you*. Seeing you in your element was incredible."

She grins up at me before reaching for my hand and nesting

hers within it.

"There was one thing, though..." I add with a half-smile, "...something that bothered me most of the night." Her hand tenses, bracing herself as she narrows her eyes to read my expression.

"I didn't get to dance with you," I say before taking a large step back, her fingers still wrapped up in mine, and then pulling her in so we're chest-to-chest. "Is it too late?"

"Dammit, James!" She tries to convey anger, but her laugh undoes the effort. Wrapping her arms around my neck, Piper rests her head on my shoulder with a sigh. I reach around her, pulling her to me tightly as we rock side to side.

"You know, this would be better with some music," she says.

*Not true.*

"I'm not sure anything could make this better."

We sway in silence, my chin nuzzled in her hair and my heartbeat keeping time. I remind myself this proximity doesn't mean anything—she's high on adrenaline and positive feelings. My body, however, only knows she's pressed against me and reacts accordingly.

I let my hands slide over the fabric of her dress as we move: up and down her back, around to her sides, to her neck, to weave my fingers through her hair, and back down to the base of her spine. I'm getting hard being this close to her, and she must feel it. Her breath catches as I bring a palm to her ass and squeeze.

"You liked that," I whisper with a smile she can hear, nudging the hair away from her ear to be sure.

"Is it that obvious?" A laugh slides out of her as she drops her arms to my lower back.

"It is if you're paying attention."

Piper lifts her eyes to meet mine and they're steady. Assured. "What else have you been paying attention to?" The challenge in her voice makes my heart race.

"This spot behind your ear, for one." I reach a hand toward her jaw and turn her face away from me, exposing her neck so I can place a wet kiss there. Goosebumps erupt on her skin when I pull away, my hand still cradling her face.

"And here." I drop slow kisses down the side of her neck, pausing after each one to build tension.

"There's this spot," my lips find her lips, softly at first, before I nudge her mouth open and tangle my tongue with hers. She lets out a small moan as we deepen the kiss, her hands pulling at my hair as the urgency increases.

I guide her backward until she's pinned against the car, exactly the way I wanted her the moment she appeared in this dress.

"What else?" Her voice is shaky with need, punctuating those two words.

"And this spot here," I bring a hand to her ribs, just under her breast to swipe my thumb across her nipple. She pulls my bottom lip between her teeth with a stilted breath.

"And my favorite spot," I whisper as I drag my hand down her side and slip under her dress, pushing away the fabric of her panties to dip inside her. She arches into me with a moaned exhale. "You're already so wet for me, P."

"That's what happens when you pay attention." The words come out choked before she strains for another kiss.

My hand works her up and down, alternating focused pressure and stretching her with my fingers until she's trembling. I can tell she's close, but I'm not done with her yet. Pulling away just an inch, I pause for a moment to adjust myself in my pants, flinching at my own touch.

"Why'd you stop?" she asks desperately, her mouth moving furiously on mine. The tension in her voice makes me want to continue this for years.

"I stopped because you were getting too close." My quiet laugh tickles her lips as I slow down the kiss until it's deep but tender.

"That's when you're supposed to *NOT* stop!" Piper gives a firm tug to my hair like it's a punishment and not a turn-on.

"Only if I want you to finish," I whisper, finding the spot where her neck meets her collarbone and sucking gently. "I am not eager for this to be finished."

She shudders and I steady her, licking kisses to her ear. "Though if *you* are, you can ask me for it." The trail of my lips continues across her jaw to her mouth.

She stops me there, meeting my gaze with no inhibition as she grabs my hand and brings it back between her legs.

"James," she says as she arches into me, "please make me come."

We dive back into the kiss, zero to sixty, the heel of my hand rubbing back and forth over her as I bring my other hand to the strap of her dress and slide it down to expose her breast. I twist at her nipple slowly until it's hard, a sharp inhale in her chest when I pull roughly.

"*Shit*, James," she whimpers into my neck. The words burn like sparks on my skin as she writhes beneath me.

"That's it, just like that," I encourage, increasing my tempo to match her small thrusts. If I move an inch, the friction of my pants would cause an explosion I'd regret. I focus on Piper's breathing as it becomes erratic, nipping my teeth at her ear. "You feel so fucking good I could come just from touching you."

She collapses into me as her pleasure spills over, her muscles tensing and squeezing, her arms tight around my back. We stay this way until our breathing slows and she brings a hand to my zipper. I intercept it with my own.

"Not tonight," I whisper, cradling her head against my chest. As much as I'm desperate for release, this night is about her. I don't want her to think the price of her orgasm is my own.

I keep Piper wrapped up, feeling her heart rate fall and her shoulders relax after a few minutes. She's melted into me, her body filling every gap in mine.

"Hey," she says quietly, looking up at me with a soft smile. I tuck a loose wave behind her ear.

"Hey," I reply, planting a kiss on her forehead.

"Thanks for giving me space. We had such a great night earlier this week and then the morning happened which made me spiral. I shut you out. I'm sorry about that."

My palms move from her waist to hold the sides of her face

gently, locking my eyes to hers. "You don't have to apologize for taking care of yourself, you know that?" She nods. "You should do whatever you need to do. You don't owe me any-thing."

## 15

*Piper*

JAMES'S PHRASE RATTLES AROUND my head as his car maneuvers the pothole-lined street leading to my house.

*"You don't owe me anything."*

Those five words pierce the bubble I've been living in, quickly deflating the protective cover I wrapped around my heart to guard against my thoughts this week. Thoughts about how reckless I am around James.

About what happened with Mr. Cargill.

About how stupid it is to let myself be distracted.

I've been pushing those thoughts aside, wrapping them up along with my common sense and tucking them away. I've been leaning into positive self-talk. I've been trying not to catastrophize. Trying not to let my fears ruin a night like tonight.

But hearing those five words slip out of James's mouth?

The bubble is gone. With one startling pop it disappears, a flashing neon DANGER sign materializing in its place. His casual reminder that we aren't responsible for or accountable to each other is a puncture wound to my heart.

We aren't a "we" at all.

James Newhouse could disappear tomorrow, and I wouldn't have any right to be hurt.

Here I am bringing this man into my life, introducing him to my roommate, showing him off at my work event, fumbling an important meeting, and for what?

*He doesn't owe me anything either.*

Shit.

Driving home after our tryst in the parking lot, the cold leather of his passenger seat raises goosebumps on my uncovered legs. My mind works overtime, spinning through the memories of the evening and wondering when and how things went so far off course.

James, on the other hand, is not spiraling. A happy hum leaves his lips as he rests his right hand comfortably on my thigh, occasionally tracing his fingers on my bare skin where my dress stops. It seems he's been able to manage what I have not—enjoying the fun of this arrangement without getting invested.

"What'cha thinking about, Pipes?" His curious blue eyes scan my face before the light turns green, drawing his attention back to the road.

"Currently? I'm thinking about what Mr. Goldstone said at the end of the night." I swallow hard, not knowing where I'm going with this but needing to address it. "About us being a good example for the women I serve."

He nods slowly, keeping his eyes fixed on the windshield. "Do you want to talk about it?"

"I don't know what to say, really." (This is the most honest phrase I've ever spoken to the man.) "It just has me thinking."

James gives my leg a quick squeeze, the warmth of his fingers sweeping away the lingering goosebumps.

"You're a pro at thinking," he says softly, and I'm not sure if it's a compliment, an observation, or a subtle dig at my anxiety. "Do you want to hear what I think?"

I keep my face turned toward the window as I nod.

"I think you threw a great party, raised a ton of money, and impressed everyone in the room. Don't let an offhand comment overshadow all the good you did tonight. Mr. Goldstone might not have gotten every detail right, but you *are* a fantastic role model, and those families *are* lucky to have you."

Somehow, James ignores the elephant in the room—the part we've yet to say aloud—about how this charade has gone beyond the train, beyond the police station and the threat of a trial to bleed into our real lives.

Or maybe it's just my life and my career? Whatever is happening between us isn't impacting James' job; he keeps me compartmentalized. And yet I've failed at that. Twice now.

"Thank you," I offer weakly. "Though I guess the exchange with Mr. Goldstone is evidence our fauxmance passes the stranger test. Seems we've become very convincing."

I don't tell him it's because I'm not pretending anymore. I want him to tell me it's not a fauxmance.

"Seems we have." A small smirk graces his mouth as he pulls up to the house in front of mine. I reach to open the door before turning back to give a last "Thank you."

He responds with his usual, "Of course."

Not knowing what to say next, "I'll text you!" spills out of my mouth as I wave goodbye. What will we text about now that the gala is over and a trial is still up in the air? Hell if I know.

"I'll be waiting," he replies as he mirrors my wave and then pulls into the street.

Waiting for what? Another half-baked reason for us to keep seeing each other that we both know is a farce?

I don't think I have it in me.

It's nearly ten o'clock when I walk through the door to find Sami waiting for me in the living room.

"How'd it go, lovey?!" She releases a squeal as she rushes over for a hug that almost knocks me down.

"It was perfect!" I exclaim, trying to reactivate my excitement from the event to cover my messy feelings about James. "It went off without a hitch. The speakers were compelling, we sold every auction item, and it looks like we exceeded our donation goal, though the official count will happen Monday."

"Ah, I'm just so proud of you! Could not be prouder. Want some champagne?" Sami walks around the couch to grab a bottle off the coffee table. Three-quarters of it is already gone. "I can grab you a glass!"

"Thanks, but I'm good." I flop myself onto the sofa and peel my stilettos from my feet. The relief feels *almost* as lovely as the orgasm earlier. "Want to guess who showed up for the fundraiser?"

"Let me think..." Sami taps her finger to her lips like she's pondering, "Beyonce?"

Cue my rolled eyes.

"I mean... Ann Patchett?"

And again.

"Okay I've got it. George W. Bush!"

I burst out laughing, the intensity of it breaking up some of the pressure in my chest.

"You were sooooo close," I snark, "but alas, it was not a singer or an author or a former President."

"It was James?" Sami grins as she settles deep into the chair across from the couch and curls up like a cat, her glass newly refreshed with bubbly.

"It was James," I sigh.

"And how do we feel about that?"

It's always "we" with Sami. She is so committed to Team Piper she'll adopt any possible emotion I might express. Gratitude blooms in my chest when I hear that "we."

"Well, I expected him to show up, drop off the boxes, and then leave. I thought it would be a blip." I run my hands down my face, stretching the skin of my cheeks up and down as I recall the events of the night.

"But instead, he was his usual helpful, respectful, so-infuri-atingly-handsome-it's-almost-painful self the entire night. He pitched in with set-up and clean-up, he charmed our donors, he served drinks when the bartender didn't show up. Then, when the event was over, he made sure I was... taken care of."

My hand finds a throw pillow and I bury my face in it, as though the gesture could stop Sami from prying.

"Taken care of," she says as she swirls her champagne like red wine, "that sounds *interesting*." She adds a wink for effect.

"It wasn't *interesting*, Sami, it was ridiculously hot. By far the best sexual experience I've ever had while being fully clothed. And in public." I peek out from behind the pillow to see her eyes grow wide and her smile grow wider.

"Piper Elise Paulson, I couldn't be prouder!" She walks over to the couch and snatches the pillow from my face before snuggling up beside me. "I know I said that earlier about the gala but honestly, this might take the cake. It's nice to see you enjoying yourself for once."

"Enjoyment was *certainly* had."

My chuckle surprises me, joined by a flood of gratitude for what my life has become—this apartment with Sami, our friendship, my job, the successful event tonight, and even these last few weeks with James (concerns notwithstanding).

I feel like I'm living again.

"So, what's the problem exactly? I'm not hearing a single problem about James or this evening." Sami scoots to rest her back against the armrest, digging her toes under my leg for warmth.

"Where do I start? Problem number one is I was distracted all night. The biggest event of my brand-new career, the possibility of a promotion and a raise on the line, and I'm glancing over constantly to see what James is doing, what expression he's making, what person he's charming. When he's around I can't think—all reason goes out the window. It's going to get me in trouble."

I don't tell her it already has with the lost scholarship money.

"Problem number two is people in my life are starting to get attached to him. You, obviously, but also my coworkers—they think he hung the moon after tonight. Problem three is *I'm* starting to get attached to him, and he doesn't seem to share the sentiment."

I swipe the glass from Sami's fingers and take a long sip before handing it back.

"What makes you say that?" She shrugs. "I can't think of a guy who pays for shit, willingly runs errands, and gives mind-blowing orgasms who's not interested." She has a point, especially considering the quality of men she's been dealing with recently.

"It's this arrangement. He's playing the role of a doting partner and he's doing a great job of it. But I keep laying down opportunities for him to admit we're not playing anymore and he doesn't take them. James seems perfectly happy to keep hanging out and hooking up and pretending to mean something to each other without any strings."

I throw my head back against the cushion and slide down, letting the couch support my weight as my feet dangle near the floor, legs outstretched. Sami nods, sitting up to rest a hand on my knee.

"I want to be the kind of person who can keep this casual, Sam, but that's not me. I also can't pressure him into a commitment that would end terribly for both of us. Most importantly, I won't risk losing focus on the life I'm trying to build and the promotion I need. Not because of some man who doesn't care enough to admit he likes me."

"You know I love you, right?" Sami cocks her head to the left while she waits for me to meet her hazel eyes. I nod.

"If you want me to tell you to cut and run, I will. Your getaway car and getaway girl will await whenever you need. But, Piper, you're treating James like he's Henry. He's not. He's been giving of himself from day one, which is something Henry NEVER did, even when he claimed to love you. James isn't an arrogant asshole who only wants you for what you can offer him."

She softens her tone as though she wants me to really hear this next part.

"Piper, you don't know things would end terribly between you two, or that James doesn't care about you. Besides, you're not the same Piper you were a few years ago. Even if things with James go south, it won't wreck you. You've welded yourself back together—you're not as breakable as you think."

Gosh, I don't deserve Sami.

"So, what do I do, then?" I scootch back up on the couch, moving from my wallowing position to sitting.

"You don't *have* to do anything if you don't want to. It's only been a couple of weeks. You could let the relationship continue to play out organically and try to temper the anxiety that says you need an answer now."

That is a terrible plan. Absolutely awful.

"Or you could tell him you're falling for him for real and see if he reciprocates."

I like this plan even less.

"Or," I interject, "I could call the whole thing off and go

back to being a focused person who has her shit together."

Sami gives a hearty laugh, rumbling out from somewhere deep in her chest. Whatever she's about to say will be true.

"Piper, the day you met this guy you were only wearing one shoe. You have never been a focused person who routinely has her shit together and *that's okay*. Your people love you despite that *and* because of it."

She pulls me in for a side hug, and I lean my head against hers with a sigh.

"You don't have to decide what to do this second or this month," Sami says softly. "If you need to take a step back, you can do that while you figure out what you want."

She straightens and clears her throat, putting on an air of authority before she continues. "And if you want to bail, I'll happily be your escort while you do it."

The image of Sami dressed in head-to-toe black with a stern expression appears in my mind, making me grin.

"Thank you, Sam. I think I'll sleep on it. The whole day has been tiring, and some of this anxiety is probably left over from the event. You always know how to keep me in line."

I steal her champagne and finish it off before sliding the glass to the coffee table.

"Stealing the rest of my drink is a heck of a way to say thank you!"

Our giggles fill the room, and I feel ten times lighter than I did when I walked in. Sami reaches for the remote, and we settle into our usual Saturday night routine, spending forty minutes debating which movie to watch before deciding on

*Titanic.*

My phone buzzes with an email from my boss, stealing my attention away from Leo. I open the message with trembling fingers. My relationship with her has been tense since I fumbled the meeting with Mr. Cargill the morning after my night with James.

**Sherry Adkerson, Executive Director, Hope First: Piper—just a quick note to congratulate you on an excellent event. We needed the fundraiser to overperform, given the loss of the funds we had expected from Mr. Cargill, and we certainly made up the difference.**

**Great work tonight. Loved seeing what you're capable of; can't wait to see more.**

Once I'm able to pick my jaw up off the floor, I let the compliment settle into my bones. Maybe the promotion *isn't* off the table? Maybe it *could* be possible to see where things go with James and not entirely ruin my life and career?

A thread of hope weaves around my heart, but my anxiety knows not to trust it. This entire night has been a whirlwind. It's going to take a few days to wrap my head around all of it.

# 16

## James

Sombreros is not where I want to be right now but then again, it never is. And yet I'm here, listening to Kyle talk about the game this weekend, the bet he plans to win, and his ideas for the prize money.

I smile and nod, waiting for my fajitas and wondering if Piper will text to ask why I missed the train this morning. With a father-son date in the suburbs after work, it made sense for me to drive today. She doesn't know that though.

"Dude, are you with me right now?" Kyle waves a hand in front of my face, and I refocus my eyes until I'm present.

"Sorry, was just in the zone," I reply, blinking as I take a drink of water and wishing it was a margarita with a Casamigos floater.

"What's got you so distracted today? Are you trying to figure out how to increase cash flow for the Athena project?" He smiles as he says it, knowing that's not what's on my mind.

"If only that was something I could do," I say with a laugh, swirling the straw in my glass. While I still maintain that Kyle is not my friend, per se—we've never once seen each other outside of work hours—he's the closest thing I've got. He is also the only person besides my dad who knows about Piper.

Pressure builds tight between my teeth as I clench my jaw, steeling myself to share.

"It's Piper." I lean back in the booth, the peeling plastic sticking to my blazer and groaning as I shift my weight. "I'm not sure what's going on with us. We had a great night last Monday with a terrible morning after, and then an amazing time on Saturday with a weird, awkward ending. I haven't heard from her since. It's two steps forward, one step back—sometimes two steps back—with her."

"Gotcha." Kyle nods, eyes narrowed seriously. "That doesn't sound like a problem, though, since you swore nothing was going to happen between you two."

"Hmm, I did say that didn't I?" I reply, twisting my neck in a stretch. "Guess I'm not just a hard-ass but also a liar."

The words come out with a huff, my trademark self-deprecation firmly in place to keep Kyle from getting too close. He sees through my bullshit and gives me a look, raising an eyebrow and leaning forward on the table as if to say, *"Really, man?"*

I can appreciate that Kyle isn't ribbing me right now. He seems genuinely interested in talking this out, and while it may be a ploy to avoid the analysis awaiting us back at the office, I'm grateful nonetheless.

"So, what's the issue then? That you like her?"

"Yes, I like her, but it's also... more complicated than that."

"Seems pretty binary to me." Kyle's shoulders shrug. "You

either like someone or you don't. It doesn't have to be complicated."

A puff of air fills my cheeks before I push it out slowly through puckered lips. "Remember the last time we came to Sombreros? The day when I was flustered after talking to Piper on the train? I wasn't... I wasn't totally honest with you about the interaction we had."

He nods with a curious expression, waiting for me to continue.

"It's hard to explain—I promise there's a lot of missing context here—but we decided to sign up for a Family Fares pass so she could save money on her commute. I added her as my wife on a joint account."

A panoramic view of Kyle's teeth assaults my eyes, his jaw dropping to his chest.

"It was supposed to be no big deal, a small fib on paper, but then the smoke bomb incident happened. The police started asking questions and they referenced my MTA account as they were building a passenger manifest. They expected us to give witness statements as a 'married couple' because that's how we appear in the portal."

My fingers add air quotes around "married couple." Kyle's jaw is still on the floor.

"Piper and I decided to lean into the charade in an attempt to avoid being outed for fraud. It's been... complicated ever since."

"Holy shit, dude. Why didn't you tell me this sooner? This is wild."

"You haven't even heard the wildest part, Kyle—we may be called to testify if the case against the attacker goes to trial. Under oath."

The skin at my hairline tickles as I recount this scenario. It feels like someone is breathing down my neck and not in a metaphorical sense.

"So, we've been spending time together, getting to know one another, in case we need to pull off this 'married' act in front of a judge. It started low-key, sharing stories and trading quips, and we successfully gave our depositions at the downtown station. None of the officers seemed to suspect anything.

"But after a while, seeing Piper stopped feeling like the means to an end. Somewhere along the line, it started to feel like a beginning."

My stomach twists as I say the words, admitting them aloud, and also to myself, for the first time. A wave of nausea tumbles through me as Kyle and I stare at each other, two emotionally stunted men trying to talk feelings over cheap Mexican food.

Kyle leans back in the booth, stretching an arm over the curved back. "Okay. I agree this is a complicated situation."

"Told you."

"But I still don't understand why having feelings for her is a problem. So what if your make-believe relationship turns real? Sounds like it might make things easier."

"It's a problem because I'm not good for her. I keep telling myself I could be—that if I'm helpful enough or attentive enough she won't realize I'm just like the ex that destroyed her a few years back. Do you remember Henry Sierra? The guy from Fundament who was caught embezzling money?"

Kyle's eyes grow wide as he starts piecing the story together.

"Yeah, him. He dated Piper for years thinking she'd cover for him because she's nothing but heart. When the whole scheme blew up, after *she* found the error in the books and reported it, Henry berated her in front of the whole team and then left her. She never went back to work after that."

Kyle is incredulous, his body perfectly still as I relay this story. Pressure rises in my chest, pressing angrily against my sternum. If the bastard walked in right now, I would deck him in a heartbeat.

"Okay but listen," Kyle says. "It's not like you're going to use her, shame her publicly, and dump her like Sierra did. You have integrity. You might hurt Piper at some point, sure, but we all hurt people we care about, even unintentionally. You're nothing like that asshat."

Kyle smiles sheepishly at the waitress who appears with our food, the word "asshat" hanging in the air as we all exchange glances. We thank her profusely.

"While I appreciate the compliment, this whole scenario feels too close for comfort." I pick at the fajitas with my fork, pushing around limp slices of bell pepper as I talk.

"Her life fell apart because a guy pretended to be something to her, knowing it could impact her heart and her job, and he did it anyway. Sound familiar? *I'm* pretending to be something to her. *I'm* risking her heart. And now it's clear *I'm* impacting her job.

"I made her late for an important meeting last week because

she slept over at my place. And Saturday? One of her donors said something about us that wasn't true and the discomfort it caused her cast a shadow over an otherwise wonderful night."

It would be wise to give Kyle a chance to speak if only so I can shovel some of this food into my mouth, but I can't stop myself from continuing.

"When I'm around Piper I can't control myself. I say and do things based on what I want at that moment while ignoring every possible consequence for her. I thought I'd be able to keep myself in check, let this arrangement be fun without anyone getting hurt. I don't think that's possible anymore."

I bring my hands to my head and massage my temples, my fingers kneading out some of the tension that's been building for days.

"So, now what?" Kyle mumbles the words around the piece of enchilada occupying his cheek, sauce threatening to drip off his chin.

"I don't know, man. She hasn't reached out since Saturday. Maybe I'll text her that I'm busy this week—I'm driving up to visit my dad later—and that I'll see her on the train. Try to pull myself back so I stop putting her in situations where she risks a bad outcome on account of my influence. I can't keep doing that to her."

My lunch is as cold and disappointing as expected when I finally take a bite.

The day is drearier as we head back to the office twenty minutes later, gray clouds hovering in the sky and threatening rain. My phone buzzes the minute we reach the lobby, and I know before I look it's a text from Piper. It's a standard vibration, the one for all notifications, but I swear I can feel a difference when a message arrives from her.

"Hey man, I'm going to hit up the restroom real quick." Kyle doesn't blink given this is a common stop after Sombreros. "I'll meet you upstairs in a few."

Instead, I duck around the corner to an armchair off the lobby and take out my phone.

Piper

> I missed you this morning! How'd you survive with no breakfast?

A pain twists in my chest, radiating outward until it prickles my skin. I missed Piper this morning too. I've missed her since the moment we met, I think—an anticipatory ache born from the knowledge that she will never be close enough.

Because I won't let her.

My fingers type something breezy instead, something that sounds nothing like the words I'd like to say.

James

> Hey, sorry, I took my car to work this morning because I'm driving up to my dad's house later. Anything exciting happen on the train?

Something about the text feels like a lie even though it's not.

Piper

> Are you asking if I witnessed a crime and spent an hour spooning with a near stranger? Surprisingly, I did not. 😂

James

> Happy to hear it!

I leave the response emoji-less. I wait for a few seconds while she's typing, three dots fluttering occasionally at the end of our thread.

Piper

> Soooooo I know the trial stuff is up in the air and I don't need you for any more errands at the moment (lucky you!), but I would still like to see you this week if you're up for it

She ends the sentence without punctuation like it's a suggestion and not an ask, an open-ended thought that doesn't need a specific answer.

I want to see her this week.

I want to see her in my bed every morning for the rest of my life.

I heave out a loud exhale before sucking in another deep breath.

James

> I've got a lot going on with work and my dad right now. I need to figure some things out. Can I circle back later?

The typing bubble appears again and then stops. It's back for a second and then it's gone. Piper wants to say something but decides not to, settling for a thumbs up on my message to end our exchange.

Shit. That's what I feel like (and it's not just the fajitas). Putting some distance between us is the right call, I know that, but it doesn't stop sinking dread from settling in my gut.

I can't let myself get further down this road knowing how I feel about Piper versus how I should. She deserves someone who will do what's best for her, and what's best for her is not me.

And who knows, perhaps I *can* circle back after I get my head and my dick in line. That little thread of hope is all I have at the moment.

I turn into the driveway and fill my lungs with air, psyching myself up for the evening ahead. While it's nice to spend time with Dad, it's hard being back at the house. This place is full of things that haven't been touched in a year—belongings that are where they are because that's where Mom left them. The thought of packing them up to sell or donate heightens the lingering nausea I've felt all afternoon.

Dad comes out to greet me in the driveway and for once, he looks good. Not quite so sullen. Is he starting to find his footing?

"Hey, James!" He shouts like my car is soundproof and he's determined to break through.

"I can hear you, Dad!" I gather my wallet and phone from the center console and step out of the car, stretching my legs before approaching him for a hug.

No one talks about how weird it is being taller than your parents. It's a reversal of the natural order.

"How've you been?" I ask, pulling away to study him. His face has more color and is a little fuller, a roundness starting to grow in his cheeks. I wonder if he's cooking for himself these days.

"Better now," he answers with a slap on my back. "Come on in, we've got a lot of planning to do before the donation pick-up."

We meander inside, slipping into the same routine we've had for years—my shoes cluttering the entryway with my jacket lying on top, his footsteps marching toward the kitchen where he'll sit at the head of the table, and I'll take the seat adjacent. A+B=C.

The routine is a welcome relief.

"You called the organization about a pick-up?" I ask. I'm pleasantly surprised. When I gave him the postcard that showed up at my apartment, I assumed it would sit untouched for months.

"I did, and they're coming next Saturday." Dad's eyes roam over my face to read my expression; he wants encouragement that this is a good idea, and I'm careful to give it to him. He shouldn't witness any of the grief that lives alongside my pride in him taking this step.

"That's amazing, Dad. In that case, we *do* have a lot to work through." I drum my fingers on the table as I think about the best way to sort through Mom's stuff. "How about we go room by room and tag items with masking tape that we... that can be donated?"

I had started to say, "... that we want to donate," but neither of us *wants* this. We want Mom here to continue to use her things for another two decades. It's a matter of need, not want.

"Sounds fine, Jamie. I've already got some ideas." He stands and makes his way to the junk drawer to grab a roll of masking tape and a permanent marker.

We're really doing this.

"Should we start here?" My hands gesture toward the kitchen and end with a slap on the table where I currently sit. The apartment Dad's eyeing in the city can't hold a piece this large.

"Sold!" He cheers, writing DONATE on a piece of tape and smoothing it on the table. "The chairs should go too," he says, adding labels to each of the five chairs surrounding me and the one I'm occupying.

I try not to think about my memories at this table: working with my dad on middle school math homework, my mom attaching a boutonniere to my suit before prom, Christmas dinners and Easter brunches, opening my college acceptance letters, and the other pieces of my life that existed right here.

I hope whoever gets this table makes fond memories with it.

"What about the hutch?" I ask. The large antique sits on the far wall, holding my parents' wedding china and a collection of honeycomb goblets. We never use any of it.

"It should go," Dad replies, glancing over to the hutch longingly but with conviction.

This process is unexpectedly seamless. No need, thus far, to discuss the improbability of stuffing a home's-worth of furniture into a one-bedroom city apartment.

Dad and I continue throughout the first floor, tagging furniture pieces and discussing happy memories as we go. It feels light, the way it did when we used to pull weeds when I was a kid, working and talking and spending time together. The only thing missing is the dirt under my fingernails.

"So, James," Dad says while tagging the armchair that sits in the corner of their—*his*—bedroom, "what's the latest with that woman, Piper? Did you listen to my advice, or did you ignore it as usual?"

My eyes roll before the question leaves his mouth. Dad knows I'm captive; of course he's using this time to follow up on my dating life. "I've seen her a few times since we last talked."

On the train, in my car, at work, naked on my couch. I've seen the look on her face when she comes, and the memory dumps adrenaline straight into my veins. I've seen a lot of Piper these past few weeks, and it hasn't been nearly enough.

"And?" Dad asks eagerly, as though I've been holding out this whole evening and now I'm going to confess we're in love.

"And I don't think it's going anywhere," I reply, pulling my bottom lip between my teeth at the corner. His face falls, shaking his head in disappointment.

"Dad, I told you not to get your hopes up. I told you when we talked that I couldn't pursue her. I know I told you that."

"I guess I thought you'd change your mind. I'm sorry you didn't." He moves to the nightstand at Mom's side of the bed and rolls a clean piece of tape over the top.

If only he knew that I *did* change my mind, or maybe she changed my heart, and that's the crux of the issue.

"I'm just trying to stay focused, and you should too," I reply. "Let's make it through this process with the house and get you settled downtown and then we'll talk. You could be my wingman at the bar; I have a feeling the ladies would love you."

The sentence hurts as it comes out of my mouth, pain rising from the depths and stinging my lips as the words leave. I meant *young* ladies would love him, the kind he could set up with his hopeless, heartless son. I didn't specify this, though, and the insinuation was that he could find another lady.

It's too soon to talk about that.

"I'm sorry," I mutter with quiet sheepishness, not meeting his gaze. "I just meant I have a lot on my plate, and it isn't the right time to get wrapped up in a new relationship. That's all."

He nods and walks over to me, placing a hand on my shoulder. "You know, James, that's the funny thing. Fate doesn't care if it's the right time."

He's implying something about Piper, but I don't push. Enough of today's energy has been spent thinking and talking about the woman I'm trying to ignore.

I give Dad a tired nod and he gets the hint, changing the subject to his rumbling stomach and musing about dinner options. It's a welcome distraction—from Piper, yes—but also from the emotional work of tagging things to donate.

My back rests against the dresser while I take in the tape-covered space. It already looks so different than it used to. It's going to be bizarre seeing the house almost empty next week, watching this stuff go out the door as a last goodbye to Mom.

Dad will need me to be here for it. I think I'll need him too.

"Hey, Jamie?" Dad's voice breaks through my daze. "Think you could bring me to that pizza place in town?" A smile breaks out on his face as he sets the tape and marker on his bedside table. He acts like "that pizza place" isn't the restaurant we've frequented twice a week since 1996.

"You mean Antonio's?" I joke back, straightening from the dresser and nodding my head toward the door. "We should definitely go to Antonio's."

Dad walks my way, and I swing an arm over his shoulder, a physical acknowledgment that we did good work today since neither of us will say it.

"You think there'll be any ladies there tonight I can charm for you?" He needles a finger into my side, prompting a yelp as I twist away from him. He's joking about my slip earlier. I'm glad he didn't take it to heart.

"Hmm, at this rate I'm not sure you'll find out. Maybe I should leave you here and go alone." I grab my keys from my pocket and spin the keyring around on my finger. Dad rolls his eyes and I smile softly as we continue our march to the car, still linked shoulder-to-shoulder.

We never wanted it to be this way, the two of us instead of the three of us. Even so, there's something beautiful about what we've become this last year and a half.

We may not know what we're doing, but the Newhouse men are alright.

# 17
## Piper

THANK THE LORD IT's finally time for my middle-grade painting class. Art is a great outlet for big feelings (that's the mantra I tell the kids) and goodness knows I have plenty of those right now.

I make my way down the stairs to the office lobby and hang a right until I reach the workspaces we use for classes and workshops. The art room is full of windows, the sun spreading cozy warm streaks on the tables each early afternoon.

With ten minutes to set up before the kids arrive, I work without thinking—pulling the supply cart out of the closet and placing a mug full of brushes on every table, a cup of water beside it. Each spot gets a small canvas thanks to the ongoing support of Art's Art Supplies, and I arrange paper towels throughout the space. I also cue up my music, a mix of eighties rock, film scores, and whatever new stuff I was convinced to download last week.

Doing something with my hands is a welcome relief after wallowing in my mind these past few days. I'm tired of living in my own brain, of fighting against fears and feelings that threaten to drag me into a dark room and then lock the door.

I may not know what's going on with James Newhouse, who I haven't heard from since he turned me down on Monday, but my hands know how to paint.

More importantly, I can be here for the kids who will show up any minute now.

An apron slides from the back of the art cart, and I grab it before it hits the floor, throwing the loop over my neck and tying the side strings behind my back. While I wouldn't care if I got paint on my Ramones t-shirt, the apron projects professionalism and models good habits for the kids. I throw my hair into a messy bun right at my crown and sit for a moment before the door swings open and Cassandra steps inside.

"Cass!" I squeal, running over to give her a hug while she tucks into herself like thirteen-year-olds do. "How are you? You haven't been here for a while."

She shrugs and finds a seat, pulling an apron to her lap but not putting it on—she's waiting to see if anyone else does.

Six other students file in and take their seats, filling the room with a hum of energy that's half hormones and half youthful audacity. It immediately brightens my mood—while others beg not to teach the middle-grade classes, I beg to have them. There's something about the confidence of a seventh grader who believes they have the world figured out when they can't even drive yet.

It rubs off on me.

The students work without much instruction which is purposeful. Often, there's very little in their lives they can control, and this space exists for them to do what they want. I mill about the room giving praise, filling requests for different colors, and replacing muddied water with fresh. Sometimes the kids will open up about their lives and sometimes they won't—either is okay.

We don't have any rules or expectations about what happens in this room, only that we paint.

After everyone is settled and working independently, I grab a canvas and pull out a chair next to Cassandra. "Mind if I sit here?"

Even though she's a closed book today, it doesn't stop me from trying as she scooches over to make space for me. I know she and her mom have been in and out of the shelter, and that it's incredibly hard for her. Her head shakes back and forth gently, and I reach across to grab a brush from the mug, leaning into her for a brief touch of affection before pulling back.

I start my work like I always do, brushing wide strokes without a plan for what the piece becomes. Red acrylic stripes the white canvas as I circle my brush to the top and down the center. Next, I add yellow, weaving the color amid the red and around the perimeter, slowing to carefully line the edges with precision. I dot on a few blue stars, not the five-point kind but little bursts of color pricking the white, red, and yellow to draw attention.

The piece feels right, like nothing is missing. I lean back in my seat to look at it from a distance, pleased with the result. This project will end up in a pile somewhere, but I got what I wanted out of it: an escape from the incessant thought that

James is avoiding me. Probably because I'm too much.

Because I'm always too much.

Cassandra's painting, to my left, is a mass of colors flowing out from a dark center, or perhaps the dark is drawing them in. She is attentive as she works, her tongue peeking out the side of her mouth in concentration. She's doing great work, and I tell her that, though she doesn't acknowledge the praise.

"Damn, Miss Paulson!" Tyree comes up behind me with a shuffle to point at my canvas. "You made a good one today."

"First, mind your language, Ty." He rolls his eyes before smiling at me. "Second, I appreciate the rare vote of confidence. Are you saying my others have been bad?"

A voice emerges from the table behind us as Xavier prepares for a roast—his specialty. I'm always his target and happily so; the kids are aware they have to be kind to each other in here.

"You think that's good? You should check mine out," Xavier turns his canvas around and the whole thing is solid blue. "Ms. Paulson's looks like an Elvis costume."

The group erupts in laughter and Xavier beams, pleased with his assessment of my work. My smile tells him I'm cool with his critique. How he knows about Elvis, much less what he wore, is unclear. Even so, he's not wrong.

Turning back to my painting to view it with new eyes, I push down the memories that spring up of KingCon. Sitting next to James, the deal we made, and all that's happened since. Those memories tangle into a lump that sits in my throat for the rest of the class.

"Alright, alright, enough with the laughter, thank you," I

say, motioning to the group to clean up their spaces as I collect cups and bring canvases to the rack to dry.

When the room is clean and the supply cart restocked, I shepherd everyone toward the door before stepping in front of it. "How're we feeling?" I shout, just like I do every Thursday afternoon.

"Feeling good!" They reply in unison, lining up to give me a hug or a fist bump on their way out. Each student receives my praise and encouragement which most return with an eye roll.

The world that awaits them outside of this building can be cruel. I want them to know they have a champion here.

It's 3:45 p.m. when I make it back to my desk. My shoulders feel lighter and my brain less cluttered after the painting class, even with Xavier's comment about Elvis. I'm working hard to keep myself out of that particular rabbit hole.

The rest of the afternoon should be easy—sifting through emails and making sure the logistics are in place for our monthly donation pick-up this weekend. I open my computer and tap my fingers lightly on the keys as I think through where to start. The pitter-patter of my fingertips on the squares focuses my attention as I pull up the file with Saturday's schedule.

I review each piece of the document carefully, stopping first to confirm that the truck is reserved, and two volunteers are booked. Looks like Tommy and Jamal are taking this one.

Three pick-ups are scheduled in various parts of town, one marked XL to indicate a large donation and the rest marked M for just a few pieces. Jack at the warehouse is assigned to meet the truck at 4 p.m. to upload. Everything seems ready to go.

Until the first name on the list stops me, my eye and my breath catching on the black font printed at the top of the page.

*Jeffrey Newhouse.*

The address is about forty minutes north of the city.

My mind tumbles back to the night in James's kitchen. The Hope First flier tucked near the fruit bowl. Didn't he mention his dad is moving? Maybe that's why he kept the postcard. Jeffrey Newhouse, James's dad, must be trying to clear out their house.

My thoughts spin, a tornado of questions and ideas bull-dozing past logic... or maybe trying to find it.

James must have known I'd see his dad's name on the sched-ule. Right? He might've been the one to schedule the pick-up. He said he was busy this week—it was probably this, getting the house ready.

God, it all makes sense now.

James isn't trying to brush me off; he knew he'd see me again this weekend and needed time to get the house in order before then.

*I'm an idiot.* Not everything is about me.

My heart rate jumps by twenty as I think through the opportunity—to spend time with James again, to meet his dad, to walk through the house he grew up in. It makes me giddy. I pull out my phone to text Sami who's been begging for a James update since our conversation after the gala.

Piper

Pleased to report that I figured it out! 🙌

Sami

Our dishwasher? The new stationary bike reservation system at the community center? World peace?!??

Ridiculousness is what I always expect from Sami. Her guesses make me smile as I swivel my chair away from my desk and toward the side wall, my back to the office door.

Piper

No, silly, this thing with James. I get it now.

She sends a gif of an old woman with her hand up to her ear, straining toward the camera.

Piper

> He scheduled a furniture pick-up from
> Hope First at his dad's place on Saturday.
> Remember when he said he was busy this
> week and I thought I'd scared him off? I'm
> sure he's been in the 'burbs for days trying
> to get everything organized. Would it be a
> terrible idea to join the truck and surprise
> him at the house?

Sami wouldn't tell me if it was but I want her approval regardless.

Sami

> I mean, since he's clearly obsessed with
> you, I'm sure he won't protest. But also
> keep in mind that this might be a hard day
> for him. I bet a lot of the furniture was his
> mom's.

Piper

> Gah, you're so right.

Sami

> Always.

Piper

I knowwww.

I twist in my chair as I think for a moment, considering what I could do to make the morning brighter. Of course, I'll bring sausage balls for James but... I could also bring some for his dad. I'm sure his mom used to make them for the whole family, and if James loves them so much, Mr. Newhouse might too.

Piper

What if I bring them both sausage balls?

Sami

That would be sweet. I bet they'll like that.

Piper

Is it weird that I'm going to meet his dad? It feels like a big step, especially when we haven't talked about the state of this "relationship." What if James doesn't want me at his house? What if his dad hates me?

Sami

> Stop it right now, Piper, or I swear I will eat every last piece of sausage in the city. Don't spiral and make up scenarios about how this meeting will be a disaster. It'll be fine. And also, no one can hate you because you're perfect and if they do, I'll leave a bag of steaming shit on their porch.

Having Sami to talk me down when I get escalated (and to threaten anyone who might hurt me) is such a gift.

I consider texting James to say I'll see him Saturday but don't. He was so good about giving me space when I needed it, and I want to return the favor. There's no need to act clingy with a guy who is my husband on paper (according to the MTA) but only slightly more than a friend in practice.

And, yes, "slightly" isn't the right word... and neither is "friend"... but I guess that's what we are for now.

Surely I can convince him to give me a ride to my place after we load up the truck, and I can use that time to tell him my feelings. That I want to give this a try for real, whether or not this stupid trial comes to fruition.

If he's as obsessed with me as Sami believes, it could be the start of something good.

# 18
## James

DAD AND I ARE waiting on opposite sides of the driveway when the truck pulls up, a full-size U-Haul riddled with dents. It backs carefully toward the house with a shrill, consistent beep, and then a sturdy guy, looks to be mid-twenties, hops out of the driver's seat and makes his way over to me.

"Are you Mr. Newhouse?" He glances down at a donation request form and then up to my face.

"Technically, but you're looking for *that* Mr. Newhouse." I point over to Dad whose smaller frame is obscured by the truck.

A second guy leaves the passenger seat and comes around to roll open the back panel, exposing the empty box minus a few moving blankets.

In an hour or two the truck will be full.

My mind launches a game of Tetris to figure out the most efficient way to maximize the space. I've never packed a truck like this, but it makes sense to start with the biggest items first. Maybe items that are of uniform shape. I turn to head inside, eager to move smaller items closer to the front door.

"James?" A small, soft voice echoes out of the truck. My head swivels to see Piper climbing down from the cab where she must have been squeezed between the movers.

Piper's here.

At our house.

In the flesh.

My compartmentalized worlds collide and the dust from the crash clouds my brain, making me dizzy. I blink and blink and blink, expecting she'll either disappear or I'll come to my senses and be able to speak.

I can't conceptualize what's happening right now.

*What is she doing here?*

"James? Hey." Piper gives her customary wave and there's no denying she's in my driveway, walking toward me with the same frayed jeans from the day of our errands, plus an oversized Hope First sweatshirt. Her hair is pulled back in a neat bun.

*Why is she here?*

Flashes of memory pummel my mind as I string together a series of events, each that felt unrelated:

The mailer from a non-profit seeking furniture donations with picture of a mom with a baby on the front.

Piper tells me she works for a non-profit that serves single-parent families. Did she tell me the organization's name that day at the park? I don't think so.

I pass the postcard to Dad and tell him to schedule a furniture pick-up when he's ready.

I attend Piper's fundraising gala and become acquainted with Hope First.

And now Piper's here, with volunteers, to pick up the stuff my dad called to donate.

I am the densest person alive for not putting this together. Of course the flier belonged to Hope First.

Of course Piper is here for the donation pick-up.

"James?" She's standing in front of me now, bobbing her head to try and catch my eyes. The heat from her hand, which she rests gently on mine, draws my attention back to reality.

Piper's here. At the house. Right now.

"Wow, Piper, hey." Wouldn't feel right without the 'wow.' "I... didn't know I'd see you today." Had I known, I wouldn't be wearing a pair of sweatpants, an old T-shirt, and a jacket from Dad's closet that is two sizes too small.

"Well, you are aware of where I work..." She tilts back on her heels and glances around. I can tell she's nervous by the way she rubs her hands up and down on top of her legs.

"Oh, I... I didn't set this up." I clear my throat awkwardly, running a hand over my unkempt hair, hoping to tame it. "My dad scheduled the pick-up. I didn't know it was with Hope First."

Piper nods, and a wave of disappointment crosses her face before her expression turns neutral. She must've thought I set up this appointment to see her, that this was another one of our excuses to keep orbiting each other.

Damn it. I spent the last week pulling away so I wouldn't hurt her and here she is, hurt regardless.

"Gotcha. I hope it's not a problem that I'm here?" Piper's voice is thready and her face flushed, like she's one second away from running back to the truck to hide.

I want to scoop her up and steal her away to my childhood bedroom, to tell her—and show her—how *not a problem* this is.

But I don't.

Because even though the image of her standing in my driveway makes me picture an entire life with her, and even though my heart is practically reaching out of my chest to grasp any future she'll give me, I can't do it. Not to her.

"I'm glad you came."

I summon a tentative smile and pull her in for a hug. If she's here, she's here. Might as well make her feel okay about it. I can handle a hug.

Wrong.

Piper's body folds into mine like every part of her was meant for every part of me. She's warmth and comfort and desire, familiar and unexpected. Her hair brushes against my jaw, her hands climb up my back, and my body floods with heat.

It's a mistake, letting myself touch her, but I can't let go.

"Well, what. do. we. have. here?" Dad's words match his footsteps as he plods in our direction, a distinct staccato as he emphasizes each syllable.

Startled, Piper pulls away, though I keep a hand loosely at her waist as we turn toward the voice. I take a deep breath in and give a noisy exhale as Dad looks us up and down, lingering on the point of contact between us.

Piper beats me to the punch in responding. "Hi, you must be Mr. Newhouse!" Her face lights up, a smile inching up so high on her cheeks it creates crinkles at the corners of her eyes.

She turns anyone into a friend with that face.

"I'm Piper Paulson, Program Director at Hope First. We are so thankful for your donation today; it's going to change the lives of a few women we serve. Thank you for thinking of us!"

I interject before Dad can ask questions. "Dad, this is Piper. The woman I was telling you about, the one I met on the train." A flush of pink creeps up her neck hearing I've talked about her with my dad.

"Ah, Piper! What a lovely surprise." He sticks out a hand and she grabs it eagerly, giving it a firm shake. His other hand comes on top of hers and he keeps it there as he talks. "Jamie didn't tell me you worked at Hope First. It's wonderful to meet you."

"Well *Jamie* here..." Piper glances over with a hint of evil in her eyes, relishing the fact that she knows this new nickname, "... isn't the best at communicating."

Her words sock me in the gut. She's not wrong to say them, not after I went radio silent this week.

"... But we'll forgive him for that." She shoots me a wink, and the tension winding through my chest relaxes some.

"Sounds about right!" Dad says it with a laugh and Piper joins in as they drop their hands. They are like old pals, these two, sharing this chuckle together. I'm the third party at this moment.

Piper slides out of my grip to swing the tote bag from her shoulder. "Hope it's okay that I brought you both something." Her sweet smile deepens further as she pokes around in her bag. My nerves stand at attention because I know what she's looking for.

"Aren't we the ones who are giving things to you today?" I joke, trying to slow the rising tide of anxiety that's crawling up my throat. My palms are getting sweaty. Neither she nor Dad laugh.

Her hand emerges from the tote with two bags, each tied with a ribbon at the top instead of the usual zipper seal. She put extra thought and care into this gift. Dad's eyes go wide as he sees them before quickly getting misty.

"Are these..." He glances between Piper, the bags, and my expression. "Are these sausage balls?"

"Yep!" Piper nods, looking to me for reassurance I can't give her. My gaze is trained on Dad whom she turns to next.

"James mentioned your wife used to make them. I figured today might be a hard day for you, donating things she likely picked out for your home. It's not much, but I hoped these might make it a little bit easier. James's mom sounded like an absolutely incredible woman."

Piper shifts on her feet with a small shiver, and while it may be from the October chill, it's likely because I'm gaping. The expression on her face asks whether this was a good idea. I'm not sure if she means the sausage balls or coming here in the first place.

Dad walks slowly toward her without a word and wraps her in the tightest hug I've ever seen. She tucks her head in the nook of his shoulder, a contrast to where she falls against my chest. She meets my eyes, and we linger there as Dad lingers in the hug, surrounded by a silence so full it may collapse under the weight of everything unsaid.

The movers return with the dining table, one of them walking backward until they come across the embrace and prompt its end. Piper and Dad scurry apart to make room as the men walk the table up the ramp of the truck to load it. It's the table I used to sit at each morning eating mom's sausage balls and talking about the day's high school drama—often about a girl and my inability to believe I'm a person worth having.

It's too much, the juxtaposition of these two women, one gone and one here, tied together only by their care for me (and, I suppose, an affinity for midwestern breakfast).

Grief crashes down my body, as visceral and startling as a cold bucket of water thrashed over my head. It's the kind of sorrow I haven't let myself feel in more than a year.

A stinging pain builds behind my eyes and claws at my throat as I consider how much my mom would've delighted in Piper. I let my mind consider, for just a moment, the kind of relationship they could've had. How much of a pain in my ass they would've been together.

How I would have pretended to hate it but would have secretly loved it.

The most gut-wrenching part of grief, I've learned, is that you don't just grieve what you had. You also grieve the moments, the relationships, and the experiences that will never be. Death leaves a trail of present *and* future loss. There's always a new moment that's missing something, missing someone, and sometimes those moments, like this one, knock you straight to the ground.

My only consolation is that Mom must have met Piper, in some alternate dimension, because there's no other way she'd be standing here with sausage balls. The universe isn't that kind.

Mom is.

Blinking and squinting, I scrunch up my face to cage in the tears, but it's futile. They come running, a herd of bulls set free after months in a pen. I wipe my face with my sleeve, or rather, the arm that's sticking out of Dad's too-small sleeve, and I duck toward the back of the house, not making eye contact with Piper or Dad who are still watching the movers.

I find the bench that sits at the base of the deck, the one facing the tree with the initials I carved before life got so hard. My head falls between my hands and my hands between my knees as I let gravity pull my tears onto the ground. They split apart at the impact.

I know how that feels.

A hand presses into my shoulder, and I feel the presence of Piper's body as she approaches me, sits next to me, rubs her fingers back and forth over my neck.

"Hey," she murmurs.

"Hey," I return, refusing to look at her. She doesn't try to catch my eye. She seems content to sit here with me, the same way she did in my car when our conversation turned heavy. Bearing witness, not fixing.

We sit like this for who knows how long, me heaving into my hands and her stroking my back, waiting for me to be ready to talk. A choked "sorry" is all I can muster.

"It's okay to cry, you know." She says it kindly, a soft permission I didn't know I needed. It makes the tears fall faster. I want to rest my head in her lap and let her play with my hair.

I also want her to leave and let me navigate this embarrassing show of emotion alone.

"Thanks, I wasn't aware," I reply. My shoulders collapse and I give a tense laugh, but it doesn't land right; it sounds snarky. It's my brain's attempt at pushing her away, at protecting my wildly exposed and tender heart. "Sorry, I just... this is a lot and I'm not sure how to manage it."

"I can't imagine. I haven't lost a parent, but I'm sure it's impossibly difficult, especially if you were close." She's being too sweet. Somehow it makes me feel worse.

"It's that, obviously," I peek at her face which is etched with compassion. She is turned toward me, attentive and filled with something like care, maybe love. It guts me. "But it's.... it's also you being here."

Her eyes narrow with concern and she straightens a bit, her hand pausing on my shoulder as I turn my head to hers, my upper body still hunched over my knees. It's ironic that this position is universal for vomit given the nausea that's tearing through my core.

"What do you mean?" she whispers, her face falling as she waits for my response. A thread of anger weaves around my grief, and while it's not justified, I'm mad she's making me say this out loud.

"It's too much." My emotion turns volatile, the energy behind the tears finding a new outlet in my mouth. I sit up and turn toward her, the words barreling out and landing sharply in her lap.

"You can't come here and give me that fucking smile that drives me fucking crazy and bring my dad breakfast like you're the damn sunshine after the rain. I don't need you to take care of me, Piper. You being the way you are—nothing but kindness and optimism—is making this morning harder, and I don't need any more hard. As you can see, I've got plenty."

"Sorry...I'm... I'm just trying to be helpful," she says. "You showed up for me ten different ways these past few weeks and I'm trying to return the favor. That's what friends do. Why is that a problem?"

Her escalation is starting to match my own as her words come faster, her hands gesturing wildly as she speaks.

"Because it makes me want to marry the shit out of you, Piper, and I can't do that. Is that what you need to hear? That I can't stand to be close to you anymore because I want you and know I can't have you?"

I rise from the bench and turn my back to her, not daring to look at her face. My hands find my hair and tug roughly, the pain failing to distract from the ache in my chest.

"I don't need you to marry me, James!" The location of her voice tells me she's standing, but I don't move. "I only need you to talk to me. We don't have to be anything more than what we've been. Can we just be that again? We were good like that. I don't know what happened that's making you act like this."

"*This* is why I pulled back. Don't you get it? *This* is the person I am—messy, detached, and broken. I've spent the last few weeks pretending to be someone I'm not—someone who's helpful and attentive, someone who doesn't lie, and who is selfless enough not to mess up your life. I know what you need. I'm never going to be that guy."

"You don't get to tell me what I need." She must be crying now, the way her words are breaking on their way out. "I don't need you to be someone else. I want you and your mess for me and mine. That's why I came here—to tell you that. I don't want to pretend anymore either. I can't pretend not to care anymore."

"That's the problem, P." I turn around, and the sight of her makes me want to collapse. She looks so small, like a wounded puppy pleading to be loved instead of kicked.

The threat of vomit rises precariously in my throat but I keep talking. "I care too. I care too damn much. I can't control myself around you, and it puts you in situations that risk everything you've built.

"You worked so hard to climb out of the hole fucking Henry Sierra left you in; I won't let myself throw you back down there. Fuck, even right now you're supposed to be working and instead, I've got you back here dealing with my shit. You deserve someone who won't lie to spend time with you, who will return your texts, who won't ask you to cover up their fucking criminal behavior *again,* and who makes you better at your job, not worse. That's not me. I can't add the pain of hurting you on top of the pain I already have. I'm at capacity.

I can't take any more."

"Damn it, James!" She's crying hard, and I'm not sure how we got here, exchanging my tears for hers. "You're hurting me *now*. Can you just listen to me, please?"

"There's nothing you can say, Piper. This isn't about you. It's about me and how I know this will end if we let it begin. I can't do that to either of us. That's it."

I am such an asshole. I want her to know this is for the best, that I'm being an asshole for her sake. There's no way she can see it like that. Not right now.

Piper nods and pulls her mouth taut, both lips tucked under her teeth. She wipes the tears from her cheeks and takes a deep inhale, sniffing up the wetness from her nose that threatens to drip.

Without another look, she turns and heads back to the driveway where I pray the movers are finishing up. The thought of her sitting captive in the truck is agonizing. She needs to be beyond my reach before I change my mind.

I sit back down on the bench and the weight of the morning pins me lifeless. I knew better than to let myself develop feelings for her. Instead of heeding the warning, I followed my heart instead of my head. It never works.

This is exactly why I don't engage—so I can avoid feeling like this and avoid hurting others in the process. This is why I stick to known outcomes, A+B=C, because it keeps everything in my control. Clearly, I make a mess of things when they're not.

Dad comes around the corner and stops at the sight of me. He's wearing a mask of empathy, but it doesn't hide his frustration. Seems I've missed the whole load-up between my breakdown about Mom and my breakup with Piper.

My guess, though, is that's not what he's frustrated about. I steel myself for the conversation to come.

"What the hell, Jamie?" He's imposing, standing in front of me, and it's an interesting reversal, him looking down at me while I sit. Like I'm a kid who's about to be punished. "Why did Piper just sprint across our yard and dive into the truck? She's crying, James."

"It's not your problem, Dad. It's fine. She'll be fine."

"It's not fine." He runs his hand through his hair just like I do when I'm stressed. It would be endearing in another circumstance.

"I don't know what happened here," he says, "but I can guess it's more of the same—you pushing people away who try to get close, you believing they're better off without you, you hurting them before they can hurt you, before they can leave you like Sydney did. Is that what you want for your life, James? To continue to be alone?"

"What if it *is* what I want, Dad? I'm not you. I never learned how to love someone and keep their heart safe. Turns out I can't manage it for a few weeks, much less decades, and even if I could, I don't want to invest the time and then lose them.

"That whole saying, 'It's better to have loved and lost than never to have loved at all?' Bullshit. It's better to be alone by choice than to be abandoned without warning. It's better to have a cold heart than a broken one. Piper deserves to have someone who can love her well. I can't do that."

"You're not incapable, James, you're scared. You're pulling this 'white knight' act, pretending you're saving her from yourself and believing it makes you the good guy. That's what's bullshit."

Dad storms back to the front yard and the silence that's left is suffocating.

*Done.* I'm done. The anvil on my chest cannot bear another ounce of anyone's hurt or disappointment. Not today. Maybe not ever.

# 19
## Piper

Slippery tears gush from my eyes, stinging the raw skin of my cheeks before dripping unceremoniously onto my jeans. Tommy and Jamal, the sizable men who flank me on either side in this too-small front seat, are gracious enough to ignore my sobbing. Jamal shuffles through the radio to find something to fill the silence, to mask my heaves, before settling on something jazzy.

Somehow it makes the seconds tick slower.

I don't know these guys well enough for any of this—inviting myself on the run today, squeezing between them in the cab, abandoning the loading effort to get broken up with in James's backyard, and then bawling this entire ride back.

I'd be embarrassed if I had any emotional capacity left.

I try my best to sniff away my tears, taking deep breaths in and releasing loud exhales as we pull onto the highway. The furniture rattles in the back of the truck, reminding me that the Newhouse home is a bit emptier. My heart is emptier still.

It's a small kindness, the only one I can find right now, that I don't have to unload this U-Haul later. Seeing the furniture pieces and being aware of all the stories they hold, stories I'll never get to hear, would rip any remaining composure from my body.

I reach forward and grasp the volume dial, turning it up with shaky fingers until the saxophone is louder than my breathing. It's only been eight minutes. We have thirty-two to go.

The conversation with James turns circles in my mind and I try to make sense of everything he said. Or any of it, really. How did we go from "I'm glad you're here" to "I can't do this" in the span of an hour? Where was the James I know, the one who is supportive and attentive, kind and helpful?

Some other James stood in his place, cold and resigned.

*"It's too much."*

That particular phrase rings in my ears, a painfully familiar refrain on loop. It pounds on my chest in rhythm like CPR, each aggressive pump bruising my ribs and pressing on my aching heart.

What he means is *I'm* too much—too anxious, too eager, too needy with my requests for favors, too conscious of my meager bank account. The damn bank account that got me into this mess.

*I'm always too much.*

My brain flickers back to the Fundament office, to the last time I cried in front of a man who told me the same.

*"Why couldn't you leave this alone?" Henry screams, the whites of his eyes bulging as he fences me in with his shaking hands, my back against his desk. "God, Piper, it was always going to be like this, yeah?*

*"You not being able to be the person I need you to be, not being able to smile and nod, sit still and look pretty. You're always trying to help, to do more. I should have left you once I realized you'd always be too much—that was years ago, Piper—before your eager-to-please conscience took me down and the company down with it."*

Henry's monologue ripped a fissure somewhere deep in my being, tearing open a wound I'd spent years hiding from. It had exposed nerves, that part of my heart, frayed from decades of never feeling good enough. Henry's words landed like a hot spark on each one. And while his words seared with pain, they also cauterized the vessels of vulnerability I once had, sealing them shut.

It worked for me. For two years, it worked.

But then I let James pull at the seal. And his tugging was so gentle, so wrapped in care, I didn't notice the new, tender flesh appearing where the scar once was. I didn't feel the fissure re-opening, becoming exposed and available for new hurt.

Until today. When James became Henry, another cold and callous banker, just like I feared he would. And I stayed Piper, the woman who always cared too much.

The truck bumps into the parking lot of the office before screeching to a stop. The noise jostles me from my thoughts, having neither heard nor seen anything during the last thirty minutes of the drive. Tommy hops out of the driver's seat, and I scoot my way across before stepping carefully down to the asphalt.

That I can stand is surprising when my soul has all but

collapsed. The ground feels mercifully solid under my feet.

"Thank you both," I turn toward Jamal, still sitting in the cab, "for letting me join you this morning. You did great work today." This half-hearted attempt to slip back into my Piper-At-Work persona is all I can manage.

Tommy nods and steps back into the truck, pulling the door closed and entering the address for the next pick-up into his phone. I raise a hand in a weak wave as they pull out, leaving me in the parking lot alone.

Home. I need to go home. I request an Uber, money be damned. I can't face the train and all the memories that ride it, the ghosts from these past few weeks occupying every seat. Facing the train can wait for another day. Right now, I need to get home.

Sami is waiting when I arrive at the restaurant, laid out between my two favorite chairs, her feet pushing against the opposite seat and swiveling back and forth. I sent her an SOS text the minute I walked in our door, and she didn't press for details. Just gave me a time (5:30 p.m.), a place (Tempest Tapas), and the promise there'd be a drink waiting for me (white wine).

I'm greeted with the usual sights and sounds of the space as I make my way to Sami. The smell is a familiar comfort, a mix of spiced sauces, alcohol, and a hint of old books from the haunt's bookstore days.

Somehow, I pull my face together to greet her, wrapping her up in a hug as she squeezes me tight. The tears have stopped for now though they'll start again soon. I can tell by the way she is hugging me.

I ease down into the seat opposite her, moving slowly as though one sudden move might break my fractured self completely open. Sami hands me a glass of white.

"Alright, lovey," she starts softly, "tell me everything. But before that, what's the vibe? Are we hurt tonight? Disappointed? Angry? You let me know and I'll match it. Personally, I'm pulling for vengeful."

She takes a sip of her red, and the smile that peeks beyond the glass is everything I need from her.

"Hmm... mostly upset. Sorry to disappoint." I return her smile, though mine falls as quickly as it appears. The tears spring back to my eyes and they sting the chafed skin at the corners, a parting gift from my afternoon dripping fresh hurt all over our house.

Sami reaches over and grabs my hand, meeting my gaze with gentleness and earnest concern.

I force a swallow through the tension gripping my throat. It presses in on all sides, a thick knot that won't budge.

"James... we... he ended things today. At his dad's house. Sorry, I don't even know why I'm crying!" (Every woman who has ever said this knows exactly why she's crying.) "It's not like we were actually dating. Maybe that makes it worse? It's hard enough getting dumped by a person who used to like you, at least. But being broken up with when you're not together? That's a new low, even for me."

Sami increases the pressure of her grip. "Piper, it was clear James liked you. Whether or not things were defined between you two doesn't change that," she says with resolute confidence.

"He made it very clear he cared about you. Don't believe for a second you misread the situation. James led you down a road toward an obvious outcome until he flipped the script today. You weren't wrong to believe he wanted you too."

"The worst part is he said he still does." I try to blink back some of my tears but it's a useless endeavor. "He said he cares *too* much and that's why he can't keep seeing me."

"God, I hate that 'It's not you, it's me' bullshit. It's like going into a job interview and saying your worst trait is being a perfectionist. It's a total cop-out." Sami rolls her eyes, indulging for a moment in her building anger before resuming a stance of patient listening.

"I don't think it was an excuse, Sam. I really believe he's too scared of hurting me, and himself, to risk putting our hearts on the line." My teeth scrape against my bottom lip as I think about what he could be doing right now, whether he's as much of a mess as I am.

"*That's* the reason he started backing off, not because he was busy. James was trying to figure out how to move forward and keep us both from getting hurt. And what did I do with his request for distance? I bulldozed through it. I leaned as far in as he leaned out, removing every ounce of breathing room between us.

"I showed up at his fucking *dad's house*, Sam. James told me he needed space, and I backed him into a corner. Of course, he felt like it was too much. That I'm too much."

"Did he say that? That you're too much?" Sami asks this question tentatively, knowing this is the most tender spot in the conversation. The most painful part of my heart.

"Basically." I think through bits and pieces of the exchange, trying to isolate James's words. All I hear in his voice is *I don't want you*.

"You're not too much, Piper. You don't need to shrink down to fit into someone else's life. The thing about love—friendship, family, partnered—is it's meant to make your life bigger. It's supposed to give you more of what's good. Love expands and multiplies and grows in the nurture of it. Anyone who can't embrace everything you bring, all the big that you are and are ready to give, can find less. It's not your job to carve yourself into their size."

This is the pep talk I knew I would get from Sami, and she delivers it flawlessly. It's an honest gift wrapped in compassion with a compliment on top. My brain agrees that she's right though my heart rebels. My heart wants to become whatever James says he can handle, even if it's just a fraction of who I want to be for him.

My heart would accept scraps at the moment.

Sami won't let that happen.

The next concern springs up in my throat, stealing my breath as I consider how this break-up affects our stupid charade. "Okay, but Sam—what if the trial goes forward? We didn't stop our fight to consider that we may still need to act fucking married in front of a judge. Can you imagine?" I put on my best dopey James impression:

*"Sorry to be dumping you in my parents' backyard. I can't keep seeing you but leave your phone on in case we need to pretend again."*

The thought makes me want to die.

"If the trial happens, you'll deal with it," Sami says. "Be cordial, play the part, let him put his hand on your back or whatever else. You wouldn't need to act lovesick. Plenty of married people aren't happy to be together. Besides, this whole trial thing is still hypothetical; don't stress about it until you know it's on the books."

"And what do I do until then?" I ask, peering into my swiftly disappearing wine as I raise it to my lips for another swallow.

"Whatever *you* want. Don't think about James or what he wants or needs or cares about. Figure out what makes you feel good, what keeps your world spinning, and lean in there. Let yourself cry or be angry or burn anything that he touched. And then dig into the things that fill your heart that have nothing to do with him. This is what we always do, yeah? After Henry, certainly, and after my series of revolving-door Hinge guys. We'll do it again now."

I set my glass on the table and slide my hands under my eyes, the cold, soft pads of my fingers soothing the puffy skin and wiping away wetness. Sami walks over and perches herself on the arm of my chair so we're sitting side by side, her arm draped around me and her head full of curly hair resting at my crown.

What a treasure it is to have a friend like this. To have someone who senses when I'm anxious and knows to greet my nerves with pressure, leaning the weight of her skull against mine.

"We'll do it again." I repeat it a few times, more to myself than to Sami. I'll just have to do it again.

## 20
## *James*

THE SUN TAKES NO pity on me this morning, shining daggers into my eyes as I peel them open. Time to face another day hungover, the same routine on repeat for three weeks now. I could fix this by reining in the number of Old Fashioneds I drink nightly, especially on an empty stomach, but I can't seem to muster the willpower.

I don't have the fortitude to do anything other than keep myself away from Piper. That task alone is taking every ounce of my strength.

I drag my legs over the side of the bed and plant my feet on the cold hardwood, sitting for a minute to talk myself into the morning routine. The predictability of my life—clothes, tea, shoes, walk, train, work—used to be a comfort. Now it's a cage, particularly with "walk and train" removed from the equation.

My arms reach up to stretch and I roll out my neck, taking a deep breath before I make my way to the closet. Gotta throw on another outfit that looks just the same as yesterday and the day before.

I ignore the shoes tucked in the back behind a stack of empty boxes, the ones with the scuff. The leather loafers I choose instead aren't appropriate for late fall, but I simply don't care.

Grabbing the keys from the hook in the foyer, I lock up, travel mug of tea in hand, and head to the car. It's been me and my car every morning since I fucked up my life three weeks ago; I don't want to violate Piper's space by taking the train.

I tell myself I'm being kind to her by driving. That I'm not doing it to avoid seeing the hurt on her face, or worse, a lack of hurt. This is about Piper and what's right for her.

Just like my decision to end things in the first place.

A thin layer of ice covers the windshield, and I groan. Since I lost my scraper, I'll have to sit inside a de facto ice box while the car heats up. The door handle resists as I pull it open and slide myself in, the cold from the leather seat seeping through my pants as I adjust the dial to blow air on the glass.

"What are you doing?" I whisper to myself, tapping my head on the steering wheel as cold air blasts around me.

I need the distraction of driving, the diversion of something to do with my hands, my eyes, and my mind because without it, the echoes of Piper in this car creep around me, drawing up memories.

I trade the goosebumps on the back of my neck for the feel of her hand, her warm fingers kneading away the tension that is even tighter now. I see her legs in the passenger seat and my palm resting on her thigh, exactly where I want it, instead of gripping this cold steering wheel. I replace the sound of the defroster with the catch of her breath as I tilt her chin for our first kiss.

I remember the way she exhaled like she'd been holding her breath since the day we met and had finally found release.

I am such a fucking mess.

I try to shake the images from my head as an opening appears on the windshield, ice slowly retreating under air that's finally turned to heat. Putting the car in drive, and ignoring the absence of Piper's hand on mine, I make the commute to work. Today should be mercifully busy given we're deep in the sale process for one of our companies.

Being completely buried is the goal right now.

The office is quiet when I walk in and slowly unwrap myself from the layers I put on this morning. My coat slips across the back of my chair, scarf gets folded and tucked into my upper right desk drawer, suit jacket hangs in a small cubby for that exact purpose.

I stretch my arms out in front of me with interlaced fingers, resulting in a satisfying crack. Rolling my shoulders back, I drop my hands to my keyboard, an attempt to power-pose myself into a productive day.

The elevator dings and then opens, and I know Kyle has arrived by the sound of his shoes and the weight behind his steps.

What would it be like to know someone else by sound? Someone whose presence floods me with anticipation, who makes my soul perk up when they step into the house?

I never paid attention to what Piper's presence *sounds* like. The thought burns like a slap across the face.

"Sup, man!" Kyle rounds the corner to my office. "Still looking like shit, I see." He gestures in the direction of my face, which, admittedly, is worse for the wear. Especially after nearly a month of hydrating myself with whiskey.

"Thank you, Kyle, I wasn't aware," I say with an exaggerated eye roll. "What are you getting into today? More work on the CIM?"

"Hmmm," his eyes narrow, "you want me to breeze past the fact that you continue to show up here looking like your dog's died every day? Can't do it anymore, dude. It's been almost a month now."

He leans against the frame of my door, crossing his arms and his legs as he stares at me.

"What do you want me to do? I'm here, I'm working, and I'm getting shit done. Doesn't matter what I look like. Please focus on the shit on your list instead of my emotional state. Which is fine, by the way."

I turn to face my monitors and resume typing, though I don't have a document open. Kyle can't see that from where he's standing.

"I'm just saying things were better for all of us when Piper was around. Not just for you. *My* life was significantly improved when you weren't such a sad sack and would join me for lunch occasionally. I would appreciate it if you could do *me* the favor of fixing things with her before I'm forced to blow you myself."

Kyle is pleased with his last taunt, giving a sly smile as he turns to the door. He lets his fingers tap the top of the frame on the way out.

He's not wrong that I've been lifeless since the donation pick-up at the house. The narrow spectrum of emotion I kept before meeting Piper—the one I'm trying to shove myself back into so that I can feel safe again—is suffocating.

It's like reverting to black and white after experiencing color. I'm drained of all feeling except for exhaustion.

I open my computer to a spreadsheet that tracks all the tasks related to the sale process, who's responsible, and each deadline. My name tops column D, and I scan down, noting all the cells missing the letter X. Those blanks represent tasks that need to be done. I settle on one I know my boss Hunter is waiting for, which should keep me occupied for the next six hours if I keep my head down and my ass in this chair. Perfect.

My phone buzzes and I growl, annoyed at the intrusion while trying to numb out with work. The call is from an unknown number with a local area code, so I pick it up. I never know if it's going to be someone from a project calling to rip me a new one about a number they don't understand or a report they haven't received yet.

"James Newhouse?" A woman's voice lights up the other end of the line, professional but warm.

"This is he," I reply, leaning back in my chair and scratching at the back of my head while I hold the phone to my ear.

"This is Angela Friedman from the State Attorney's office. I'd like to speak with you about the incident you witnessed on the train."

My entire body pauses, every system screeching to a halt at her words. My heart starts beating again but at twice the rate. I clear my throat, trying to keep my voice steady. "Okay. Am I... being subpoenaed?"

"We're in discovery now. I need to ask you some questions about your deposition before a decision can be made about whether you will be called to testify." Her tone is matter of fact, as though her words haven't created a Grand Canyon-sized pit in my stomach.

I bet she's reaching out to several witnesses to assess who might best represent their case. My hands turn clammy as I think about Piper having this experience, of picking up the phone and being greeted with the news that a trial is moving forward. Anxiety-by-proxy tightens in my chest.

Ms. Friedman and I agree on a time to meet and she thanks me for my time before hanging up. Presumably, to return to her day without issue. Me, on the other hand? I'm spiraling.

I need to talk to Piper.

My usual seat on the train—or rather, the seat I used to sit in—lures me in as I prepare myself for the heaven or hell that will await me in eleven minutes. That's when Piper should board this car, at 7:26 a.m. The seconds tick by fervently as I think through how I will greet her, what I will say to her, and how I'll suggest we move forward given the trial news.

My thoughts swirl like a word cloud, one that promotes the most used word to the biggest font size. PIPER flashes in bold letters across my mind.

I spot her immediately as we roll into Roosevelt. As usual, she appears to have arrived exactly on time, her cheeks flushed and mirroring the red slouchy hat covering her hair and ears. My heart leaps at the sight of her and then falls to my knees. I have no right to be excited by her.

Worse, it's my own damn fault.

Piper boards the train with her bag tucked between her arm and her side, the strap hanging loosely on her shoulder, and she has no apparent concern about whether she might see me here. I realize, right now, that surprising her after three weeks with no contact might be a huge mistake.

I watch her scan the car for a place to sit, knowing her eyes will venture toward the seat next to me in three, two, one, and she's here, meeting my gaze. Her expression changes briefly, more shock than surprise, her brown eyes growing wide.

She whips around to find a seat in the front of the car and settles with her back toward me. No second glance at our set of seats or at me sitting in one of them.

Of all the possibilities I played out for this ride, I never considered that Piper might ignore me. I thought I'd get her anger, her hurt, perhaps her confusion or indignant pride. But indifference? I didn't prepare for that.

I shift in the seat, the hard plastic creaking under the weight of my frame as I balance an elbow on the small ledge beneath the window.

It was a flash of eye contact, two seconds max, before Piper turned away. But she was solid amid her surprise. Unaffected.

Intact. No hint of the heartache that's been destroying me daily.

Without me, Piper's life has maintained a bloom of color.

Without her, my life has slipped into grayscale.

She is alright. I'm the one who's not.

Clarity comes swiftly, my dad's voice echoing in my mind: *you push people away who try to get close, you hurt them before they can hurt you.*

Maybe I didn't break things off to protect Piper. Clearly, she didn't... she doesn't... need that from me. I did it to protect myself. And it was a fucking futile endeavor because it hasn't spared me an ounce of pain.

It has only meant I'm hurting alone.

The space next to me stays empty as we hurl toward downtown. I feel her absence from it so acutely, and it's a small mercy no one else sits beside me. The gentle sway of Piper's hair taunts me from several rows up, swinging beneath her hat as the train bumps along. I want to run my fingers through it, to stretch my hand along the back of her head, tucking my thumb under her ear.

It's the sort of touch I took for granted with Piper. When I held her right here as the air filled with smoke, when we kissed in my car, when she straddled me on my couch, when we danced in the parking lot after the gala. Even when I hugged her, recklessly, at my parents' place. That tenderness is what I miss most.

Those small moments when she felt safe under my touch.

I told her she would be safe with me. I showed her she could trust me when I said it.

*And then I made her look like a fool for believing it.*

My head taps lightly against the window as I gaze mindlessly, never seeing a thing outside the glass. I consider what I put Piper through, masquerading my baggage as righteousness.

Will I have the chance to tell her that forcing an ending between us was a mistake? Given her reaction when she boarded this morning, I don't think I'll get it.

The train slows as it approaches the platform, and I give myself a pep talk for the conversation about to happen. Whether or not I can salvage any semblance of a relationship with Piper is secondary to her right to know the trial is moving forward.

I start walking toward the doors before the train reaches the stop, positioning myself near the exit so everyone from the front of the car will see me as they approach. Piper gathers her things and stands, quickly swiping her hands on the front of her legs before turning in my direction. She doesn't make eye contact, and it feels purposeful, an intentional decision to leave her eyes on the ground as a more comfortable alternative to my face. My stomach tightens into a knot.

"Hey," I call softly, hoping to steal her attention without drawing the eyes of the other passengers waiting to unload. "Hey, Piper." I try a second time, dragging myself against the flow of traffic until I'm in front of her.

My hand reaches for her arm, but I think better of it as she moves to her right to step around me. "Piper, please," I beg, moving back into her path and blocking the exit. "We need to talk about the trial."

For the first time all morning, her eyes snap to mine with purpose. They contain a look of confusion mixed with regret that she will have to engage with me. She nods and gestures her head toward the platform, stepping quickly off the train while I follow close behind.

We find a spot away from the throng of people and pause there. Her body language is closed at every possible spot: narrowed eyes, drawn mouth, crossed arms, and rounded shoulders. Maybe she's not as intact as I thought. I need to start talking before I do something stupid, like wrap my arms around her and pull her to my chest.

"Hey, thank you for taking a second." My gratitude serves as a peace offering. Piper doesn't seem to accept it. "I... I got a call from an attorney yesterday. They want to vet me as a possible witness for the trial. It's happening. Did you get a call as well?"

Her eyes go wide as she shakes her head, a low exhale escaping from her chest. Relief floods through me; I know how much anxiety she'd have if she were called to testify.

"Okay, good. That's good." There's no reason to keep talking to her now that this question about our charade, and whether we'll need to revive it, has been answered. Still, my mouth keeps moving.

"I'm meeting with their office next week. I don't know what's going to happen from here, but I feel in my gut that I'll be subpoenaed. I'd bet money on it."

"That's wild." Those two words are all she says, and they betray none of her feelings about the matter. Especially paired with an apathetic expression I haven't seen before.

"I just wanted to check in; I figured if you had gotten a call too, you'd want to talk about it. So glad you didn't." Piper nods. I guess that's it.

She swings her bag from her shoulder and starts rifling through it. This particular bit of movement is so achingly familiar that hope pricks at my heart as I watch her dig. She finds what she's looking for and brings it up, sliding her blue and yellow Family Fares card into my hand, cold plastic with roughed-up corners poking at the skin of my palm.

"I won't need this anymore then." She imitates a soft smile, the kind you give when a stranger enters your elevator. Piper strides past me to go left on the platform, in the direction of her office and the people she serves, the ones whom she loves and who love her back.

I turn the card over in my fingers, studying it, this last piece of evidence that there once was an "us." Her act of returning it cleaves "us" into a distinct "me" and "you."

While I debate throwing it away—tossing this token of my fears and failures into some grimy bin with the rest of the city's refuse—I slide it into my pocket instead. Maybe I'll tuck it into my scuffed shoe at the back of the closet, a monument to the beginning and end of what was, what could have been, and what wasn't with Piper Paulson. It might make me feel worse, but at least it'll remind me what I felt was real and that I'm capable of feeling at all. It's the only consolation I can find at the moment.

# 21
## *Piper*

*Two Months Later*

I wrap my arms tightly around my chest as I clear the steps of the courthouse. The winter wind bites at my cheeks, nipping them red—the tenderness of my skin echoing my heart. I don't know why I'm doing this today, watching James give his testimony.

Getting his text last week inviting me to the hearing was like taking a shot of straight cortisol; I've been jittery ever since.

After two months, I had come to terms with never hearing from him again. There was nothing left to say after the fight at his dad's house and how I responded to him showing up on the train three weeks later. I know I was too standoffish, though the same thoughts run miles in my mind justifying my behavior:

*It caught me off guard, seeing him back on the train.*
*He didn't give me any time to prepare for the interaction.*
*I had just gotten myself to a non-teary state when he came back into my life. It's understandable I'd try to protect myself.*

While true, these thoughts don't quell the gnawing at my

conscience when I think about my last exchange with James. If I'm willing to be honest with myself, I'm here at the courthouse for a few reasons. To make sure I won't be arrested for fraud, first and foremost. To support someone who was once a friend. To hopefully get some closure, or maybe a final memory that's not me handing him my Family Fares card.

If I'm *really* honest, the buzz that accompanied his message rattled my bones, sparking the small flicker of hope that managed to survive my weeks of tears. While I don't want to let myself wish for it, I wonder if he's felt the same.

A rush of warm air tickles my face as I swing open the gilded door to the government building. I let my arms relax before I unwind my scarf and take off my coat, pushing both through the x-ray machine as I stride through the metal detector. The heat in the building stands in contrast to the aesthetics of the place, all white marble and cold metal.

I have no idea where I'm supposed to go next and I'm not about to text James. Maybe I'll figure it out… or maybe I won't and I'll tell him I tried, hopefully receiving the closure I want without having to see him.

There's still time to bail.

An officer walks by, taking pity on me standing helplessly in the lobby, and asks where I'm trying to go.

"The smoke bomb trial?" The case must have a formal name, something like "The State vs. Criminal" (as if that's more official), but I have avoided learning anything meaningful about the proceedings.

I can't dwell on that day, how it ignited the spark between us that burned too bright and then burnt out too fast. It's better to ignore it, though that's not possible now. Every memory of September 28th, and the incident that enshrines them, will be in front of me today.

The officer knows the case I'm talking about and directs me to the elevator, up to the third floor, second door on the right. I didn't realize a courthouse has many small courtrooms and not a single grand one like they show on TV. It makes me wonder what else is happening here and what other lives have been upended by a single moment they have to relive today?

The thought makes me feel less alone.

The hallway is nearly empty as I slip in the back door, the courtroom more crowded than I thought it would be. The State invited everyone who witnessed the incident to attend, though I didn't get a call—James's phone number was on the account, and it makes sense they'd assume I'd be here given *my husband* is testifying.

I recognize a few folks, people who continue to ride on the B Line and occasionally join my car, though they're people who mean nothing to me outside of the air we share for fourteen minutes each morning.

The way it should've been with James.

There are available seats in the back of the gallery and I find one, dropping my bag on the ground and laying my coat on top. My hands slide back and forth over my legs as I wait.

When does this start? How does a hearing work? My stomach rumbles, demanding a breakfast I forgot to eat.

I peer ahead to the front of the room where a center aisle

splits two tables and the judge who sits directly across. There's a witness box to the right, and seeing it sends a shiver down my spine. I cannot imagine if I had to testify today. What a gift that my statement was bad enough no one thought to call me.

Next to the witness stand is the jury box, which is mercifully unfilled since this is a preliminary hearing.

As I'm taking in the space I catch a moving head, someone rising halfway from the attorney's table on the left. James. I recognize him immediately. He turns to scan the crowd like he's looking for someone. I wonder if his dad is here somewhere, or maybe Kyle from work.

It's not every day you participate in criminal proceedings.

Why does he have to look so ridiculously good? He's wearing a blue suit, and it's tailored to perfection. He moves to button the jacket out of habit as he stands, tucking in a tie with a pattern I can't make out from here. His hair is neat, shorter than when I last saw it, and he's wearing his glasses.

The combination of the frames with the suit lights me up with desire. *Stupid body betraying my heart with this reaction.*

It's bad enough that I'm having flashbacks of our "trial practice," the memory of his mouth on my neck scattering sparks across my skin.

James's gaze trains on the gallery as he scans each row, his shoulders tight. I resist the urge to glance away as he reaches my section, though I've half a mind to slide between the seats and cover myself entirely. He catches my eye and softens, a visible exhale making his chest concave as he holds my stare.

I want to wave because that's what we do, but it's not appropriate here. Instead, I nod and he returns it. We each give a soft smile. He seems grateful I'm here, and as he turns back to his seat, I realize he was looking for *me*.

That small glimmer of hope stirs in my chest.

The judge bangs a gavel and the room quiets except for the shuffle of pants in seats. James straightens in his chair. The trial has been going for days now which means we won't hear opening statements—they will jump straight to witness examination.

A woman, whom I'm guessing is the state's prosecutor, calls a man I don't recognize to the stand. The questions begin once he's sworn in.

It's wild listening to another person recount the events of the day question-by-question. My experience was so insulated, bound from beginning to end by James and his body in relation to mine. I never considered what other people might have seen or felt—or how they interpreted the noise and the smoke—without the lens of clinical anxiety.

Hearing this man's testimony is like watching an old home video; my memories of the day collide with additional details I missed in person. The more the witness talks, the more I'm glad I missed those details. James made sure my only focus was my own breath. I wonder if my breath was his only focus too.

My palms turn clammy the minute James is called to the stand, the day's second witness. I rub them against my pants, but it doesn't stop the sweating. James takes his seat and catches my eye again.

Does he want to know I'm listening? Or is he seeking reassurance from me like I used to get from him? I give him another soft smile.

"Please state your name for the record."

He clears his throat. "James Newhouse."

"Do you know the defendant?" The prosecutor points to a man sitting next to the other attorney. He looks young, late teens.

"I don't."

"Have you seen him before?"

"Only a few times, in the same car on the B Line train during morning rush hour."

The questions come rapid-fire, quick and to the point. James doesn't look flustered as he answers them. "Just tell them the truth," I remember him saying when I spiraled about the possibility of testifying. He's taking his own advice.

"Was the defendant present in your car on the morning of September 28th?"

"I saw him on the train that morning, yes."

"What were you doing on the train on September 28th?"

"I was commuting to the downtown station where I exit to walk to my job."

"Did you notice anything amiss when you boarded that morning?"

"No, everything seemed very typical."

"What was the first indication that something was unusual?"

James shifts uncomfortably in his seat, his eyes darting between the prosecutor and my side of the gallery. He clears his throat again. They haven't asked about who he was sitting with or talking to on the train. So far, it doesn't seem like he'll have to perjure himself today.

"I heard a loud sound, like a pop."

"What happened next?"

"I dove down between the seats," he answers.

"Why did you dive between the seats?"

"It was on instinct. I didn't do it consciously."

"Then what happened?" she asks.

"The car started to fill with smoke. People started coughing. I moved from the window to the aisle to position my back toward the rest of the car."

"Why did you do that?"

"I had someone with me." James and I lock eyes again. "I wanted to protect her."

Heat rises behind my ears.

"Protect her from what?"

"No one knew what was going on, whether it was a bomb of some kind or a gunshot. I wanted to put myself in harm's way if there was going to be harm. Not her."

My eyes start to water, a sharp, stinging pain growing behind my nose as he recounts the events. I never asked what the incident was like for him. Hearing it now cracks me open.

"Did you believe you were in danger?"

"Yes."

"Why?" she asks.

"Because of the noise and the smoke. Because trains have been the site of attacks in the past."

"Is that why you ducked down? Because you believed this was an attack?"

"I..." James pauses for a second, glancing down at his lap and pulling slowly on his fingers as he thinks. "I believed it was an attack, yes, though I didn't know what kind or the possible magnitude."

"What did you think might happen?"

"I thought we might get shot, or that there may be an explosion of some kind. That something would happen to Piper, the woman I was with, whom I was trying to shield. I... knew I'd rather have something happen to me if something was going to happen. I didn't want to be in a situation where I survived and she didn't, or where she got injured and I could have prevented it."

"Were you worried you might get injured or you might not survive?"

"Moreso for Piper."

"Why was that? Did something about the environment lead you to believe she was at greater risk?"

"No, I... I didn't believe she was at any greater risk. I just... I love her..." James glances down briefly and takes a deep inhale, "... *loved* her, and protecting her was my primary concern."

My mouth hangs open as James continues, a quick glance in my direction with the most intentional, albeit brief, eye contact I have ever seen. It's a laser that sears through the scar tissue in my heart, bisecting it until the red pulsing flesh is exposed again. His words reverberate deep in my chest.

James loved me.

He *loves* me.

Whether it was a slip of the tongue or intentional, his use of past and present tense makes me sweat from more than my palms. I'm growing warmer by the second, desperately wishing I could peel off some layers of clothing. Positioning my cold water bottle against the side of my neck is the next best option.

The incident on the train occurred when? A week after we met? Three conversations deep? James couldn't have known he loved me then. Right?

All he knew of me was that I'm clumsy and poor and am consistent with my breakfast.

The attorney continues her line of questioning, but I hear exactly none of it. Thoughts and timelines swirl in my mind until I can't concentrate over the thumping of my heart. It's taken weeks to convince myself James never cared about me, to believe the mess of words that roared out of his mouth in his backyard.

But what if... what if he wasn't trying to convince me, but rather himself?

Holy shit.

Something happens and people start moving, standing to stretch, rolling out their necks, gathering their things. I wish I knew how James's testimony ended, to get a read on his expression at this moment, but I can't find him amid the crowd gathering en masse at the courtroom door.

Is this it? Is our whole charade really, truly over now? Relief settles in my chest as the weeks and months of anxiety about this trial finally dissipate. But it's met with a sinking feeling in my gut, the relief quickly turning to something else. Regret, or maybe disappointment, that the final tie between James and I is now cut.

My eyes are down and unfocused while I remain in my seat. A tornado of thoughts and feelings rips through me, wreckage of the last few months of my life swirling around in the periphery of my mind.

I blink alert when a pair of shoes enters my field of vision, Cole Haans with a large scuff on the toe. James's voice greets my ears before I see his face.

"Thanks for being here." I don't look up. "For coming down here today." He takes a step closer, and if I lift my head, I will be eye-level with his crotch which is the last thing I need right now. James turns and sits in the seat to my right and we sink into the same position we have always assumed, my knee pressing lightly into his leg.

My heart waits for his left hand to settle on my thigh. I shouldn't expect it right now, not after everything, but it's a gift when it comes. Neither one of us acknowledges it.

James turns to face me, and I swivel to meet his gaze. His blue eyes are magnified behind his glasses, flecks of gray and green catching the light, and they're filled with an emotion I can't discern. He's the picture of perfection with his hair carefully styled, his tie perfectly straight, and his suit custom fitted so it looks poured onto his body, but that's not the man I see.

I see a James who is as messy as I am, who keeps people away because he can't stand the thought of hurting them or allowing himself to be hurt. He wants a tidy outcome, and that's not how love works even *when* it works.

"We're adjourned for lunch," James says quietly, as though he doesn't want to startle me. Doesn't want to make me jump and pull my leg out from under his touch. "Any chance you'd join me? I have a few things I'd like to say if you'd let me."

My heart softens with the words, their familiar kindness and lack of expectation, the type I'd come to expect from him before he became someone else.

*There he is,* my soul whispers.

*There's my James.*

I nod, trying to temper any trace of eagerness that may spill out from my throat before I decide how to feel. I bombard my brain with positive self-talk, the strategy I've been working on with my therapist thrown into overdrive:

I can have lunch with James.

I can hear him out, maybe tally up some points for my own closure.

We can eat a meal and catch up.

It doesn't have to be a big deal.

You're not as breakable as you think.

"Sure," I reply, grabbing my bag and sliding my water bottle into it. "I'll follow you out."

## 22

## *James*

WE SETTLE AT A table in a local sandwich shop, a dive as unromantic as they come. It smells vaguely of vinegar and burnt bread, the occasional ding of a toaster interrupting the chatter of businessmen on their lunch breaks.

It's not ideal for this reunion, but it'll do.

"So," Piper offers, extending an olive branch after I gave one earlier with this invite. "What's new with Mr. James 'Banker Man' Newhouse? Other than not getting busted this morning on the stand, I mean."

The tentative smile she offers to accompany the nickname thaws some of the ice between us, allowing us to settle back into the playful but guarded banter we had when this charade started. It's comforting.

"Well, Pipes," I say cautiously, wondering if she'll throw something at me for calling her that. Instead, her eyes give a dramatic, familiar roll. "I've been working, much to no one's surprise. Dad moved into his apartment, about five blocks from my place, and that's been an adjustment. We were able to sell the house for cash."

I try to hide a grimace, but I'm sure she catches it easily. A cash offer in this area means they want the lot; they're likely to bulldoze the house if they haven't already. Her face changes, an I-know-that-you-know-that-I-know kind of look to tell me she understands how much it hurts to lose the house that way.

We both pretend we aren't close enough to acknowledge it.

"Is your dad settling in okay?"

"Seems like it. He's gotten to know several of his neighbors, and we meet for dinner at least once a week. He says he's going to start volunteering soon, but I'll believe it when I see it. We've had enough new starts for the time being."

I scrub my hand through my hair while gazing down at the menu. Not that I'm hungry. I just can't stand to look at her for too long. If I do, I might pull her chair to my side of the table. "How is everything with you?"

"Good," she says cheerfully, though when I look up, her smile doesn't meet her eyes. "Work is going well. I got the promotion a few weeks ago."

It's a decent performance, these words and this face, but I see right through it. There's so much subtext, so much we're not saying, and yet we continue to pretend like it's not there. Like we don't know each other inside and out.

"That's great, P. Very well deserved. Did Sami take you out to celebrate?"

"She did." She rubs her hands up and down her legs, the tell-tale sign she's anxious. "You said you had something to discuss?"

My stomach clenches with a level of unease I haven't felt

before. Not with Piper.

"Yes, I do," I reply. Leaning forward, I put one hand on top of the other, rubbing the skin on my knuckles with nervous energy. "I've spent the last few weeks trying to think of how to say this, and I've decided there isn't a good way to do that. So, if it's alright with you, I'm going to word-vomit it. Piper-style, if you will." The reference tugs at my heart, memories of her breakneck monologues running through my mind.

"Go on."

"I need to apologize. For the way things ended, and for the way I acted." I release a heavy exhale.

"And for what else?" she asks. The anger she must have been pushing down for months rises to the surface and twists her face into a scowl. "For leaving me crying and stranded in your backyard? For missing the train every morning after? For never reaching out until the damn hearing came knocking and forced you to re-engage with me for the sake of our ruse? Are you sorry for that too?"

*Yes, yes, and yes.*

"I'm sorry, P. For all of it. I got scared and I ran. I thought it would be easier that way. For you, at least."

"Nothing about this was *easy*, James. I told you I wanted you, and you told me I was too much."

No, no, no. God, does she really think that? Did I say that? Please, tell me I didn't say that. "That's not what I meant. Piper, please, it's not what I meant."

Rehashing our break-up in an off-brand Subway on a random Tuesday is not how I wanted this reunion to play out.

"That's literally what you said, James! That this was too much."

"What I said—what I was trying to say—was that I'm shit at handling my feelings and I'd be shit at caring about you. I didn't think I could be with you the way I wanted to and the way you deserve. It was never about you being too much."

Her face softens like she needed to hear me say that. Like she might actually believe it. I bring my hands to my face and rub the heel of my palms against my eyes, hoping it will ease the sting that's building behind them.

"And now what, you're sorry?"

"I've been sorry, P. I was sorry when you gave me back your fare card and when we were in my backyard before that. I was sorry when you showed up at my house and I was sorry when I brushed off your text the week before. I've been sorry since the incident on the train when it became clear my dumb fucking Family Fares idea put you in a compromising position."

"I agreed to it, James. I can make my own decisions."

"You can, and that was my mistake. I never honored that you can take care of yourself. That's what I'm apologizing for most of all. I chose, for both of us, that this... thing..." I gesture between us, "was too risky. Not only for me but for you. That wasn't my call to make for you."

Her body eases in her chair, tension releasing from her shoulders as she takes a deep inhale. "I forgive you," she says softly. Then silence stretches between us, taut with my hope and her fear before she adds, "but it doesn't mean I trust you."

I nod. "Can I try to earn back your trust?"

"And how would you do that?"

"I'd like to start from the beginning, to get to know each other authentically. To allow feelings to develop we don't have to ignore, and to express them without pretending. We built a whole story for ourselves around a lie, P, and that's not the sort of foundation anyone should build a relationship on.

"I don't want to omit things or give you the cliff notes version of my life anymore. You deserve to spend time with people who won't keep you at arm's length. I'd like to be one of those people."

"But, James, you're the one who broke it off when your feelings became too real. Why should I believe you won't do it again?"

If only I could crack open my chest and show her that her name is branded on my heart. While I'm trying to convey this with my words, they're two-dimensional. My love for her isn't, and therefore the words feel insufficient. I need to try them anyway.

"I've seen what life is like without you, Piper, and it's no safer. Turns out there's no protecting myself from you because you pulverized every wall I built. My guess is I did the same for you. The question isn't whether I'm all in; you have my heart either way, P. The question is whether you'll take it."

"James, these words, they're what I needed to hear two months ago. Not now, not after I've tried my damnedest to envision a life without you. To convince myself a life without you could still be good."

Her words tighten the ache behind my ribs, sharpen it, push

it deeper. "I'm so sorry. I know I'm two months too late. But if you'll let me, I'd like to try to make it up to you, to try this thing again. To show you I won't run."

Her eyes hold mine and they're full of every emotion I tried so hard, for so long, to avoid. But this time, they're not threatening. They tell me I have a chance.

"Can you give me a few days? This is a lot. This whole morning, it's just... it's a lot. I need to think about it."

"I'm here, P. I'll be here. Whenever you're ready, I'll show you."

I'm two tons lighter as I make the walk from the sandwich shop to work. The hearing is over, and with it, the concern about whether we'll get caught. Even better, Piper finally knows how I feel about her and what I want.

Not even the bitter cold can dampen the warmth that's radiating from my core; a growing hope starts to overshadow the fear she might say I'm too late.

I pull out my phone as I wait for the WALK sign to flash at the intersection, cars rolling by in stops and starts, occasionally laying on their horns.

My thread with Dad sits near the very top of my text messages, ready and waiting for my report.

James

I don't need to say more. He knows what this means because he's had to listen to me sulk for nearly three months (and because he's the one who told me what an idiot I was for letting Piper go in the first place).

His reply comes quickly and without fuss.

Dad

Three dots flutter across the screen as I wait for the rest of his message.

Dad

You did a hard thing today.

Dad

...

Dad

...

Dad

I'm proud of you, no matter how this turns out with Piper. Mom would be proud too.

## 23

### Piper

I CAN'T MAKE MY way home from the restaurant fast enough, grateful I took the entire day off and not just the morning.

My feelings bounce around my head, each one a pinball that ricochets off the obstacles I erected to prevent myself from being hurt again. They bump up against these bits of rationality, testing them to see if they're firm.

Some aren't as sturdy as I thought.

I walk through the door and drape myself over the couch, sliding down the back cushions toward the seat like molten lava. My phone rings, and I answer the call without looking at the screen, setting it on speaker as I stare at the ceiling.

"Piper! I didn't expect you to answer; I figured you'd be at work this afternoon." Mom's cheerful voice echoes in the room and I can't decide if I'm glad for this distraction or desperate to be alone with my thoughts.

"I'm actually at home; I took the day off after the hearing. Didn't know how I'd feel—whether it would be draining to relive the incident in that way." My eyes fixate on the spiky popcorn on the ceiling. I look for patterns, wondering if I can spot an animal or a flower amid the dots like a child looking for shapes in the clouds.

"And how was it? That's why I'm calling—to make sure you're okay." Margaret Paulson is nothing if not concerned for the well-being of her children. It's a blessing and a curse.

"I'm okay. It was... a lot. I'm still trying to process it, to be honest."

She nods, which I can tell through the phone, a feat that should seem impossible but is not if you know Mom.

"What was it like seeing James?" she asks tenderly. She's curious but won't be pushy. While she'd love for me to bear my entire soul over 4G this morning—she hasn't let up with her questions since I told her about him, the ruse, and the break-up—she knows my heart can't take it today.

"That was the hard part," I answer. "We went to lunch after his testimony, and I hadn't expected or planned to have any real interaction with him at all, much less a meal. He... he apologized for the way he ended things, for hurting me the way he did. He also asked if we could start over... if he could take me out and we could see what it's like to care about each other without having to pretend."

"And how do you feel about that?"

"It changes by the second. I'm angry he couldn't figure this out weeks ago. I'm scared I'll get hurt, that he'll run away when things get complicated, and I'll be splayed out on the couch crying again."

"And?" God, moms always know, don't they?

"And I wanted to tell him right then that I'd like to start over too. That I'd start tomorrow if we could."

"Then what's stopping you, sweetheart?" She must be shuffling around the kitchen as I hear an occasional drawer closing and the clang of utensils shifting inside it.

"You're scared, of course, but look at you," she says. "You didn't crumble. You worried that having him in your life would sink your job, but you got the promotion, Piper. He left, and you cried, but it didn't bury you. If heartbreak happens again, with James or whoever might come next, you'll deal with it. You're strong enough. If something in your heart is telling you to try again, you should."

The vision of someone *after James* prompts a wave of nausea that rolls from my head to my toes. I don't want an *after James*. I want James. It's as complicated and as simple as that.

It's clarity I'm glad to have.

"You're right, Mom. Happy? You're always right." I hope she can sense the smile in my voice, the way I say this with gratitude instead of the teenage angst that used to accompany these words. She loved me fiercely through that stage, without wavering, because she knew I'd come around.

She waited for me to come around.

Maybe that's the lesson I need today—that love is about letting people come to their own conclusions in their own time. I exhale something between a laugh and a sigh as James's words repeat in my mind: "I made the choice for both of us that this...thing...was too risky. Not only for me but for you. That wasn't my call to make for you."

James came around. Perhaps I can too?

"Let me know how it goes, honey. I love you!"

"I love you too, Mom."

Friday comes with unexpected sunshine, and it melts away some of the anxiety that has a permanent home in my chest. Something about a sunny day, even when it's near freezing, feels like hope—like the winter won't last forever, and my ever-changing, stressful situation-of-the-moment won't last either. I turn my face to the sun as I speed walk toward the train, dodging piles of melting, dirt-tinged snow as I focus on the station ahead.

It feels good to feel good for a moment, to shake off the stress I've been battling since seeing James a few days ago. He's given me the space I asked for, and I'm grateful for that, but it's also nerve-wracking.

What if he's not willing to wait as long as I need? What if he regrets what he said in that stupid sandwich shop? What if seeing me reminded him of all the ways I'm a bad idea, the ways I'm never going to be the type of woman a guy like him should be with?

The "what ifs" are so frequent they're starting to feel like friends.

I told myself (and Sami, who cannot get enough of this recent development) that I'd spend the weekend thinking and painting and figuring out what I want. What I don't tell her, and barely admit to myself, is I've already decided.

I can't venture back into the land of "What is this?" with James. We need to be together or not. No more in-between. If he wants to start again and can show me he's serious about it, I'll risk another try.

The steps to the platform are slick, and I'm careful not to touch the metal railing as I ascend—it will rip the skin off my hand with its frost. In the winter, I regret that the trains in this city are elevated and not shielded from the elements by operating underground. I swipe my new fare card quickly, the flimsy plastic moving from wallet to hand to the left side of the turnstile to wallet to bag without thinking.

The train pulls up as I approach and I wait for it to stop, shuffling my way to the third car where I will take my usual seat. I step over the gap, hauling my bag after me as the doors close. Glancing up to find my seat, I'm greeted by a mass of people who are all standing for some reason—a visual blockade of bodies. I try to inch my way past them, frustrated that today is the day everyone's getting serious about sitting as the new silent killer.

Ducking and weaving, my heart makes a leap so wild it stops me in my tracks. There's music playing, and it's getting louder.

It's a classic, the sort of song my parents would dance to in the kitchen, though I can't make out the words yet.

I look around frantically, but no one else seems to recognize, much less care, that there is music wafting through the car. I expect some hothead to lash out any minute at the imperti-nence of it—the choice someone made to forget their headphones for a 7:26 a.m. train and play the music out loud.

There are unwritten rules on the train and whatever this is breaks several.

With enough force, I push past the last of the standers and he's there, James, sitting in the seat next to mine. Well, he was sitting, but now he's rising and with him the volume of the music playing from his phone, outstretched in his hand.

*What is happening right now?*

I follow the line of his arm to his shoulder, his neck, his face, his hair—hair that's slicked back in a pompadour, teased up in the front. I drop my eyes to his chest, and it all becomes clear—the blockade, the music, the hair—James is dressed like Elvis. He's singing and the people behind me have joined him in chorus.

And then the lyrics fall into place. It's "Can't Help Falling in Love."

I'm dizzy as I take in the scene. He reaches for my hand and pulls me to my seat before my legs buckle; the lurching of the train does my wild heart no favors. My field of vision blurs except for James and his face, my ears trained on the words coming out of his mouth.

The magnitude of James's gesture, how far outside of his comfort zone he's gone, how little he wants to be the center of attention... it makes me want to cry and laugh and dissolve into him entirely. Then the questions begin.

*Where did he get this costume?*

*Who are these people?*

*How long has James been planning this?*

My mind goes still as the next question comes: *Does he mean these words he's singing?*

The song ends and the train is quiet, a silence I've never considered possible in an environment like this. James looks so adorable, so ridiculous, so earnest I want to wrap him up with a bow and stick him in my pocket. Frankly, it should be a crime for him to look like this. I can't stand it.

"James, what in the world..." I ask as I search his face for answers, reluctantly pulling my eyes away from the deep V of his white, bedazzled suit. As much as I like him in it, I think I'd like him better out of it.

He settles our joined hands on my leg before taking the fingers of his free hand and guiding my chin until our eyes lock. My flesh burns under his touch, sparks radiating between his skin and mine.

"Piper," he starts quietly, with as much intention as I've ever seen. "I... haven't been fully honest with you." His eyes implore me to stay with him, to not let my worried mind wander and miss this next part. "I can't ask you to start over with me, to build a foundation based on truth, unless I am willing to do the same."

I nod, catching a few shaky breaths and pushing them into my lungs as he continues. He slides his hand from my jaw to my collarbone before settling it over my heart.

"That first day you sat down next to me on the train, on this train, in this seat, when I offered to add you to my commuter account? I didn't have one." He clears his throat and maintains his gaze, searching my eyes with his. They're a deeper blue today, flecks of gray reflecting the metal surrounding us.

"The first time I saw you, about two weeks prior, my car was in the shop. I was pissed I had to take the train, that I had to take an important call on public transit. And then you stepped in with your wild hair and your vintage t-shirt, looking completely at home with yourself even while disheveled."

We both chuckle. "The atmosphere changed when you stepped into the car that morning. The universe shifted in a way I couldn't name. It made me feel like I could breathe again, or maybe for the first time ever."

Tears cloud my eyes as James talks, as his thumb grazes over the top of my hand. His throat works down a swallow.

"I paid the fare in cash each day after just to watch you for the fourteen minutes between your two stops. So I could study your face from the back of the car and wonder what it was about you that made me feel at home too.

"The day you stepped on my shoe, and I barely said two words to you? I wasn't angry, I was nervous. I was nervous to have you so close to me, to feel so acutely something like hope but that I couldn't name, not yet."

"This stupid family pass," he brings a hand to his wallet and takes out the card, worn around the edges just like my heart, "is the only pass I've ever had. I never wanted to ride the train, Piper. I wanted to spend time with you. And of course, I didn't know you then, the day we made our deal. I just knew, somewhere deep, that I needed to."

I can't force a single word out of my mouth which seems to shock us both, my usual nervous dialogue strangely silent.

"What I'm saying, P, is my soul knew from the first moment I saw you that you are it for me. I'm sorry it took so fucking long for my heart, my brain, and my courage to catch up. I'm still not sure how to do this—how to be in a relationship, and how to keep you safe from me at my worst when I'm selfish and an all-around asshole. I just know I can't lose you again."

"James," his name comes out like a croak, pushed into my throat and around the lump sitting solidly in the middle, "I don't need you to keep me safe, and I don't need you to be selfless. You're allowed to be an asshole sometimes."

It makes me laugh to hear it coming out of my mouth and it lights a smile on James's face as he listens intently. "I need to know you can handle my mess and that you trust me to handle yours. That's what you said, right? The day the smoke bomb happened? You said, 'I can handle you,' and you meant it. I can handle you too, James, and I mean it."

He tips his forehead to mine, the tuft at the front of his hair crunching slightly as it meets my skin, a testament to the amount of hairspray he must've used for this Elvis 'do. I can't stop my mouth from pulling up toward my cheeks, a cheesy smile spanning the width of my face.

"I'm all yours, P, my fear and my hope, my heart and my mess," he whispers against my cheek, his breath tickling softly against the edge of my smile. "Whether you want it or not, I'm yours."

I pull myself away just long enough to angle my lips to his, to slip into a kiss so tender it might melt me into a puddle on the floor of this train car. James's hand slides up to cup the back of my head, his fingers weaving through my hair as his mouth moves with mine, his other hand reaching around to the small of my back and sliding me closer to him.

Our kiss is interrupted by a chorus of cheers and whistles, the earlier flash mob staring starry-eyed as they look at us. I forgot, until now, that there was anyone else on the train.

"So that's a yes?" a man shouts, leaning his ear in our direction but with his face turned to the rest of the crowd, hyping them up with his arms.

"Let me ask the damn question first, Kyle!" James rolls his eyes and while I'm dying to know if this Kyle is *work Kyle*, I'm more eager to hear the question.

"Piper," James says as he bows his head, looking both sheepish and gleeful as he sucks in a breath. "Will you start from the beginning with me?"

I give him a gentle thwack on the arm before turning to the crew and Kyle... *and Sami (?!)* who is leaning against Kyle with concerning closeness... and then back to James to give a confident "*YES.*"

The crowd goes wild as we return to our kiss, melting together with a heat that could power the sun. While he doesn't say the words, his mouth communicates exactly what mine replies: I missed you. I need you. Thank God I'm yours.

The skittering of the train's wheels shakes us out of our embrace as we pull into the station. James grips my hand and brushes his lips across my knuckles before leading me toward the doors, his other arm steady across my lower back. The touch is so natural and yet it makes my stomach tumble to my knees. *I'm his.*

We come up behind the crowd and I'm shocked to see a handful of my coworkers (those whom James met at the gala), plus several folks who appear to know James based on the approving nods and slaps on the back they give him as they exit. We step onto the platform and Sami tugs us away from the flow of commuters.

She grabs my free hand with a squeal and pulls me into a hug, rocking us both from side to side.

"What are you doing here, Sam?" I ask as Kyle lingers near James with a huge, beaming smile.

"Did you think I'd miss something like this? When James called me—"

I turn to find a sheepish grin on James's face, equal parts apologetic and proud. I want to kiss his lips right off of his face.

"I had to be here. Of course, I would be here!" Sami is radiating joy and it's her own— she's not mirroring my joy for my sake. She's really, truly, happy for me.

"And this guy," she elbows Kyle, who gives a fake yelp in response, "is the most infuriating man I've ever met, and you should be aware I put up with him all morning because THAT is how much I love you. That's how much I love you two together."

Sami extends our hug to pull James in, leaving Kyle the obvious fourth wheel until he wraps his long arms around Sami and me to complete the circle.

"Damn it, Kyle, get your hands off me! And why the hell do you smell like that?!" Sami's outburst sends us into a fit as we pull apart. I am dying to hear about their morning together and learn the shenanigans Kyle pulled to get so far under Sami's skin.

These two might be exactly what the other needs... if we could convince them to tolerate each other first.

I catch my breath and take in the moment, all of us here on the platform, happy. It's everything I couldn't have imagined two years ago when my world went black. What a gift this new life is.

My stomach lurches as I tear myself away from my gratitude, knowing this is where we'll all split—James and Kyle to their office to the right, me to building to the left, with Sami taking the train back home. A vice grips my heart at the impending distance from James, at the wait until we can see each other again after so many weeks of waiting already.

James senses it and pulls me in tight, wrapping an arm around my shoulder and the other around my waist, nudging a loose wave from in front of my ear with his nose.

"Don't worry, Sweet P... can I call you Sweet P? I'm not going anywhere, and I coordinated with your boss for you to have the day off. Are you ready to go back to the beginning?"

## 24
## *James*

WE'RE NEARING OUR FIRST location, and I've got Piper
tucked into my side, one arm around her waist to guide her
forward and the other hovering over her eyes. She must know
where we're going based on the direction we walked from the
platform—and the fact I couldn't cover her eyes for six entire
blocks—but I like the idea of surprising her anyway.

I open the door and she shuffles through, clawing at my
hand and pulling it down from her face to reveal The Velvet
Stool all to ourselves. They're not usually open in the morning,
but I pulled a few strings. Two paper cups wait for us at the
bar, and I drag her over, her hand in mind.

"Did you seriously rent this place just to recreate the night I
saw you here?" she asks incredulously, scooting herself onto a
stool, her legs not quite reaching the floor.

"No, I rented this place out so I could drink coffee with
you." I turn my attention to the paper cups in front of us, each
bearing the logo of the coffee shop we visited after giving our
depositions.

"An Old Fashioned wouldn't be appropriate for just after 8 a.m., so I combined two of my favorite memories with you—sitting at this bar knowing you existed just back there," he points to the high-top tables lining the far wall, "and having a celebratory mug with you and realizing my pretend feelings weren't so pretend after all."

"Really?" Piper nods skeptically, mostly for show. "I wouldn't have guessed you had real feelings for me then."

"Pipes, I was all over you that day at the station," I reply with a laugh. "I couldn't keep my hands off you. Do you think the lady checking us in needed to see me kissing up the length of your neck?"

She blushes a soft pink and runs her hand under her ear as if she might recapture the moment with her fingertips if she's fast enough.

"I didn't want to say goodbye to you that morning," I continue. "I didn't want to lose any time I might convince you to spend with me. So we had coffee, even though you were right... I do prefer black tea."

Her mouth gapes open for a second before it turns to a chuckle. God, it feels good to be honest with her.

With that, I lift my cup to hers and wait for her to meet it, no glass or ceramic "clink" to signify the toast but she knows what I'm looking for. She brings her drink to mine and then to her mouth to take a long pull, her eyes on me as I do the same.

"To what are we toasting, Mr. Newhouse?" she asks.

"To new beginnings—"

She cuts me off. "To seven years of *great* sex!"

I sweep her into a rough kiss, my mouth meeting hers with

enough command that she knows I'll guarantee it, hopefully for a lot longer than seven years. My fingers trace along the top of her thigh, inching closer to where her leg meets her hip and where I'd like to duck between. I catch her soft moan in my mouth before pulling back with a chuckle.

"Not yet," I whisper softly. "We just met, remember?"

She rolls her eyes and turns back to her coffee, giving me a look that tells me she hates (*loves*) when I tease her.

"You know what else I realized that day in the coffee shop?" I bring the conversation back to our beginning. "That I'd love to have coffee with you every morning for the rest of my life."

"You did not!"

"You're right. I thought about a lot of other things that were... significantly less appropriate for a coffee shop first." It makes me chuckle to recall it, the mental tango I danced that morning between what I was thinking in my head and what I was letting come out of my mouth. I don't bother hiding it now.

"It was part of the same train of thought, actually," I say, "you sitting at my table with your hands wrapped around a mug and me behind you with my hands wrapped around your..."

"NOT YET!" Piper says with a devilish smile. I pull my hand from her leg and cross my arms, miffed at how easily she throws my words back at me.

"Alright then, your turn. What was going through *your* head in that café?" I ask.

"Well, first, I was thinking how random it was that you did

a gap year in Italy. Renaissance art and a daily afternoon nap didn't square with my impression of you."

"To be honest, it didn't square with me either. Though I did have the time of my life that year—at least, I think I did... a lot of my memories are hazy given the copious amounts of alcohol I consumed."

Piper tilts her head, a dreamy look warming her brown eyes. "Florence was one of the places I hoped to visit when I worked at Fundament; I had the money to go but not the time."

"I'll add it to my list."

"...What list?"

"The list where I jot down all the things I need to do to convince you to marry me someday. Item one: figure out how to date for real. Item two: book us a flight to Europe. Sounds like an excellent plan to me, Pipes."

I relish the way Piper looks at me, her pupils expanding with unspoken want as I plan a future with her. For us.

"You know what else I was thinking that day?" She rests her chin on her hand and gazes thoughtfully as she speaks. "That I was grateful for you. That I liked sitting across from you and being a couple, even if it was a ruse. That I didn't want the morning to end either; I wanted more of it."

I lean one leg off the stool and straighten to stand, smoothing out my pants before stepping behind her and wrapping my arms across her chest. There's something about the way she fits here; the way my head can sneak perfectly between her neck and shoulder to whisper in her ear.

It's my favorite way to hold her.

"You get all of it, P. Every single bit of me. Today and to-morrow, here or in Florence or anywhere else. Heck, even in another train car filled with smoke. I'd be happier there with you than anywhere else without you. I'm all yours." I nibble gently at her ear, breathing in the scent of her.

She smells like home.

Piper turns her face and plants a kiss in the crook of my arm before laying her head there. It makes the perfect opportunity to drag my lips down the opposite side of her neck.

*Pace yourself, Newhouse.*

"Is there anything else on the agenda today?" she asks. The words come out sluggish, as though she's only eager to leave this moment if we're heading to a bedroom next.

"We're going to take a walk," I reply, kicking myself for making so many damn plans.

It's much colder in the park today than it was in late Septem-ber, though the sun provides a nice cover of warmth when the wind isn't blowing. We start at the fountain, and I turn Piper to walk backward, facing me, like she did the night we met here after work.

"Don't tell me you have Sami waiting for me on the balcony of the bar," Piper laughs, gesturing to the rooftop across the street.

"I don't," I sigh. "Turns out taking the morning off was the maximum commitment she could make. Kyle too."

"Yeah... about that." She looks at me from under her lashes, eyebrows raised like she doesn't trust what I'm about to say. "Did you...set them up?"

"No, I didn't *set them up*. I introduced them via text so they could help me pull off the surprise on the train today. Whatever mischief they got up to this morning before you or I arrived is beyond me." I crack a small grin. "That said, I don't hate the idea of them together. Sami seems like the kind of woman who could put Kyle in his place. Someone has to."

"Agreed," Piper replies, "though it doesn't sound like they got off to a great start." She shrugs, unconcerned. "Besides, we should hold off on double-dating until we get used to single-dating. I plan to single-date the hell out of you if you're up for it."

"I wouldn't be here if I wasn't," I reply.

I need to keep this conversation going if I want to avoid throwing her over my shoulder and carrying her to my bed in the next ten minutes.

"Let's try a first-date question, then. What makes Ms. Piper 'Pipes' 'Sweet P' Paulson tick?" The question echoes what she asked me the last time we walked in this park.

"Hmmmm." She smiles sweetly. "Helping people. A good cup of coffee, obviously." She raises the to-go cup she's been carrying from our first stop. "The attention of a tall, handsome man with stunted social skills."

"Hey! That's my line!" I blurt, reaching forward to grab her by the waist. She squirms out of my grip so she can still face me.

"It's true, you know," she says. "Ever since I met you on the train, your presence has been like a drumbeat, quickly becoming a steady rhythm in the background of my life. It's the sort of dependable consistency that frees me to go off-beat when I need to. Because I know I can slip back into the music after, and the piece will still be beautiful because you've been keeping time. I didn't know how much I needed that, how much I loved it, until the thrumming was gone."

She glances down at her feet, not wanting to dwell on the time we were apart. Her eyes meet mine as she continues.

"You keep me in line, James. You call my heart to tick in time with yours. *You* make me tick."

The cold stoniness that used to live in my chest is now something vibrant, something unmistakably alive. Piper makes me tick too.

"Can I be honest with you," Piper asks, "since we're starting over?"

"Of course. Tell me the truth, P. Please."

A small frog springs up in my throat. I thought she *was* being honest. That last bit was the most authentic exchange we've ever had; certainly, the most vulnerable. What else could there be?

I spot the bench we sat in previously, about three-quarters down the mile-long loop and lead us there. We sit close.

"I lied to you. In the car when we were running errands. I told you I was happy working at Fundament, that I was happy when I was with Henry. I wasn't. I never was. Turns out I didn't know what happiness felt like."

I wrap my arm around Piper's back and pull her even closer. She's still not close enough. She reaches up to grab my hand that dangles from her shoulder.

"My turn to be honest," I reply, holding her gaze. "Can I tell you what I wanted to do the day we first sat here?"

"What exactly was that?"

"I wanted to wrap you in my arms just like this." I rest my chin on the top of her head and breathe in whatever magic she puts in her hair. "And then pull your legs over mine." I scoop up her legs and drape them over my lap, forcing her to twist toward me so we're no longer side by side but instead face to face.

"I wanted to cradle your jaw and push my fingers behind your ear." I lift her chin gently, bringing her mouth a centimeter from mine. "So I could kiss you like this."

My lips brush against hers slowly, tenderly. This will be the kind of kiss we shared in my car, the best first kiss I've ever had. The one we could've had on this bench if I'd found the courage. I nudge Piper's lips open and slip my tongue in to tangle with hers, deepening as we find a rhythm.

A soft, satisfied sigh escapes her throat.

"What I really wanted," I remove myself from her only long enough to say the words, "was for you to make a sound like that. For me to be the one who pulled it out of you."

She adds a thought of her own before diving back into the kiss. "I'd be happy for you to hear every one of my sounds."

My dick sends up the signal to leave, not willing to be patient for another second when she has a mouth like that. God, I love her mouth.

"How about we go... somewhere else..." Piper suggests, sensing (or feeling, who I am kidding) that we need to get somewhere private.

"Can I take you home?" I ask, immediately wishing I'd specified *my* home. Sami being at her place doesn't make it "somewhere private."

"*Please* take me home," Piper replies, grabbing my hand and yanking me up from the bench, my long legs trailing hers as she speed-walks toward the train. Her eagerness to get to the station only intensifies the situation in my pants, which is unfortunate because this Elvis costume has no give.

"I may have to find a different seat for this ride," I joke, swinging my coat to try to cover my lower half as we near a sprint. Sitting next to her on the train, her leg pressed against mine, but not being able to touch her the way I want to? Straight torture.

"I'll tell you where I want you for the ride, James." Piper smirks as she says it, her innuendo heavy in the air as we dart into the third car.

This will be the longest commute of my life.

25

*Piper*

WE STUMBLE INTO JAMES'S foyer, and it's a miracle we're alive given how little attention we paid to our surroundings on the way home. I kick off my shoes, hang up my coat, and head to the kitchen before he can pull me in for another kiss.

It's not that I don't want one, I'm just desperate to peek in his fridge first.

In fact, I want to ransack this whole place to uncover all of James's secret quirks and habits. I rip open the appliance door and find exactly what I expect: a leftover pizza, some whiskey, and two jars of hot sauce. It's a shame no one lives in this nice of a home; James basically squats here.

I spin around to face the island, a balloon bouquet perched on the counter. It's an arrangement from Shindigs—I spot Mr. Ellis's handwriting on the front of the card.

"Woooooow. Seems like someone was confident I'd end up in his house today! Is this for me?" I'm giving James a hard time and he knows it.

He walks into the kitchen and puts his hands on my hips, turning me so I'm backed into the counter. He's blocking me in with both arms, trapping me under him with my spine against the cold granite edge.

"I hoped," he says with a smile. "And if not, I figured I could take this thing and stomp on each balloon one by one. That was my backup plan." His foot nudges mine to widen my stance so he can slide his leg between my thighs, leaning into me further.

It creates the kind of pressure my body always craves but is especially delicious right now. A shiver shimmies my shoulders.

"You knew I'd love it," I whisper. "You were right."

"I want to do everything you love, P. Like I said before, you're not hard to figure out. Just takes paying attention."

"I love your attention."

James presses his weight into me, his pelvis flush against me. The stiff length of him is heavy against my leg. His nose nudges my lips before he sinks into an urgent kiss, the tenderness of our kiss at the park replaced by desire he needs to pursue *now*.

I meet him there, my hands wrapping around his waist to squeeze his ass, to glide up his back, to rake my nails down in lines that will linger tomorrow.

He lifts me onto the counter, spreading my knees so that he can step between, keeping his weight pressed against me as we meet chest to chest. My longing grows needy. I want his fingers everywhere, his mouth everywhere. I also want him to take his time.

I want everything.

A ringtone cuts through the moment like a hot knife and

James drops his head to my chest with a groan, his hands still tight on my thighs. He's never wanted anything more than to ignore this phone call.

"It's my dad," he mutters, his breath warm through the fabric of my shirt. I need his mouth about two inches lower to the left or right, but we're frozen while the phone rings.

With a groan, James peels himself away from me and grabs the phone from the opposite counter, accepting the FaceTime call a split-second before it times out.

"Yep?" James answers, his voice higher than usual and his breathing fast.

"Jamie! How did it go this morning? Please fill me in. Don't make me wait any longer."

Mr. Newhouse looks good from what I can tell, after I've slid off the counter and onto a more respectable barstool (unless you count the last time I was here).

"Wait, is that Piper back there? Hi Piper!"

"Yes, Piper is here. We're catching up, can I call you back later?" James rakes a hand through his hair, trying to expel some of the tension that built and then stopped, a roller coaster swaying at the apex, filled with potential energy.

He pivots to face me, mouthing "Sorry" with a grimace as he lowers the phone to obscure his dad's view.

"C'mon, let me say hi! I'll only be a minute."

James nods, heaving a sigh as he props the phone on the counter and steps behind me, tucking his head in the space between my neck and shoulder. Now we can both see his dad and he can see both of us. The stubble on his chin tickles my shoulder every time I breathe.

"Mr. Newhouse! How are you doing? I heard you moved?" I ask. James might want to rush this conversation along, but I don't. I want to make a better second impression with his dad than I did the first.

"Piper, dear, I'm doing just fine. I've had a lot of fun exploring my new neighborhood! Hey, would you want to join us for dinner on Sunday? We'll probably get together at my place now that the new table has arrived—"

"*Dad!*" James interrupts, trying desperately to redirect the conversation. "We're taking things slow. You promised to honor that, remember? If things went well this morning? Having family dinner forty-eight hours after confessing our feelings doesn't seem like the best idea."

"Yes, I'd love to!" I squeal, ignoring James's protests and speaking directly to his dad. "Tell me the time and what I can bring. I'll skip the sausage balls this time. I can't wait to see how the apartment is coming along!"

"See, J? It doesn't have to be a big deal."

Hearing that familiar refrain in Mr. Newhouse's voice fills me with warmth as I understand for the first time where James got it.

"I'll see you two on Sunday then. Enjoy *catching up*." Mr. Newhouse gives us an obnoxious wink before ending the call, clearly aware of our plans for the afternoon after reconciling this morning.

James collapses onto me with a whine, his body enveloping me on all sides. "I'm sorry," he repeats, a blanket apology muffled by his face in my shirt.

"Don't be sorry your dad loves me," I joke, before replacing the line with the obvious answer. "Don't be sorry your dad loves you."

He nods, releasing an exhale before straightening and pulling me off the bar stool with a spin so we're chest to chest.

"Can we start over?" he asks, cautiously optimistic that this brief interruption hasn't killed the mood.

"That's the whole point of today, James," I reply. "Yes, we can start over."

The words are barely out of my mouth before I'm staring at his ass, my body flung over his shoulder as he carries me toward what must be his bedroom. He flops me down on his bed, carefully but not delicately. He's not trying to be gentle at this point.

His covers are ideal for burrowing, and while I am almost positive James is a "no street clothes in the bed" kind of guy, I don't care. Given how he's looking at me curled up in his sheets, I don't think he cares either. Not today.

"Are you going to join me or what?" He seemed *very* eager to move into action a minute ago.

"I will." He smiles. "After I soak in the sight of you in my bed. Do you know how many times I've thought about you here? How our night together in the living room replayed in my mind as I lay in this bed, wishing you were next to me, and under me, and on top of me? I built a lifetime's worth of fantasies involving you in this room. It's going to take me a minute to choose where I want to start."

James strips off the top of his white Elvis jumpsuit, his chest firm, and I'd love to start with my hands on his pecs if he'll let me. I follow his lead and remove my shirt, keeping on a lace bralette that is uncharacteristically sexy for a workday. Good thing I never went to work today.

"Take off the bottom half, too," I demand, removing my skirt and throwing it over the side of the bed. My underwear doesn't match the bra but it's not the worst pair I own, all things considered.

James pushes the pants down to his ankles, stepping his feet out one at a time until he's standing in a pair of boxer briefs. The sight of him sends a rush through my core. I'm wet just looking at him; the anticipation of his body on mine makes me swell.

"You're not in charge here, Pipes." James slides into bed and rolls on his side to face me, his palm finding the softness of my stomach and resting there. "Let me take care of you."

He nuzzles his face to mine and kisses me slowly, so slow that the building ache between my legs becomes unbearable.

"James," I beg, arching up, trying to meet his hand or somehow inch it lower.

"I'm going to give you what you need, Sweet P. Trust me." I nod, knowing he'll come through but eager for relief *now*.

James positions himself over me until he's eye-level with my breasts, taking one in his hand and sweeping his thumb over the nipple while his mouth sucks at the other, pulling at the peak through the sheer fabric of my bra. The stimulation makes me shudder—the friction of his touch and the lace rubbing against my sensitive skin feels heavenly.

"James, yes, that feels so good. *You* are so good." I've never felt this much pleasure without any sort of stimulation below the belt. I wonder if I could come just like this, with James sucking and pulling at my nipples, whispering how sweet I taste and how much he loves this.

We're not even naked yet.

He pauses for a moment to sit on his heels, nudging the bralette up my body and pulling it carefully over my head before flinging it to the floor. I am desperate for his bare chest to meet mine, frustrated by his resistance as I try to pull him down.

Instead, he hovers, trailing a line of kisses from my mouth to my collarbone, to the underside of my breasts, to my belly button, and then lower.

When he reaches the edge of my panties, he stops, grazing his lips lightly before pulling the top of the fabric between his teeth with a tug. I want them gone *NOW*. Five minutes ago would have been better. I try to shimmy my legs to help the effort, but James is no longer tugging.

He glances up at me with searching eyes—they match the wildness burning in mine.

"Can I kiss you here?" He drops his mouth to the fabric between my legs, right where I want him most, and I jolt. I'm already so sensitive. There will be a substantial disconnect between what I want and what I can take.

"Do you want to kiss me there? You don't have to," I whisper, threading my fingers through his hair as he hovers over me, waiting for permission. Oral sex is a no-go for some folks, and I don't want him to feel compelled for my sake.

"I want to kiss you *everywhere*, P. I want to know you inside and out. I want to touch you and taste you and hear you moan and watch your thighs shake and go limp when you come. I want to spend the rest of the day learning every possible way I can make you break apart and spend all of tonight putting you back together. So, yes, please, let me kiss you here."

*This must be what it feels like to be worshipped.*

"Yes. James, yes." My body is buzzing with anticipation and desperate for his touch.

He grabs the top of my panties and drags them down to my ankles, slipping them over each foot before they join the pile next to the bed. James stops to take in the sight of me, his gaze traveling up and down my body, lingering at my face, my breasts, my stomach, and lower.

He's cataloging every part of me, taking mental pictures for a growing gallery of all the pieces he desires. I feel certain he captures every single one. My heart wants to burst.

He moves himself to the foot of the bed and pulls me down to the edge, kneeling to place both of my legs over his shoulders.

He starts gently, sliding his tongue through me as I sink into his face, wrapping my legs around his back and crossing them at the ankle to pull him closer. The heat of his mouth draws every ounce of my attention to where he's working, the entirety of the universe existing between his lips and mine. His tongue slips inside me briefly before dragging up, slowly at first and then with increasing pressure.

"*James.*" His name escapes my throat, breathy and needy as he begins to suck, pulling me into his mouth and nipping lightly with his teeth. The sound he makes in response, one of deep satisfaction at making me feel *so. fucking. good* ratchets me into another echelon.

He brings his hands to my breasts, his fingers twisting my nipples in rhythm as he sucks harder. The sight of him like this—bathed in early afternoon light, unapologetic in his fierce desire to pleasure me—is almost too much.

I'm nearly there as I arch into his face, begging him to keep going, just like that, to make me come. He glances up to me, keeping his mouth exactly where I need him. The eye contact throws me over the edge.

I gasp for air as he continues soft strokes with his tongue, teasing out every wave of pleasure within me until my mind and body are nothing but Jello. I can't make a coherent thought, much less offer him the praise I'd like to, because I no longer have a brain. The only thing in my head is a jumble of pure oxytocin.

James fills the space that I cannot.

"Holy shit, Piper. That was... you are... absolutely incredible." He slides himself onto the bed and lays next to me, curling himself around me as I bask.

The idea that this experience was incredible *for him* is incomprehensible. What kind of mystical man thinks giving a mind-blowing orgasm is better than receiving one? I don't hate it. That's the understatement of the century. I love it.

"*You* were incredible," I manage to say. "I've never... that's not a thing that usually works for me."

"I'm always happy to work for you." James kisses my shoulder with a tenderness that almost hurts. "Working you up is my very favorite kind of work."

I roll over him until I'm straddling his legs and he's lying on his back, noting the flush on his cheeks from either heat, friction, or being here with me. It's his very best look.

Finally, I drag my hands along his chest, admiring every individual muscle that lines his abdomen. He shivers as I inch my fingers closer to the waistband of his briefs.

"Do I get to be in charge now? I'd like to put in some work of my own."

James smiles, his lips pulling high in each direction as he nods. He releases a groan as I grind against him, his head flopping back against the pillow.

I lift myself off him so I can strip him down, removing the last layer of clothing between us, nothing left but skin and sweat and need. Grabbing a condom from his nightstand, I roll it onto him before lowering myself to his lap. I place him between my lips but not yet at my entrance, and I rock back and forth, my wetness covering the length of him in a steady rhythm as I glide up and down. He bucks into me, moaning, whenever I near his tip.

"Piper, if you keep doing this..." he spits out the words in gasps and starts, "I'm not going to even... make it inside of you."

I stop for a moment while he catches his breath.

"Then let's get you inside me," I say, leaning forward to suck on his neck, my hand grabbing him from between my thighs and positioning him where he belongs. I lower myself onto him inch by inch, allowing time to stretch so I can take him fully.

When he's there, filling me entirely, I sit myself up and begin to rock. It takes a minute to find a tempo and angle that works, one that allows him to hit where I desperately need him and has him digging hard into my hips as I slide up and down.

"Look at me," I ask, though it's not a request so much as a demand. Our eyes connect before his fall to my breasts, one in each of my hands as I push and pull, pinching my nipples between my fingers until it makes me arch into my own touch.

"Fucking hell, Piper," he gasps, his hands reaching around to palm my ass.

"You like that," I muse, recalling the night in the parking lot when he said the same to me.

"I really, *really* do." The words break as I take one hand and slide it down, dragging wetness from where our bodies meet and bringing it to where I'm most sensitive. My thumb lingers there, sweeping circles that bring me closer to release. I increase my speed, riding him as he works to keep his eyes on me, on my tits bouncing with each thrust.

It feels so damn good. The position yes, but also the ability to make James feel this too. I'm inching closer as I continue the rhythm, spurred on by a wave of James's praise.

"*Look at you taking me so well*" pushes me to orgasm, my body squeezing him in waves that bring him to his own finish.

We ride out the pleasure until I collapse onto him into a heap of sticky skin on skin, our hearts beating as fast as our breath.

I want to stay here for the rest of my life.

After a minute, maybe five, I slide myself to his side. We're still intertwined, my leg flung over his hip, his knee resting between my thighs, my arm draped across his back, and his under my pillow, right beneath my neck.

"Hey, P?" His voice is just above a whisper. He brings a hand to my face, lightly pinching my chin between his thumb and pointer finger, gliding his palm under my jaw.

"Yeah?" Once again, my deliriously satisfied brain can hardly form a sentence.

"There's one more thing I've never said to you, not directly, and I need to. It's three words."

My heart rate picks up and my palms start to sweat as I wait for what he'll say next. If he plans to say, "I love you," I'm ready to hear it.

James takes a deep breath in. "I forgive you."

My head rears back in confusion, my eyes narrowing. "You forgive me for what?"

"For scuffing my shoe."

I grab the pillow from behind my head and smack him with it, half planning to smother him before he yanks it toward the floor, pulling me along with it until I'm on top of him again. I can't help but kiss him, even if he is infuriating.

"Sorry, let me try that again." James says with a smile, and I'm back on the train all over again, sitting next to him, just learning his name. But this time his words come out differently.

"I love you, Piper Paulson." His eyes, usually a cool blue, are filled with warmth. "I love your old T-shirts and the way you flail when you're nervous. I love your sausage balls and I love this..." he reaches up to rub his thumb under my ear, "this spot on your neck. I love how you serve the people in your life, and how you throw your whole heart into the people you love—"

I can't help but interrupt. "And I love, James Newhouse, that you're one of them."

# epilogue
## *James*

*Two Years Later*

"Hey, what time are the folks coming to deliver the new chairs?" I'm trying to get Piper's attention, but she's lost in her phone, texting with Sami about something more important than the logistics of our furniture delivery.

I nudge her knee with mine, the cold plastic of the train's seat squeaking as I move. It snaps her to attention.

"Sorry, what?"

I can't be mad with the face she gives me—not the expression but her actual face—wild hair framing her brown eyes and full lips. It's a consistent problem for me.

Aren't husbands supposed to be angry at their wives occasionally? I wouldn't know.

"The new chairs—are you able to be home during the delivery window?" We've had this conversation seven times over, ever since Piper moved in and made it her mission to make my sad, blank house into a home—our home. The only downside has been coordinating the painters and builders and delivery folks.

"Yes! I should be free. I'll ask my boss about working from home on Friday." Piper says this with a glint in her eye, still thrilled she has free rein to make the house livable. "It'll be nice to have the chairs before your dad comes over on Sunday."

We get together with Dad every weekend, alternating between his apartment, local restaurants, and our place. While I want to think we do this because Dad needs me, the truth is he loves Piper so much he can't be away from her for more than six days.

I'd be offended if I didn't share the sentiment.

Piper laughs, her gaze still glued to her phone, and a twinge of jealousy runs through me that someone else made her chuckle.

"What's so funny with Sami this morning?" I prod, using my arm around her shoulder to pull her in tighter so I can see the screen.

"She's making a list of what she needs to do before her artist-in-residence program starts. One is to schedule a bikini wax. You know, in case she decides to take an Italian lover during her first week there." Piper giggles again and the sound tickles my ears. I lean my head against hers and breathe her in.

The fact that Sami will be in Florence for the next six months is bittersweet. Piper is going to miss her like crazy, and it will mean more days like this one—having to share my favorite girl with her favorite girl.

Even so, it's not all bad; I was able to reconnect with the host family from my gap year, and they're letting Sami stay with them. In exchange, I made her listen intently to my suggestions of all the things she should eat, see, and do while she's there.

An Italian man wasn't on my list.

The train slows to a stop as we approach downtown. I stand, gathering myself to head to work. Piper doesn't make a move, so I step around her to the aisle, extending my hand for her to take.

"You coming?" I ask, knowing Piper will be anxious if we're the last ones off the train.

A mischievous smile graces that pretty face of hers as she takes my hand and presses it to my chest.

"Are you asking me if I want to *get off*, James? Because the answer is yes. You know asking me to come *always* makes me come."

Heat creeps up my neck as Piper stretches onto her toes to kiss me, sliding her tongue to tangle with mine just briefly. Not briefly enough, apparently. I move our joined hands to cover myself while we approach the doors, willing my body to remember it's a fucking workday.

You would think after a few years that a kiss and some innuendo would no longer be novel. You'd be wrong.

We step onto the platform like we have hundreds of times now, still dreading the moment we have to split directions. I wrap her into me tight and kiss her lightly, careful not to make my pants any tighter than they already are.

"I'll meet you later at Hope First?" I ask, knowing it's silly. Of course she'll be there. She's the one who arranged the financial literacy class I teach every week. It feels good to have a legitimate excuse to leave work early and even better to empower Hope First's clients with economic know-how. Seeing Piper in her element is the cherry on top.

She pulls away, her hand lingering in mine until the very last second as she walks backward in the direction of her office.

"Wouldn't miss it!" Piper replies with a grin and a wave. "I'll see you then, *hubby*!"

I walk toward the stairs before turning back to look at her one last time.

"Can't wait, *Mrs. Newhouse*."

# Mrs. Newhouse's Bisquick Sausage Balls

## Ingredients

- 3 Cups Bisquick

- 1 Pound Pork or Mild Italian Sausage

- 2 Cups Shredded Sharp Cheddar Cheese

- 1/2 Cup Milk

- 1 1/2 Teaspoon Italian Seasoning

## Instructions

1. Preheat oven to 350 degrees. Grease a baking dish.

2. In a large bowl, combine all ingredients. Shape into 1-inch balls. Line up on a baking sheet.

3. Bake until brown, twenty to twenty-five minutes. Serve warm, freeze for later, or package in a Ziploc for a stranger on the train.

# Acknowledgements

The day I turned 37, I went to Barnes & Noble and bought twelve romance novels in a fit of birthday indulgence. I sat in the Starbucks cafe with my free drink in hand and let myself muse on this season of life and what I wanted to do with it. The idea for *Somewhere Along the Line* came like a direct deposit to my brain; I started writing it a week later. I had absolutely no idea the undertaking that is writing, editing, publishing, and marketing a novel, and had I known upfront, I probably wouldn't have done it (I'm like Piper this way). It is because of the support of the lovely humans below that this story was able to get out of my brain and onto the page. Thank you, thank you, thank you.

Monica, for telling me I needed to "get a life" when I decided to write this book but then saying how proud of me you were seventy-five thousand times throughout the process. Thanks for being my Sami.

William, for sharing your insights about self-publishing.

The Bookish Babes—I'm so thankful for our little IG message group for support, brainstorming, commiseration, and sharing photos of kids, pets, and desserts. Y'all make me feel less like a crazy person.

Courtney Corlew for your support, encouragement, logistical help, and marketing know-how, which allowed me to get this book off the ground. You are a gem of a human!

Hannah and Clare, for taking a chance to Zoom with an

unknown new writer who didn't even have a picture up on her Instagram at the time. Your generosity in sharing your insight and experiences was invaluable.

Allie Samberts, for your kind words, direction, and encouragement when I had a breakdown over email and thought about scrapping this whole project.

Kristen Hamilton, for turning all my hyphens into em dashes, for fixing the punctuation on every dialog exchange in the whole book, and for leaving notes that said DO NOT UNDER ANY CIRCUMSTANCES CHANGE THIS when you saw something you liked.

Beth Heyn at e.h. editorial for the last, most important set of eyes before printing.

Andrea Somberg and Lauren Billings, for your suggestions and guidance throughout the querying process.

Laolan Art for the beautiful, stunning cover that I am absolutely obsessed with and is everything I imagined and more!

Sadye, for watching my children past my (day job) working hours so I could sneak additional words in, and for telling me about your dream (y'all, it was an actual literal sleep dream!) that I would be an author someday.

Livvy, for being brave enough to be my very first reader, and for agreeing to never mention this book's spice since I'm married to your brother.

Sara, for immersing me in the world of romance novels (aka slipping me Bridgerton paperbacks in Starbucks) and for being the most steadfast and supportive friend of every version of me since 2006.

Grandma, whose absence has taught me what grief feels like. I know you'd be tickled I wrote a book like this, and you'd love every second of it. 100%.

My family, friends, in-laws, and current and past co-workers who have buoyed my spirits during this process and have championed this book to the people in their lives. I am too lucky!

Tyler—you have never once, in fifteen years, treated my impulsive, wild ideas as silly. Your encouragement and unwavering belief in me is the reason this book happened. Thank you for being my James. I love you.

T and M, you're too young to read a book like this and frankly, I never want you to read it even when you're older. Being your mom is an incredible privilege but so is having you watch me be more than "just" your mom. May you grow up to do whatever impulsive, wild thing your heart is leading you toward.

And lastly, you! Yes, you specifically. Thank you for reading this book of my heart. If you loved it, please consider:

- Tagging your location at whereisyoursomewhere.com for our traveling book project

- Leaving a review on Goodreads and Amazon (even if you acquired the book elsewhere). As an independent author, reviews from people like you are invaluable!

- Posting a photo with your book on social media with #whereisyoursomewhere and tag @mallory-thomas_writes

- Loaning the book to a friend, stashing it in a Little Free Library, or gushing to your book club, coworkers, family members, strangers on the street or the Internet about how they have to read Somewhere Along the Line

Review on Amazon:

# About the author

Mallory Thomas is a writer and reader of soft love stories that make you swoon, squeal, and blush. When she's not writing, she can be found picking up after her two kids, joking with her handsome husband, and planning trips to the beach. She's also a baby formula expert and content creator. She strives to write books that are better than your phone—she hopes the time spent reading her books will leave you happier and more hopeful than time spent on social media. If she accomplished this, please leave a review at Goodreads.com and wherever you purchased this story.